sklg

D0938871

MAR - - 2022

Much Ado About a Latte

Center Point
Large Print

Also by Kathleen Fuller and available from
Center Point Large Print:

A Double Dose of Love
The Farmer's Bride
Hooked on You
The Innkeeper's Bride
Matched and Married
The Promise of a Letter
The Teacher's Bride
Words from the Heart
Written in Love

**This Large Print Book carries the
Seal of Approval of N.A.V.H.**

Much Ado About a Latte

A MAPLE FALLS ROMANCE

KATHLEEN FULLER

CENTER POINT LARGE PRINT
THORNDIKE, MAINE

This Center Point Large Print edition
is published in the year 2022 by arrangement with
Thomas Nelson.

The text of this Large Print edition is unabridged.
In other aspects, this book may vary
from the original edition.
Printed in the United States of America
on permanent paper.
Set in 16-point Times New Roman type.

ISBN: 978-1-63808-210-1

The Library of Congress has cataloged this record
under Library of Congress Control Number: 2021948534

To James. I love you.

Chapter 1

You never forget your first kiss . . .

At sixteen years old, Anita Bedford had never broken her parents' rules. Now she had violated at least two of them, maybe three. She always did what she was told . . . except for tonight. But how could she stay away from Tanner Castillo's party when he was the one who'd invited her?

She bit her bottom lip, unsure what to do. She'd been so excited to attend her first high school party that she hadn't thought about what would happen if she got caught. Now, in the dark of Tanner's coat closet, waiting for whatever was supposed to come next, she couldn't think about anything else.

She put her hand on the doorknob, then drew back. If she chickened out, the teasing would be relentless. She'd been the butt of enough jokes at school, and she refused to give her classmates more ammunition. Instead, she took a deep breath and stepped away from the door, only to lose her footing, grabbing at the coat behind her. When she felt the leather, she knew exactly what she was holding. Tanner's jacket.

She'd seen this jacket on him enough times to know exactly what it looked like—a deep mahogany color with zippered side pockets, the leather worn to the point that it fit him perfectly in all the right places. Even now she could imagine him walking into the library where they met twice a week, his thick, light-brown bangs brushed to the side, small white gauges gleaming in his ears. He'd been the first kid in town to get them, and now there were several students who had followed suit. His look was a combination of traditional and edgy, making him irresistible.

Sigh.

Without thinking, she pressed his jacket against her chest. Had he noticed her brand-new scoop-neck yellow top and light-blue denim jeans when he opened the door to his house and let her in? Or that she had gotten her braces off last week? He hadn't said anything about her braces yesterday during their tutoring session, but she thought he might have noticed tonight, because he did sit next to her as they and their friends played the Truth or Dare game that had landed her in his closet. Tanner was nice like that. But he sat next to her every Tuesday and Thursday after school as he tutored her in math, so sitting next to her at his party obviously wasn't a big deal to him.

Only to me.

This was stupid. How long were they going to make her wait? Maybe that was the point—no one was coming after all, and they were laughing at her in the Castillos' living room. Tears burned in her eyes. She should have known better than to try to be a part of the cool crowd. Was Tanner laughing with them? *I think I'm going to throw up.*

Suddenly the door opened. Anita squinted at the light shining in her eyes. The glare wasn't that bright, but compared to the dark it might as well have been a spotlight. Before she could speak, someone shot inside the closet and shut the door.

"Anita, it's me," a male voice said.

She almost fainted with relief. "Tanner!"

"Shh." He pressed his finger lightly against her mouth.

When he removed it, she responded, "Why are we whispering?"

"Everyone's standing outside the door."

"Why?"

"Why do you think? They want to make sure we're together in the closet long enough."

That didn't make any sense. She'd had no idea high school parties were so confusing. "Long enough for what?"

A pause. "Anita, please tell me you're joking."

She wasn't, but this wouldn't be the first time she'd misunderstood a situation.

"We're supposed to kiss," he explained softly, his tone even. "If we leave the closet too soon, they're going to push us right back in."

"Oh." Then she realized what he was telling

her. "Oh!" Butterflies performed a shaky ballet in her stomach.

He chuckled quietly. "What did you think was going to happen?"

"I wasn't exactly paying attention." She'd been too focused on watching Tanner's every move.

"Then why did you take the dare?"

Her face burned. "I don't know." Now she felt dumb, a sensation she was more than familiar with. "I've never played Truth or Dare."

"Never?" She could almost imagine one of his ash-blond eyebrows rising above his sage-green eyes in surprise.

"No."

He blew out a long breath. "I shouldn't have let Corey talk me into having this party, and I definitely shouldn't have let them play Truth or Dare. Nothing good happens with that game. My mother is going to flip her lid if she finds out about tonight."

As he talked, she smelled the scent of mint-flavored gum. Fresh, as if he'd recently started a new stick. She was surprised he'd had to be persuaded to have the party. He was one of the popular kids and had a lot of friends. She had assumed he partied all the time like they did.

"I've learned my lesson," he continued. "Hopefully not the hard way." Another pause. "I was surprised to see you here."

"You invited me, remember?"

"Uh, yeah. I didn't think you'd actually come, though."

So he had invited her out of politeness. She should have known that at the time. Then again, she was always slow on picking up cues. "I'm sorry," she said, hugging his jacket.

"No, I didn't mean it like that. I'm just saying this isn't exactly your type of scene."

"What do you mean?"

"You know." He shifted away from her, giving them a little more space from each other. "Parties."

"I've been to a party before," she said, forgetting to whisper.

"Like this one? Do your parents know you're here?"

She was about to tell him they did but stopped herself. Everyone in town knew her father, who was a cardiologist, and her mother, who was a therapist. Both of them worked in Hot Springs, and they, along with her and her brother, Kingston, and sister, Paisley, never missed a church service. They were paragons of the community, and Tanner would never believe they'd let Anita go out past curfew. "No. They don't."

"You snuck out, then."

Anita nodded, then remembered he couldn't see her in the dark closet. "Yes."

"Enough talking!" A sharp banging sound rattled the door.

Anita jumped and lost her balance again, Tanner's jacket slipping from her grasp. Instantly his arms went around her waist.

"You okay?" he whispered in her ear.

"Yes." The butterflies were now a whirlwind in her stomach. He was at least five inches taller than she, and if she wanted to—and she definitely wanted to—she could lean her head against his chest.

"Kiss! Kiss! Kiss!" The kids outside banged on the door again.

"Just ignore them."

How was she supposed to ignore them? They were chanting so loudly it was like they were in the closet too.

"Don't worry, we don't have to kiss," he said, letting her go. "If we both stay quiet, they'll eventually shut up."

Her shoulders slumped a bit. "Oh. Okay."

"Huh," he said.

"What?"

"You sound disappointed."

So much for hiding her feelings. And since she was honest to a fault, she had to make things worse by saying, "I've, uh, never been kissed before."

He didn't say anything for a moment. A long moment. Then he finally spoke. "Would you like . . ." He cleared his throat. "Would you like to be kissed?"

Her heart nearly exploded in her chest. Ever since he had started tutoring her three months ago when she signed up for the after-school tutoring program—on top of the tutor her parents had already hired—she had thought about kissing him. She'd always thought he was cute, and over the time he had tutored her, she had developed a secret crush on him. She wasn't the only girl at Maple Falls High School who was enamored with him. He was easy to crush on. He was smart, nice, and patient, something every tutor who worked with Anita had to be. On top of everything else, he always looked and smelled good. He was the complete package.

"Uh," he said. "Forget I brought it up—"

"Yes!" Then she put her hand over her mouth. "I'd like to be kissed," she whispered through her fingers.

Tanner was in big trouble.

Not just because of the party, although right after he and Anita were finished here, he was going to kick everyone out of the house—something he should have done before the party started. His younger brother, Lonzo, had spilled the beans to Corey's younger brother about Lonzo and their mother being out of town this weekend to visit family in Texas. Corey must have heard about it, because the next thing Tanner knew, fifteen people had been invited to come over.

Tanner should have nipped it in the bud right then, but somehow everything had gotten out of control, enough that when Anita had asked him what he was doing over the weekend—something she asked every Thursday for some reason—he absently mentioned the party. He'd never thought in a million years she would come. Not Goody Two-shoes Anita Bedford. He wasn't exactly a rebel—although getting gauges in his ears had made his mother think he was until he explained he only did it because he liked the look. But he was a year older than Anita, and he had definitely kissed, and been kissed by, a few girls in his time.

Well, now that he thought about it, only two. School and work had put a crimp in his dating life.

But those girls weren't Anita. Why had he opened his big mouth about the kiss in the first place? He knew she was naïve; that's why he had volunteered to be in the closet with her before any of the other guys had the chance. But he hadn't expected her to be this innocent. He had to admit it was kind of nice to be around a girl who wasn't trying to date him. They were friends. Not close friends, but during their tutoring sessions he'd gotten to know her a little better. Math was extremely difficult for her, but she always tried her hardest, and he tried his hardest to teach her. He admired her persistence, and soon it hadn't just been about the extra twenty bucks he made each week tutoring her. He wanted to see her succeed too.

"Tanner?"

He heard the hope in her voice, and he was surprised to find that he was nervous, something he'd never been around Anita. That had to be the reason his thoughts were all over the place. Surely there was nothing wrong with a little kiss between friends, right? And he was her tutor after all. He'd had a lot of practice teaching her math, so why not do her a solid and help her out?

"Okay," he said, moving close to her again. He rested his hands lightly at her waist. "Put your hands on my shoulders."

"Like this?"

He could barely feel her hands resting on him. "You can touch me, Anita. I won't bite."

"Oh." Her giggle sounded strained. Awkward. And kind of cute. When she settled her hands on his shoulders, she said, "What do I do now?"

What should she do now? He'd had his first kiss when he was twelve, and that hadn't been much of one—more of a peck from one of the girls who had been at the one and only summer camp session he'd ever attended. Looking back, he could see now that the counselors should have been fired for the stuff they let the campers get away with.

His other kisses had been with Kayla Smith, a girl he'd dated for four months when they were sophomores. She had moved last year, but they had broken up before that.

He took a step closer to Anita, breaking out of his rambling thoughts before she decided he'd changed his mind. Now he was close to her ear. "I'm going to kiss you now, Anita," he murmured, then moved his head until he found her lips.

It took a second for her to respond, but once she did . . . Wow. Kissing her was nothing like he'd experienced before. Her lips were sweet, and that soft moan she made . . . His hands tightened at her waist, drawing her closer to him—

"Hey!" Corey yelled, banging on the door.

They jumped away from each other.

"Stop hogging the closet!"

"Shut up, Simpson!" Tanner gave his head a hard shake, trying to regain his senses.

"Did I do okay?" Anita asked, her voice small.

"Uh, yeah." More than okay. He'd never had to catch his breath after a kiss before. But he wasn't going to tell her that. She saw him as a friend. Her tutor, to be more accurate. "I think you've got it."

"Open the door, or I'm going to break it down," Corey shouted.

"That's it." Tanner was done with this guy and everyone else. He threw open the door, his eyes squinting as they adjusted to the bright light. "Party's over."

Corey stood back and held up his hands. "Hey, dude, why ya mad? You should have said something if you wanted to be alone with Anita all night."

"I *don't* want to be alone with her." His temper was getting the best of him, not to mention he was still reeling from the kiss. "Get out of my house." He turned and went to the front room. "All of you, leave now!"

"This party's lame anyway." Corey came up behind him, then walked over to Madison Baker and put his arm around her shoulders. "No booze, no fun."

Tanner rolled his eyes and pointed to the back door. "Out."

Everyone grumbled and groaned but complied. He barely knew most of the kids here, and he was relieved when they left.

Then he remembered Anita.

"Anita?" He searched the front part of the house where the closet was, then went outside. He put his hands on his hips and frowned. She had left along with everyone else, and he hadn't had a chance to see if she was okay or even tell her goodbye. She probably thought he was the biggest jerk on the planet. He sure felt like he was.

But a small part of him realized he owed Corey

a favor. Because if Tanner hadn't left the closet when he did, he might have kissed Anita Bedford again.

No, I definitely would have.

On Tuesday, Anita sat at her and Tanner's usual table in the school library. She squeezed her hands together and made sure they stayed in her lap. She'd thought about canceling today's session, but she would've had to come up with an excuse to tell her parents, who always wanted to know how her tutoring went. If she canceled today, they would want to know why. She was still so out of sorts, she knew she couldn't come up with anything believable.

Her stomach twisted into a tight knot. All weekend and Monday she had remembered what Tanner said right after their amazing kiss: *"I don't want to be alone with her."* Those words had hit hard, and as soon as she'd heard them, she'd left his house and snuck back home. Her mother and father had no idea she'd been gone, and neither did her siblings. Not that she would have cared if she'd been caught. Nothing could compare to the pain her heart was going through right now. Her first kiss had knocked her off her feet, and she had felt Tanner pulling her closer right before Corey had interrupted them. But instead of savoring every second of their kiss, she wanted to crawl into a hole and disappear forever.

She glanced at the clock in the library. Almost three o'clock. Tanner would be here any minute. She looked around the room. Usually there were several other people here, including the librarian, but today the library stood empty. Great. He would probably bolt once he saw they were the only ones here.

"I don't want to be alone with her." No matter how hard she tried, she couldn't force his words out of her mind.

Unable to sit still any longer, she yanked her math book out of her bag and opened the pages to the day's homework assignment. Yuck, geometry. While she was in intervention classes for both math and reading, math was her worst subject. Today the teacher had talked about a coordinate plane, and she'd had no clue what it was. If Tanner did show up, he would think she was dumb as a bag of rocks, if he didn't already.

"Hey."

Anita looked up, and her breath caught. How was she supposed to keep her composure when he looked so hot today? A navy blue V-neck T-shirt, bootcut jeans, and his ever-present leather jacket.

He smells good again.

"Looks like everyone else bailed." Tanner sat next to her, putting his books across the table from her backpack. He took all AP courses, and his statistics and advanced chemistry books sat on top of a red spiral notebook.

Anita shrugged, unable to look at him. Instead she stared at the graph in her math book. She couldn't make heads or tails of it, but she wasn't thinking about math anyway. Somehow she had to get through this session, and then she would tell her parents she needed a different tutor. The only reason she hadn't done so over the weekend was that her father was working a hospital shift and her mother was busy with Paisley at a cheerleading tournament. She was sure Tanner would be relieved.

"Um, before we get started, can we talk for a minute?" he asked.

She looked at him, surprised. "What about?"

"Friday night." He glanced away and fidgeted with the metal spiral holding his notebook together. "I'm sorry about what happened at the party."

She already knew he regretted the kiss, but it hurt even more to hear him say it. Fighting tears, she started to stand. "It's all right," she said quickly. "This will be our last session."

His head jerked around. "What? Why?"

"I don't want you to feel like you have to tutor me. Or be around me."

"Oh boy." He ran his hand over his face. "You heard what I said, didn't you?"

Nodding, she reached for her backpack. "Don't worry, you don't have to be alone with me anymore."

He reached for her wrist, stopping her. "Can I at least explain before you leave?"

She looked at his hand on hers. He even had nice hands—long fingers, short, square fingernails, and lightly tanned skin due to his Spanish heritage. Her own hand was small underneath his, and her perpetually pale skin looked almost bleached next to his.

"I was really mad about the party," he said, releasing his grip. "I didn't want that bonehead Corey to get the wrong idea about us. That's why I said what I did."

Anita sat back down, already missing the warmth of his touch. *I'm hopeless.*

But he seemed genuinely distressed, so she had to hear him out.

"We're friends, right?" His gaze met hers.

Anita hesitated. She wished they were more than friends, but obviously he didn't feel the same way. Finally she nodded. "Right."

"I don't want to ruin that. Or our tutoring sessions. You got an A on your last test, and I think you can get one on the next test too."

"I don't know." She pushed her book toward him. "Coordinate planes."

"A piece of cake." Tanner smiled.

She almost melted in her seat right there. But she managed not to. She and Tanner were friends, and she would rather have that than nothing.

"Let's forget about Friday, okay? Then we can

focus on this." He tapped the page. "Not some idiotic party that never should have happened."

She was sure he meant the kiss too. The embrace they'd shared would be their one and only, and wishing differently wouldn't change anything. If Tanner could forget the kiss, then so could she.

But deep down, she knew she never would.

Chapter 2

April
Ten years later

"I hate the name the Four Musketeers."

"We *know*," Harper Wilson and Riley McAllister said in unison.

"You bring it up every Tuesday, Olivia." Riley's cushion-cut diamond engagement ring glinted under the fluorescent lighting as she waved her hand. Shortly after her fiancé, Hayden Price, had proposed during the grand reopening of Knots and Tangles—the yarn shop Riley co-owned with her grandmother, Erma—he had replaced the pink-yarn ring Erma had fashioned for him with the beautiful understated one she wore now. Anita held back a sigh. The proposal had been so romantic, with him dropping to one knee in front of the Bosom Buddies, Erma's long-time group of friends. Anita, Harper, and Olivia Farnsworth had been there, too, and afterward the four of them had formed their own group—one that after eight months still didn't have a name.

"Shouldn't we be talking about something more important?" Harper said. "Like your wedding, Riley. How are the plans going?"

"Good. Everything's moving right along."

Olivia nodded. "You're not worried about Tracey showing up?"

Only Olivia would be straightforward enough to bring up Riley's mother. But when Anita exchanged a glance with Harper, she saw she and Olivia weren't the only curious ones.

Riley shook her head. "No. Mimi said she was back in jail again."

"This might sound heartless, but I'm glad." Harper scowled. "You don't need her showing up and ruining everything."

"I agree. At least she's safe in jail, too." Riley sighed. "Tracey's made her choices. I've made mine. Mimi and I are our own little family, and Hayden will soon be a part of that." She smiled. "There is one little hitch, though."

"What?" Anita asked, concerned. She wanted everything perfect for Riley.

Riley took a sip of the chai tea she had fixed earlier. "Mimi is still insisting she can wear her prom dress as a grandmother-of-the-bride dress."

"You're kidding," Harper said, a horrified look crossing her face.

Riley rolled her eyes. "I wish. Fortunately, she can't find it. Her attic is full of stuff, and she's barely made a dent in the boxes. But she's *absolutely, positively* sure it's up there some-where."

"What does it look like?" Anita asked.

"You know the vinyl tablecloth she has on the

kitchen table? The one with the avocado-green and egg yolk–yellow flowers on it? Like that, but worse."

"Oh no." All three girls groaned.

"I'll take her shopping," Harper said. "I'll convince her to pick out something a little more contemporary." Harper, the fashion queen of the group, had also contributed some advice on the bridesmaids' dresses, at the bride's request.

"That would be great." Riley grinned. "I still can't believe I'm getting married."

Harper frowned. "You're not having any doubts, are you?"

Riley shook her head. "I can't imagine life without Hayden. It's surreal how much has changed since I came back to Maple Falls last year. I went from being an introverted struggling artist to being a partner in Knots and Tangles with Mimi, selling some of my work online, getting engaged, and finding the best friends a girl could ever have."

"You're still pretty introverted." Olivia crossed her short legs and looked directly at Riley. "Then again, so am I."

"Me too," Anita interjected.

"Except when you're at work," Harper pointed out. "That's when you unleash your inner extro-vert."

Anita frowned. "Is that wrong?"

Harper chuckled. "Of course not. The customers

love it. Everyone knows you're the best waitress at Sunshine. And as for me, I don't have an introverted molecule in my body, and I like it that way."

They spent the rest of the evening talking about the wedding, interspersed with reluctant discussion about choosing their group name. At nine o'clock—always at nine, the time Olivia had established when they first started their weekly meetings—they cleaned up the snacks and left the shop.

"Do you need a ride, Anita?" Olivia asked as they walked into the parking lot.

"Not tonight." She had a car, but she rarely used it. One of the perks of living in a small town was that everything she needed was within walking distance of her house—her waitressing job at Sunshine Diner, the church, and the grocery store, among other places.

As her friends got into their cars to go home, she waved goodbye to them. When they'd gone, she turned and headed around the corner to the storefronts on Main Street, the opposite direction of her house. The rubber soles of her gray slip-on tennis shoes were nearly soundless as she walked along the sidewalk past Knots and Tangles and two more empty buildings, then stopped in front of the third one, next door to the diner. When she was growing up, it had been called the Trimble Building, but now everyone referred to it as empty building #3, or just #3. A crooked *For Sale* sign sat in one of the large picture windows.

Streetlamps lit up the dark street, but she didn't need light to know every outer detail of #3, from the picture windows on each side of the dark wooden door to the splintered wooden façade that was in desperate need of repair and fresh paint. During her childhood, an antique store had lived here, run by the Trimble family, who no longer lived in Maple Falls. They'd sold the building to a bank, but during her freshman year of high school the bank had moved to another location outside of Maple Falls. Since then #3 had been empty.

She pulled her lightweight blue jacket close to ward off the spring chill. This wasn't the first time she'd stopped in this spot and contemplated her future. Once Riley and Hayden had begun their campaign last year to revitalize the town, Anita had started paying more attention to her surroundings. This old building wasn't the only thing going downhill in Maple Falls.

But what if . . .

Six months ago she had come up with a crazy idea: opening a café in #3. Not only would it be a great addition to the downtown, but it was also right next door to her current workplace. People wanting a quick cup of coffee and a snack could go to the café, and for meals they could go to the diner. The two could promote each other and maybe work together as one in the future—although it would be a challenge to get George, Sunshine's owner and her boss, on board.

But she always talked herself out of the idea, and tonight was no exception. She didn't have the brains or skills to run a business. She wouldn't even know where to start.

Then again, Riley had been a reluctant business owner too. Yet once she renovated Knots and Tangles, she had grown to love running it. The yarn shop was popular, and people from all over the state came to buy her products. She also sold yarn online to customers all over the world.

Could a café possibly be the next hot spot in Maple Falls?

Yes, if someone else opened one.

She touched the cold concrete, then turned to go home, dashing her own hopes once again.

A few feet from #3, however, she stopped. Looked in the direction of the diner. Saw the glow of the lights from the large window facing the street.

Is he still there?

Unable to stop herself, she walked the short distance to the diner, pausing at the edge of the window to peek inside. The place closed at eight, and usually the staff had clocked out and left by eight thirty. But through the wide serving window she could see Tanner, the assistant manager and Sunshine's main cook, still working in the kitchen. His head was down, and he wore his usual green baseball cap, a beat-up thing just sturdy enough for him to tuck his shoulder-length ponytail underneath.

Sigh.

Suddenly Tanner lifted his head, paused as he saw her, and waved.

Darn it. He'd caught her. When he gestured for her to come inside the diner, she couldn't refuse, not without him getting suspicious.

Act natural. She waved back and went to the front door, ignoring the *Closed* sign prominently displayed above a smaller sign showing the days and times the diner was open. She pushed against the heavy glass door and walked inside, immediately hit with the enticing smells of cumin, peppers, and cilantro mingled with the usual fried-diner-food smell. Sunshine Diner had a fifties décor, right down to the barstools and jukebox—a jukebox that hadn't worked in over a decade.

"Hey, Tanner," she said, walking toward the front counter.

"Am I glad to see you." He walked out of the kitchen. "I need a taste tester."

Not only was Tanner the best cook Sunshine had ever had, but two months ago he'd somehow convinced George to open a catering business

29

with Tanner in charge and Bailey, one of the new waitresses, assisting him. Anita knew he spent several nights a week after work tinkering with his catering menu. Sunshine Catering had booked only two small parties so far, but he worked so hard and was so good at his job she knew he would soon be adding to his client list. Just like she knew whatever he was cooking right now would undoubtedly be delicious.

Still, she hesitated. She couldn't deny that she felt nervous around Tanner. Shortly after that kiss they'd shared way back in high school, he'd stopped tutoring her to take a busboy job at a restaurant in Malvern, and she'd rarely seen him outside the scattershot times he attended Amazing Grace Church. Absence hadn't made the heart grow fonder, and she'd gotten over her crush on him. In the years that had passed since then, she'd moved on.

Or so she thought.

Three years ago, when George hired Tanner as a cook at the diner and he and Anita started working together, it hadn't taken long for those puppy-love feelings to return. Only this time it wasn't puppy love, and she had no idea what to do with the intense attraction she felt toward him—other than hide it from him. That was difficult enough for her to do when they were surrounded by coworkers and customers. This would be the first time they'd been alone.

"Unless you're busy," he said, uncertainty entering his sage-green eyes. "I don't want to impose."

Never one to turn down a request for help, she shook her head. "You're not imposing." She placed her purse on one of the round red-and-silver stools and sat down on the empty one next to it.

"Awesome." He smiled, his gorgeous eyes meeting hers.

Double sigh.

"I'll be right back." He spun around and dashed to the kitchen, then returned holding a large white plate filled with a variety of small appetizers. "These are for Harper's party," he said, putting the plate in front of her. "I thought I would add a Spanish twist to the menu and serve some of my grandmother's recipes."

She had forgotten he was catering Harper's cocktail party next Saturday night. Or rather, she'd been too surprised to find out Harper had invited her but not Olivia or Riley to think about anything else. Then again, both Olivia and Riley were busy, Olivia with her job as head of the Maple Falls library and studying for her second master's degree, and Riley with work and wedding plans. So Anita had been the one to get the invite. She still didn't know what she was going to wear. Being invited to cocktail parties didn't happen very often.

More like never.

Tanner pointed at each sample. "There's ham, cheese, and olive empanadas; Spanish tomato bread; roasted pepper–stuffed mushrooms; *patatas bravas*; and *bandarillas*."

"I didn't know you spoke Spanish," she said. He'd even rolled his *r*'s.

"I don't. Not much, anyway. My mom's family is third-generation Puerto Rican transplants, and Dad's was from Spain. I picked up some words growing up, mostly from Dad, but not many. He insisted we all speak English."

She'd known Rosa and Alonzo Castillo growing up; the Castillo family had attended the same church Anita went to. She hadn't been aware of their backgrounds, though, and Tanner had never mentioned his father to her until now. Their tutoring sessions in high school had always focused on the subject matter—or at least Tanner had. Anita couldn't say the same. Why would she pay attention to reading comprehension when she could stare at him for forty minutes?

She was aware that there was another reason he didn't talk about Alonzo. His father had died from leukemia when Tanner was eight. She was surprised, and a little honored, that he'd said something about him tonight.

"Anyway, *bon appétit*." He gestured at the tapas again.

"Isn't that French?"

"Yes, and one of only three French words I know."

She smiled. "What are the other two?"

"*Oui* and crepes. Does that make me multilingual?" He winked at her.

Her heart did a little backflip. "I think it does."

She needed to focus on the task at hand instead of how attractive Tanner was, so she examined each appetizer more closely. The patatas bravas looked like small crispy potatoes, and the bandarillas were long thin skewers of tiny pickles, pearl onions, mini sliced carrots, pieces of roasted red pepper, and various sizes of green olives. "These all look so yummy. I don't know what to try first."

"I suggest the bandarillas." He picked up a skewer and held it out to her. "I hope you don't mind anchovies."

She hadn't noticed the tiny slivers of anchovy meat in between the veggies. "I've never had them before."

He pulled the skewer back. "Maybe you should start with the potatoes, then."

"No, I don't mind trying the anchovies. And I do love olives."

He grinned again. "A woman after my own heart."

Her cheeks heated, and she focused on the bandarillas and not on her racing pulse. Two bites in, and she discovered she did like anchovies.

After several more nibbles she declared it a winner and reached for the potatoes. She paused before she picked up one of the small pieces with a toothpick. "I feel weird eating in front of you."

"Don't worry about it." He leaned against the counter, a white apron covered with food stains tied around his slim, athletic body. "I'm stuffed from snacking on all this food. I'll have to double my run this week to burn off all the calories."

"That sounds like torture."

"It's not. You should join me sometime."

She froze, the potato poised above the plate. In the three years they had worked together, he had never asked her to join him for anything. Then again, why would he? Even though they went to the same church, had played on the new church softball team Hayden had started last summer, and worked Wednesday shifts together, they interacted only superficially. Was he ready for that to change? She sure was.

"Not that I'm insinuating you need to lose calories. Or, um, weight. Because you don't. Not at all." He threw up his hands. "Forget I mentioned jogging. I'm going to shut my trap while I'm ahead."

She shoved the potato into her mouth, hiding her disappointment as she mentally noted the morsel was even more scrumptious than the skewer. She hated running, but she'd suffer through a marathon if it meant being with him.

Not that she would be able to keep up if they did go on a jog together. Tanner was the type of guy who was good at everything. Tutoring, cooking, athletics . . .

Sigh.

"Those patatas bravas must be really good."

Had she actually sighed out loud? She crammed three more bites into her mouth. "Mmmf, good," she managed before she swallowed the large mouthful. "Your grandmother must have been an excellent cook."

"The best. I never met her because she lived in Spain, and we weren't able to go over there for a visit before she passed away. I think I got the cooking gene from her, though." He tilted his head. "So what were you doing lurking around the diner?"

Oops. He was suspicious after all. "I wasn't lurking." She eyed the empanadas and picked up a small square. "We had our usual meeting at Knots and Tangles tonight."

"And you decided to walk by the diner. The exact opposite direction of your house."

Uh-oh. She was stuck. If she admitted she'd been watching him, she'd have to explain why, something she wasn't completely sure of herself. Talk about awkward and embarrassing. Maybe she should tell him about her business idea and see what he thought about it. No, that wouldn't work either. She didn't want him to think she was ready to start a café when she was 99.9 percent sure she wouldn't, shouldn't, and couldn't.

Before she could stumble through a reply, the oven timer went off, and he disappeared into the kitchen.

Whew. Saved by the bell, literally.

When he returned with a dinner plate filled with small, seasoned pieces of cauliflower, she kept him distracted. "What's this called?"

"Pan-fried cauliflower." He chuckled and pushed the plate closer to her. "I think it should have a fancier name, but that was what was on Abuela's recipe card."

Then he brought another small plate from behind his back. "Of course, we can't forget dessert."

She grinned at the piece of pecan pie topped with a dollop of whipped cream. "I didn't know this was Spanish," she said.

"It's not. Just good old southern comfort food. You deserve a reward for being my guinea pig."

The food, not to mention the time she was spending alone with him, was reward enough.

Although he'd said he was full, Tanner finished off the rest of the bandarillas while she sampled the cauliflower, which unlike its name wasn't plain at all. Tasty, like everything else he made.

"This is nice," he said, leaning against the counter again. "Why don't we hang out more?"

Anita almost fell off the stool, and despite

trying to temper her hopes, they flew sky high. *Please let him be serious this time.*

His phone buzzed, and he held up one finger and pulled it out of the pocket of a pair of khaki shorts that had seen better days, part of his Sunshine Diner uniform. He looked at the screen, frowned, then put the cell back.

"Everything okay?"

"Yeah. Maybe."

Concerned, she said, "You can return the call. I don't want you to miss something important."

"Nah, she can wait."

She?

"My girlfriend," he added.

Anita froze, her sky-high hopes crashing to the ground. He had a girlfriend. She should have known that. Someone as talented, gorgeous, and nice as him would be taken. Obviously when he had mentioned hanging out, he'd meant as friends. Or even just coworkers. The same thing he'd wanted when they were in high school.

"She's actually my ex," he said, piercing one of the pieces of cauliflower with a toothpick but not picking it up. "We started dating about a year before I got hired on here. She lives in Arkadelphia, and I met her when I was working at one of her father's restaurants in Hot Springs." He shrugged. "I'm surprised she contacted me after all this time."

At least the ex wasn't someone in Maple Falls.

But Anita wasn't exactly relieved, either. "Does she want to get back together?"

He nodded.

"Do you want to get back with her?" She held her breath, waiting for his answer.

"Not really—"

Yes!

"But maybe I should give her a chance. Just to see if there's still something there." He paused. "What do you think?"

I think you should be with me. But she couldn't tell him that, not when he was considering getting back with this girl. Woman. Whatever. She couldn't believe he was actually asking her for advice. Anita Bedford, the last person on the planet who should be giving romance tips.

Knowing the oven timer wouldn't save her again, she decided to take his question seriously. "You should only go out with her if you really want to. There's nothing worse than stringing someone along."

I should know.

Although that wasn't fair. Tanner had no idea she was attracted to him. Even the kiss they'd shared in the closet back in high school had been under duress, for him at least. It had been magical for her.

"You're right. I'll let her know I'm not interested. I don't have time to date anyway. Between working at the diner and the catering business and . . ." He paused again. "Thanks, Anita. I guess I'd better start cleaning up now. I've been working since noon, and I'm pretty beat."

Although she wondered what the "and" was on his list, she had been nosy enough for one night. "Yeah, I'm *really* tired too," she said, faking a yawn. He'd given her an out to leave and nurse her disappointment. But it wasn't in her DNA to leave a mess behind without offering to clean up. "Do you need some help?"

"Nope. But I can wrap that pie to go if you want."

Even though her appetite had disappeared the moment she heard him utter the word *girlfriend,* she nodded, not wanting to reject the offer. It only took him a few minutes to put the pie in a plastic container, and he came out of the kitchen and handed it to her across the counter. "See you tomorrow," he said.

"See ya."

She picked up her purse and hurried out of the diner, not stopping until she reached the end of the corner. She glanced at the pie container. The words *Thank You* were scrawled on the top in black Sharpie. Despite herself, she smiled. On top of everything, he was thoughtful too.

As she walked home, she felt restless. Why was she still holding on to these feelings for Tanner? If he could talk to her so casually about dating someone else, then it was obvious he wasn't romantically interested in her. Even if he was, he'd straight out said he didn't have time to date. Although if he was considering getting back with his ex, he would find time if the right person came along.

Clearly Anita wasn't that person.

Her restlessness wasn't only about Tanner, though. She enjoyed being a waitress, loved her little house that she rented from Mabel, who also worked at the diner, and cherished the preschool Sunday school class she taught. But she was twenty-six and lately had been feeling like her life was standing still. Maybe that's why she couldn't get the café idea out of her mind, even though she didn't have the courage to pursue it.

When she reached her house, she unlocked the door and started to go inside.

Meow . . . meow . . .

Not again.

For the third time this week she looked up on the roof and saw Peanut, her little white, orange, and black calico cat, perched on the edge. Actually, Peanut wasn't really her cat but a stray who had started hanging around Mabel's house two months ago. Anita had put out a bowl of food one evening a few weeks ago when it was cold. Unfortunately, she was allergic to cats and couldn't bring him inside. Which was too bad, because when he was on the roof, he wouldn't stop wailing until Anita got him down.

She went to the backyard, and as expected, he scurried over the pitched roof and met her there, the light from the streetlamp shining behind him. "This isn't funny anymore," she said, planting her hands on her hips. "I'm tired of climbing up to get you."

He lifted a paw and licked, completely unbothered.

She trudged to the shed she and Mabel shared, a wooden structure that held the lawn mower, tools, and a ladder. The shed was never locked, and a few minutes later she was scrambling up the ladder.

"Come here, you little furball." She held out her hand and Peanut walked over to her, positioning himself to be carried down the ladder. "I swear you do this on purpose."

Meow. He tucked himself into the crook of her arm and purred.

After she'd climbed down and set Peanut on the ground, made sure his food and water dishes were full, and put the ladder away, she went inside her house and set her purse on the round table in her small kitchen, her mood tanking even more than before. Even her little home, decorated with the things she loved, wasn't welcoming tonight.

She thought about #3 and the café again. About Tanner. About her friends accomplishing things with their lives while she sat in a rut. She'd had exactly four dates since high school, all of them forgettable, and zero since Tanner started working at Sunshine. That number wasn't going to change anytime soon.

The most exciting thing in her life right now was rescuing her cat.

Anita went to the sink, filled up a glass with water, and drained all of it. Something needed to change. *I have to change.*

The question was . . . could she?

Chapter 3

"Did I cut it short enough?"

Tanner blinked at his reflection in Artie's mirror. As soon as he'd sat down in the barber chair twenty minutes ago, he'd rested his eyes and let Artie do his thing. Now he couldn't recognize the guy staring back at him. "That's me?"

"Yup." Artie brushed stray hairs from Tanner's neck with a dry flat brush. "All that hair . . . poof! I bet you're disappointed about not saving your ponytail for posterity."

"I'm fine with donating it." He moved his head. What a difference. He couldn't remember the last time his hair had been this short, and his head felt lighter than it had in years. "Why did I wait so long?" he mumbled.

"I have no clue what goes through you kids' minds." Artie set aside the brush and took off the black cape from around Tanner's neck. "Like those white things you're wearing in your ears. Back in my day, men didn't wear earrings."

"Pirates beg to differ." Tanner winked.

"I ain't that old." Artie sniffed but admired his handiwork. "Who knew a good-looking guy was under all that hair?"

Tanner got up from the chair, taking one last

look at his sleek new haircut. He had the same wavy light-brown hair his father had had, straight from the Castillo Spanish heritage. "Good job, Artie."

Artie grinned, his own hair long gone except for some gray fringe at the back of his head. "Glad to have another satisfied customer."

They walked to the front of the shop, empty other than Tanner and the other barber, a young guy Tanner didn't know, who was sitting in his chair scrolling through his phone. Artie's shop was located just outside of Maple Falls and had a good reputation. But like everything around here, his business was declining.

He paid his bill and gave Artie a hefty tip.

"Don't be a stranger," the older man said, waving as Tanner walked out of the shop.

Tanner didn't intend to. After years of keeping his hair long, out of convenience more than anything, he'd finally taken the plunge and had it lopped off.

He brushed his hand over the back of his head as he headed for his red Jeep in the parking space in front of Artie's shop. After he climbed into the driver's side, he flipped down the sun visor and looked in the small mirror on the back. This time the gauges grabbed his attention. Over the past few years he'd thought about taking them out and having a dermatologist stitch up the holes. He'd seen one of his friends do the same thing a few years ago, and the scar was barely noticeable. Maybe it was time to finally make that appointment.

But not today.

He hurried home, planning to take a quick shower and wash any leftover hair off his face and neck before he went to work. When he entered the house, he could hear the sound of a telenovela blaring from the TV in the living room. What little Spanish his mother knew she had learned from watching her stories. She couldn't seem to get enough of them.

"Hey, Mom," he said to her as he walked into the living room. She was sitting in her worn-out recliner, her feet in a basin of soapy water.

"Hi, honey—" She grabbed the remote and turned down the volume. "Your hair! Where did it go?"

He laughed and sat on the couch across from her. The piece of furniture had more than a few lumps, courtesy of his younger brother, Lonzo, and his friends jumping all over it when they were preteens. When he'd caught them, he'd been so angry he chased them out of the house. Lonzo had never jumped on the couch again. "I got it cut today."

"I can see that." Mom smiled, her plump cheeks hitting the bottom of her rimless glasses. She had worn her own hair short for years, and despite being in her early fifties, she didn't have a single strand of gray. "I can't believe you finally did it." She stared at him and clasped her hands. "Oh, you are so handsome."

"And you're biased, but thanks." He glanced at her feet in the basin. Today was her day off from her full-time job at the bottling company, but on those mornings she picked up an extra job from the cleaning company she worked for part time. He'd noticed she was soaking her feet more often lately. "How was your morning?"

She leaned back in the recliner, a chair almost as old as he was. "Long."

"You don't have to work two jobs, Mom—"

"We're not having this discussion again." She gave him a sharp look.

He was used to seeing that expression whenever they talked about the subject, but he didn't let it stop him from saying his piece. "Lonzo is almost done with college, and I make enough money for us to live on."

"Because you work two jobs, right?"

She had him there. He got paid more as an assistant manager than a regular cook, and they could get by with him working only that job. But taking on the catering business meant the extra cash cushion he was counting on for his future plans—plans he wasn't ready to reveal. "I don't mind," he said, knowing he was losing the battle before it even started.

"And I don't mind either. What if Lonzo

decides to go to graduate school? He's been talking about it lately."

"I'm sure he'll find a way to pay for it. He's at the head of his class, and they'll probably give him a scholarship. He won't have a problem with school, and he'll for sure find a job as a chemical engineer when the time comes."

Mom lifted her chin. "What if you lose your job?"

Tanner almost smiled. *If only she knew.* "That's not going to happen."

"How do you know? Bad things happen, Tanner. We must always be prepared."

Good grief, the woman could be stubborn. He couldn't blame her, though. She had raised him and Lonzo on her own after their father died at thirty-four, almost nineteen years ago. Since then she had worked at least two, sometimes three, jobs to make sure he and his brother had every-thing they needed to succeed. But it was past time for her to take a break. "At least quit the cleaning job."

She snatched the remote and turned the volume back on higher than it was before.

Shaking his head, he rose from the sofa. "I have to get ready for work."

When she didn't respond, he headed to the bathroom upstairs. He quickly showered, then dressed in his work clothes and headed for Sunshine for the late lunch/supper shift. When he arrived at the diner, he stepped out of his Jeep and saw Bailey carrying a large bag of trash out the door, destined for the dumpster.

She paused, the midday sun glinting off her neon-red hair. "Tanner? Is that you?"

"Yep." He hadn't expected everyone to be so surprised.

"Nice," she said.

"Thanks." Reaching for the black garbage bag, he said, "I'll take that for you."

She handed it to him and went back inside while he headed for the dumpster. He flipped up the lid and tossed the trash in, then went into the diner to wash his hands before clocking in. When he was finished, he went to George's office and grabbed his card from the slot next to the time clock. Unsurprisingly, George wasn't around. Over the past six months or so, he'd seemed disinterested in the business he had run for almost forty years.

Tanner punched his card and went into the kitchen. Fred, the morning cook, was flipping burgers on the griddle.

"How's business today?" Tanner asked, his usual greeting at the beginning of his shifts.

"Kinda slow. Not that I'm complaining . . . Whoa." Fred's heavy-lidded eyes widened. "Who's this clean-cut guy? You join the army and not tell me?"

"Ha-ha." The ribbing was going to get old

quick, but he could handle it. "I'm not the military type, so you're stuck with me."

"Wouldn't have it any other way." Fred turned and slid a spatula under one of the sizzling burgers. He had started at Sunshine right after George took over running the place from his father and was happy with his job. When Tanner was promoted to assistant manager, Fred supported the decision, even though he'd been passed over. He'd assured Tanner that managing Sunshine was the last thing he wanted to do.

Mabel bustled into the kitchen and nearly skidded to a halt. "Well, I'll be. Mark this day down as a miracle. Tanner Castillo finally got a haircut."

"Now you can stop bugging me to get one."

She inspected Artie's work. "Looks good. You'll be shooing away all the single ladies now."

He doubted he'd be shooing away anyone. "Thanks, Mabel."

"Does this mean I can burn your ratty cap?" When he nodded, she opened up a cabinet near the kitchen entrance, pulled out a hairnet, and handed it to him, chuckling. "Now you have to wear this."

Tanner rolled his eyes and slipped the hairnet onto his head. "I'll be scaring off the ladies with this thing, not attracting them."

"Doubt it." She moved past him to the other

side of the kitchen, where she made the pies Sunshine was famous for. "I'm plumb befuddled that a young man like you is still single."

He grabbed an onion and started chopping. "Haven't found the right girl," he said.

"Maybe she's right under your nose."

Tanner looked up and saw that Anita had walked into the kitchen to start her shift. He couldn't help but smile. She had showed up at just the right time last night, and he appreciated her input not only on the tapas but also on his ex. As he was cleaning up after she'd left, he'd thought about something that hadn't crossed his mind in years: the kiss they'd shared in high school. Even now he remembered how intense it was—by a seventeen-year-old's standards. She'd said she had never kissed anyone before, but he'd had a hard time believing that, considering the way she kissed him.

Since then, they seemed to live in different orbits. He'd worked in restaurants in other cities until the cook job at Sunshine had opened up, and after he'd been hired, he'd been busy learning the job, getting promoted, and convincing George to start the catering business.

But spending time with her last night had been nice. More than nice. He appreciated the way she hadn't hesitated to help him taste-test food she'd never tried before, and her gastronomical bravery in trying the anchovies—an ingredient most people either loved or loathed—was impressive. Best of all was her sigh when she tried the patatas bravas. That had been one of the sexiest things he'd ever seen *and* heard.

Muy caliente.

Then he'd gotten that text from his ex, and Anita's mood had shifted, as if she had closed herself off, leaving him confused and disappointed. She had also seemed uncomfortable when he asked her for advice, so he'd cut that conversation short and ended the evening. He probably shouldn't have brought up his ex with her, but he'd really wanted to know what she thought.

He stilled. *Oh no.* He'd completely forgotten to call Heather last night. His thoughts had been more on Anita and the past than on nipping things in the bud with Heather. He'd have to do that after his shift was over.

Bailey entered the kitchen and poked Anita in the shoulder. "What do you think of Tanner's haircut?"

Anita turned, and their gazes met. She had the most beautiful amber-colored eyes, something he'd noticed both when they were in school together and last night too. Back then she'd been cute in an awkward way, and the braces she wore hadn't helped. But when she had showed up at his party and smiled and revealed she'd had them taken off, he'd been a little knocked out. Kind of like he was now. Why hadn't he noticed until last night how pretty she was? Had he been that distracted? Apparently so.

When she didn't say anything, he remembered the hairnet he'd shoved on a few minutes ago. "I know, I know," he said, "I look ridiculous."

"No," she said, still staring at him. "You look very handsome."

Her compliment made him beam, and he wondered again why they didn't spend more time together. They'd known each other most of their lives, and they had worked together for the past three years. She was single, as far as he knew.

And I'm single. Maybe Mabel was on to something.

"Uh, I mean, you look okay. The haircut, I mean. It's okay." Anita turned and kept her back to him, fussing with the white apron she wore over her pink uniform, even though the bow she'd tied at the back was already perfectly straight. "I'd better check on the customers."

And just like that, the idea of suggesting they go out disappeared.

He continued chopping, his eyes immune to onion tears due to the thousands he'd diced and sliced over the years. What had he been thinking, considering asking Anita to hang out with him? She'd never let on that she was interested in doing anything with him.

Except for the kiss.

But that had been when they were kids, and peer pressure hadn't given them much choice. It wasn't like he had time to do anything other than work, anyway.

Man, he was tired. That had to be why he'd had that wayward thought. Working two jobs, picking up extra shifts, and taste-testing his grandmother's recipes over the last week were all taking a toll. Then there was his worry about his mother working too hard. How ironic. He needed to follow his own advice and take a break.

I will . . . someday.

After the lunch rush was over and Fred, Mabel, and Bailey had clocked out, Tanner glanced through the serving window and was surprised to see Jasper Mathis walk through the door. Normally he could set his watch by Jasper's punctuality, since the man arrived every week-day afternoon precisely at four thirty, but for some reason today he was two hours early. Tanner nodded at him as he took his seat on the left side, facing the front door so he could watch who came in and out. The eighty-something-year-old man spent almost all his time in down-town Maple Falls, whether working at Price Hardware as a volunteer employee or hanging out at Sunshine to jaw with the customers. But the diner was dead right now. Maybe he had come in to kill some time before he ordered his early-bird special.

Tanner went back to work, placing unbaked rolls on a large tray.

"Tanner?"

He turned as Anita walked into the kitchen. The *something* that had sparked the idea of asking her out had disappeared, thankfully. The last thing he wanted was for things to be awkward between them. "What's up?"

"There's someone who wants to see you," she said, her brow furrowing.

He slid the tray into an empty slot in the rack next to the oven. "Who is it?"

"She said her name is Heather."

He froze.

Anita moved closer to him, her frown deepening. "She also said she was your girlfriend."

He almost muttered a curse under his breath, but he tried to watch his mouth around women, something his mother had drilled into him almost since birth. "What's she doing here?"

Anita shrugged. "Is she the one you were talking about last night?"

"Yeah." He started to shove his hand through his hair, only to get his fingers tangled up in his hairnet. "I forgot to text her back last night. I was so tired I collapsed into bed."

Anita's expression was blank. "What do you want me to tell her?"

To go away. But that wouldn't be right. He should have told Heather he didn't want to see

54

her again, and he should have said it when she first started contacting him a month ago. "I'll be right out."

After Anita left he stared at the raw rolls in front of him. He didn't like that Heather had told Anita she was his girlfriend. They'd only texted a few times, although lately she had been sending messages more frequently. He'd have to set her straight, that's all. At least they didn't have any customers, other than Jasper. All Tanner had to do was tell her the truth, and Heather would have to accept it. Easy enough.

Anita forced a smile at the woman standing on the opposite side of the counter. "Tanner will be out in a minute."

Heather sat down on one of the red barstools. "I take my coffee black, by the way."

"Yes, ma'am." Anita was always polite to customers, even the very few rude ones she'd encountered over the years—but most people in Maple Falls were friendly. She grabbed a mug from under the counter, filled it with coffee, and set it in front of Heather, who was scrolling through her phone, her long red fingernails clacking against the screen. She didn't acknowledge Anita when she picked up the coffee and took a sip.

"Yuck." She set the coffee down and pushed it away, then resumed scrolling through her phone.

Anita tried not to take her attitude personally. The diner coffee wasn't as delicious as a high-end coffee shop would offer.

She covertly studied Heather a moment. Although the woman looked to be around her and Tanner's age, her juvenile behavior implied something else, and so did her wardrobe. She wore a too-short black miniskirt with fishnet tights, a low-cut red blouse, and a formfitting and cropped black leather jacket. This woman was Tanner's type?

Her thoughts screeched to a halt. She wasn't in the habit of judging people, and she didn't need to start now. "Do you need anything else?" she asked before heading over to Jasper. She liked to visit with him when she had time, and right now he would give her an excuse to escape.

Heather set down her phone. "I thought you said Tanner was on his way."

"That's what he told me."

"Go get him again." She rolled her eyes. "Gah, the service here sucks."

Anita's teeth clenched until her jaw hurt. *Be polite . . . be polite . . .*

"Anita!" Jasper called out.

She relaxed her mouth and looked at him. "Yes, Mr. Mathis?"

"Can you bring me some extra sugar?"

She hadn't even brought him his tea yet. "There's sugar at your table—"

"Please."

She nodded and turned from Heather, who was now holding up her phone and making the peace sign in front of her face while she took a selfie.

Anita grabbed a few packets and took them over to Jasper. "You shouldn't be having these, Mr. Mathis," she said, lowering her voice as she handed them to him. "You need to watch your sugar."

He motioned for her to sit down, then brushed the packets to the side. "Who's that hussy at the counter?"

Her mouth twitched, and she almost smiled before glancing to see if Heather had heard him. But she was still taking selfies, this time holding up her coffee cup and pretending to drink it as if it were a latte from heaven. Anita, feeling more than a niggle of guilt, whispered to Jasper, "That's not very nice."

"Who cares if it's nice. It's the truth," he said as she sat down across from him. At least he was speaking in a semi-whisper this time. "She needs to put some clothes on."

Anita agreed, but she kept her mouth shut.

Tanner finally walked out of the kitchen and over to Heather. She noticed he stayed behind the counter, and he started to put his hand on his head, then dropped it to his side as if he remembered he was still wearing the hairnet. He had to be the only guy who made a hairnet look good.

Ugh, she was doing it again—pining. An old-fashioned word, but one that perfectly explained what she couldn't stop doing.

"Can't imagine why Tanner would have anything to do with that—"

"Mr. Mathis," Anita warned.

"*Misguided* young woman." He scowled and waved a large-knuckled hand in Tanner and Heather's direction.

She should get Jasper his tea, but since he hadn't asked for it yet and he seemed to be engrossed with Tanner and Heather right now, she stayed put. She tilted her head toward them, trying to hear what they were saying. Or rather what Heather was saying. Tanner simply stood with his arms crossed, nodding his head as she continued to talk.

The bell above the diner door rang out as two couples she didn't recognize walked inside. All Sunshine diners seated themselves, and as they decided on a table, Anita stood. "I'll get your tea," she said to Jasper. "Do you need anything else?"

"Supper," he said, still staring at Tanner and Heather. "I skipped lunch, and I'm peckish."

Anita nodded. But as she made her way over to the two couples on the opposite side of the diner, her heart sank. Heather was leaning forward and showing Tanner not only her phone but almost everything the good Lord had given her from the waist up. If that wasn't bad enough, their heads were almost touching.

"Excuse me, miss?" One of the women lifted her hand. "Can we get a menu, please?"

"Oh, of course. I'm sorry." Anita hurried to the end of the counter and grabbed four menus, trying to ignore Tanner and Heather as she went over to the table. "Our specials are on the board," she said, handing them their menus. "Can I get you something to drink?"

She tried to focus on their orders, something she could do in her sleep. But when Heather giggled behind her, her pencil tip snapped against the menu pad.

"Did you catch our order?" a man with a white straw hat said, looking at the broken pencil point.

"Yes. Two iced teas, one Diet Coke, and a glass of water."

"Thank you."

Anita shoved the broken pencil behind her ear and headed for the drink machine.

"See you later, Tanner," Heather said, sliding off the stool. She swung her long brown hair, streaked with blond, behind one shoulder and slipped the strap of an expensive-looking purse over the other one.

"Uh, see you." Tanner gave her a quick wave.

Anita scurried to the kitchen and filled the drinks before anyone noticed she was lingering. When Tanner followed her, all she said was,

"Jasper's hungry." He nodded and started on the man's supper—one slice of pot roast, green beans, a dinner roll, and mashed potatoes, no gravy. She filled Jasper's tea glass, set it on the tray with the other beverages, grabbed another pencil from the cup by the door, and went back to the dining room.

Envy swirled within her, along with a fat dose of irritation. Tanner obviously hadn't taken her advice last night, or even today since Heather had said she would see him later. Had he even seriously considered what she said, or was he just being polite when he thanked her? And what about him being too busy to date? Was he lying about that too?

None of this lined up with the Tanner she knew . . . or thought she knew. She reminded herself that there were years of his life she knew nothing about. But still, she'd never imagined a woman like Heather would be a part of that life.

For the rest of the afternoon and evening she tried not to think about the two of them as she completed her shift with Pamela and Kevin, who had clocked in at four. It helped that Tanner hadn't said much. No doubt he was thinking about being with Heather, while Anita was struggling not to picture the two of them together.

After the diner closed, she dawdled in the kitchen while everyone left except for her and

Tanner. He had taken off his apron and hairnet and was smoothing down his newly short hair. He didn't need to bother because the light-brown waves were still perfect. She'd always liked his long hair, but now that it was short . . . *Swoon.*

Stop it! She needed to leave now, while she was still upset and confused. All she had to do was go to George's office, clock out, and put Tanner and that *misguided* woman out of her mind.

Tanner walked up behind her. "Anita?"

Warmth traveled her spine at his low, husky voice. *I'm hopeless.*

"Would you mind closing up for me? I'm kind of in a hurry."

His words hit her like a bucket of cold lemonade, a Sunshine Diner staple in the summertime. "Sure." Trying to be nonchalant, she turned around, twirling the pencil she was holding between her fingers. Two twirls in and it flew out of her hand, hitting the floor.

"I got it." Before she could move, he had already swooped it up.

When he handed it to her, she blurted, "Do you have plans tonight?"

"Last-minute ones, yeah."

That confirmed he was going to see Heather.

She'd better appreciate you.

His brow furrowed. "What?"

Had she said that out loud? She had to stop doing that in front of him. "Nothing." Her forced laugh sounded like she was choking on a basket of fries.

"Thanks for locking up. You're the best." He dashed out of the kitchen, obviously in a hurry.

She stood alone, surrounded by the scents of grease and bleach. The green monster had appeared in her heart again, no matter how many times she told it to go away. But really, what right did she have being jealous? Tanner could do what he wanted. Date whom he wanted. Maybe Heather was a nice girl. So what if she wore too much makeup and left too little to the imagination? If she was what Tanner wanted, then Anita had no choice but to accept that.

She searched her purse for the spare diner key she always carried with her. As she shut off the lights, she shut down her last hope for romance with Tanner. Even if he and Heather didn't work out, Anita wasn't anywhere close to his type, now that she knew what his type was. She didn't wear makeup, she loved her pixie haircut, and when she did dress up it was usually in pastel, feminine colors. There was nothing flashy about her, and she wasn't going to change for him or anyone else.

But she could change for herself.

As soon as she locked up the diner, she fished her phone out of her purse and called Harper.

Her friend answered on the first ring. "Hey, Anita."

She drew in a deep breath. *Now or never.* "I need you to do something for me."

"Sure, anything."

"Help me open up a coffee shop."

Chapter 4

This is what I get for being a nice guy.

Tanner ran his hand through his hair and grimaced. He smelled like a grease pit, and all he wanted to do was get home and take a shower. Instead he was helping Heather fix her Jeep. But the more he looked at her engine, the more he suspected she didn't have a problem at all—at least not with her vehicle.

He kept his gaze on the machinery in front of him. If he weren't so irritated, he would take his time and appreciate all the features of her brand-new, top-of-the-line vehicle. He could only dream of a car like this. He had bought his own Jeep secondhand, a ten-year-old vehicle that had a decent exterior and ran almost like it was brand new thanks to his and the previous owner's meticulous care. He was happy with his car, but it was nothing compared to the latest the Chrysler company had rolled out this year.

"Are you sure there's nothing wrong?" Heather moved next to him, leaning so far over that if he even glanced to the right, he would get an eyeful for the second time that day.

He stared at the shiny radiator cap. "Nope. Nothing that I can tell. But I'm not a mechanic."

"I swear it was making a funny noise earlier

tonight. The other night you said you had a Jeep—

"I did?"

"In one of your texts. Anyway, I thought you could figure out the problem." She moved closer to him, touching his shoulder. "I also remember how good you used to be with your hands."

Cringe. She hadn't changed much over the years, except for wearing more makeup and fewer clothes—and both distracted from her attractiveness. She didn't have to try so hard or be so insecure. That insecurity was one of the reasons he'd stopped dating her.

"You should take this back to the dealer and let them take a look." He closed the hood of the Jeep, regretting he hadn't texted her last night like he'd told Anita he would.

"I don't know how to thank you," she purred, slinking even closer to him. "I was worried there was something really wrong with it."

Sure you were.

He couldn't believe she had driven all the way from Arkadelphia to ask him to look at her Jeep, and he'd agreed to do so only so she would leave the diner and stop showing him her selfies on her phone. They'd met as Rusty's Garage, and even though it was closed, the bright parking-lot lights were perfect for looking at the engine. It was also a neutral location. He'd half expected her not to show up and was disappointed when she did.

Where had she been the last five hours while he finished his shift? He was starting to wonder if Heather was a little off her nut.

"Why don't you and I go get a drink and celebrate?" she asked, pursing her red-lipped mouth.

He backed away. "Uh, celebrate what?"

"That my car is all right." She patted the hood. "I really love this baby."

She loved it so much that when he'd checked the oil it was almost two quarts low. "Make sure the dealer puts some oil in the engine."

"I will, promise." She made an *X* with her fingers across her chest, right where he shouldn't be looking. He had to admit she had nice . . . assets. Always had. But a toned body didn't make up for incompatibility. "Now, about that drink—"

"I've got an early shift tomorrow," he lied, hurrying to his car.

She quickly followed him, her high heels tapping against the concrete. "Tomorrow night, then?"

He paused, seeing where this was going. He could keep running away from her, or he could set her straight. "Look, Heather," he said, meeting her gaze. "I don't think we should see each other again."

A spark of anger flashed across her face, only to morph into a sweet smile. "Why not? We had so much fun together when we were dating, didn't we?"

Now that he was fully remembering their relationship, the fun times had been few and far between. What could he tell her that would make her leave him alone but wouldn't hurt her feelings?

She moved closer to him. "One date, Tanner. That's all I ask. For old times' sake. I'll definitely make it worth your while."

Panicked, he blurted the first thing that came to mind. "I'm, uh, kind of seeing someone."

Her heavily mascaraed eyes hardened. "You gave me the impression you were single."

Uh-oh. "I did?" He racked his brain. Had he said that in any of his texts? He couldn't remember. He needed to pay more attention to what he texted—and to whom he was texting it.

"Yes. Your Facebook profile says it too."

Facebook? He rarely posted anything on his profile, and when he did, it was usually about a special at Sunshine or the catering business. Even then he'd been lax in using social media. Had she been stalking him virtually? He didn't like lying, but desperate times and all that . . .

"I'm sorry you got the wrong idea, but my girlfriend and I have been together a long time—"

"You just said you were *kinda* seeing her."

Yikes. Time to regroup. "We started dating recently," he said, searching for a valid response. "But we've been friends for a long time."

"What's her name?"

"Anita."

Uh-oh. Why had he said *her* name? He could have said anyone else, even Bailey. But no, without hesitation he'd said Anita.

"The waitress at the diner?"

If he could sink into Rusty's oil-spotted parking lot, he would. But he couldn't turn back now. "Yes. She's my girlfriend."

Rolling her eyes, Heather crossed her arms over her chest. "I find that hard to believe, Tanner."

"Well, believe it. We're serious too." Why tell one lie when he could tell a dozen? Anita was going to strangle him for dragging her into this mess.

"Right." Heather shook her head. "A waitress. You're choosing a homely waitress over all this." She gestured to her body and then patted her expensive Jeep.

Tanner's jaw jerked. She could insult him but not Anita. "You're out of line, Heather." He opened the driver's side door before he lost his cool and said—or did—something he would regret.

"You can do a lot better than her," Heather shouted as he slammed the door.

He started the car, yanked the gearshift down, and spun out of the parking lot. His house wasn't far from Rusty's, and when he pulled into his driveway and put his car into Park, he drew in a deep breath. What a mess. Not only because of

Heather, who was positively a hot one, but also because he had used Anita as an excuse. His hands gripped the steering wheel. All he could do was hope Heather had gotten the message—and that Anita didn't find out he had lied about their relationship.

But what if Heather ended up coming into the diner again? He banged his head against the back of the headrest. How was he going to explain all this to Anita?

Maybe he wouldn't have to.

He took out his phone and blocked Heather's number. She'd been so furious when he left, she likely wouldn't contact him again, especially when she found out she couldn't text him any-more. So there was no reason to tell Anita what he'd done—not right now, anyway. And if Heather did show up, he would deal with her on his own. Something he should have done in the first place.

When Anita arrived home after her shift at the diner, and after she'd rescued Peanut from the roof again, she went straight to her snack cabinet and grabbed the box of Little Debbie brownies—with colored sprinkles—she'd stupidly bought at the grocery store earlier that week. She walked into her living room, plopped on the couch, and plowed through two packages before she had a single coherent thought. There were still four packets left, and she was tempted to eat them all. Knowing she would probably end up throwing up if she did, she refrained. But only barely.

Her gaze darted to her living room floor. The empty wrappers and half-eaten box of brownies lay on the cream-colored carpet next to her sofa. Ugh, her stomach hurt.

I shouldn't have done that.

She got up and took a shower to wash off the diner smells from her skin and hair. Normally she did that the moment she got off from her shift, but after setting the café in motion she'd needed her caloric comfort. By the time she finished talking with Harper—who, bless her, had agreed to help her with the purchase of #3—her nerves had been shot. And whenever that happened, Little Debbie always came to the rescue.

But the café wasn't the only thing she was stressing about. Not only was she starting a new career chapter in her life, but she'd be changing her personal life too. Leaving Tanner behind was for the best, especially now that he was getting back with, *ew,* Heather. But how did someone shut off feelings? Especially when those feelings had apparently simmered unrequited for years? She had to have held the record for the longest case of futile infatuation in the universe. One thing she did know: she was done spending the rest of her life wanting someone who would never want her back. How she'd accomplish that was still a mystery.

Once she finished her shower, finger combed her damp hair, and put on her nightshirt, she cleaned up the wrappers, put the uneaten brownies in the cabinet, and settled on the couch. Desperate for a distraction, she found her favorite TV channel, Animals 24/7. But even the cute little puppies chasing each other around didn't help, and her thoughts continued to ping-pong between the café and Tanner. She feared that calling Harper on the fly had been more of a reaction to Tanner and Heather than a carefully thought-out decision. Should she call her back and cancel? They'd spoken less than two hours ago, and her friend would understand that six months hadn't been enough time to consider her plan.

Anita jumped at the sound of her ringtone, a song about letting go, then grimaced. She'd purchased the phone a month ago and thought it would be fun to have her favorite movie song as a ringtone. The fun had lasted about a week, and now every time the phone rang, she promised herself to change the tone—and every single time she forgot, since she communicated mostly by text. In fact, the only person who actually called her was . . . Uh-oh.

She reached for her cell on the coffee table and looked at the screen. *Mother.* Great. She wasn't in the mood to talk to her or anyone else, and she was tempted to skip the call—something she had done before. But the last time she had, her mother had called and left voice mails every twenty minutes until Anita picked up. She wasn't prepared to hear her phone ring more than once tonight.

"Hi, Mom."

"Hello, sweetheart. How are you? I haven't heard from you in days."

"I talked to you yesterday morning."

"Oh? Well, time flies, doesn't it? I'm just calling to see if you're coming to brunch next Sunday."

"I always come to brunch, Mom. Kingston is picking me up."

"Again? I don't understand the point of you having a car if you never drive it. Although considering your car, that's probably a good idea."

Anita closed her eyes. Her older brother, Kingston, had been taking her to their monthly brunch for the past four months now, unless he was on duty at the hospital. Giving her a ride had been his idea because they were rarely able to spend time together anymore. "I like riding with Kingston," she said, not bothering to explain the reason. "And my car is fine." At least it had been up until this morning. Before her shift she had decided to drive to Malvern to check out the two cafés in town. Just for fun. Then she'd discovered her car wouldn't start. Her mother didn't need to know that either.

"Very well. But if you ever decide to get a new one, your father and I will be glad to help. We've attended several social events with Mr. Cochran and his wife."

"Who are they?"

"He owns three Ford dealerships. One in Hot Springs, one in Benton, and one in North Little Rock."

"That's nice." Anita pinched the bridge of her nose.

"I'm sure he'll sell us a nice car at a good price."

She didn't miss the *us* in her mother's statement. And that was the problem. She didn't want her parents to buy her a car, or anything else. She might not drive a Lexus like her younger sister, Paisley, or live in an expensive condo like Kingston, but she had bought her car on her own.

"Shall I talk to Nate?"

"About what?"

"Your new car." Her mother huffed. "Are you even listening to me?"

"Sorry, Mom. It's been a long day."

"Did you work a double shift? I told you not to be on your feet so long. It would be a shame if you got bunions at your age."

"I didn't work a double, and I don't have bunions. I'm tired, that's all."

"I have the perfect remedy for sleep. First, you brew some organic Provo blood orange tea.

Oh, wait, you probably can't afford that. It's expensive. I'll give you a box when you come on Sunday."

Blood-orange tea? Blech. "Thanks, Mom."

"Has Paisley talked to you about the bridesmaids' dresses?"

Her mother could change subjects with whiplash speed, and lately her favorite topic was Paisley's wedding, even though it was more than a year off. Both Paisley and her fiancé, Ryan, were in their last year of law school in Texas. "Not yet."

"Hmm. I'll have to give her a nudge to do that soon."

"I'm sure she's been busy."

"Of course, but that doesn't mean she should shirk the wedding planning. I managed to work full time and get my master's degree in counseling and raise the three of you, all while being voted president of the PTA six years running. It's all about time management. I'll be happy to show you my planner. I couldn't live without it."

"I thought we were talking about Paisley?"

"Ah, yes, we were. I'll have to show *her* my planner. *Again.* I have every wedding planning appointment scheduled. In *ink*."

Anita rolled her eyes. *If* she ever got married, she was totally going to elope.

Fortunately, her mother switched the conversation to her latest volunteering venture at Garvan Gardens, a large, beautiful botanical garden in Hot Springs National Park that was a popular attraction with both Arkansans and tourists.

"All right, dear," she said after describing several of the items she had helped sell in the garden's gift shop. "I'm eager to see you next Sunday. So is your father."

Anita's heart softened. Her mother was overbearing and a little high-strung, but she meant well. And Anita was happy she'd see her father, who was often as booked as Kingston was. Both were doctors—her father a cardiologist and Kingston a pediatrician. "I can't wait," she said sincerely.

"Ta-ta for now."

"Bye, Mom." She hung up, shaking her head at her mother's trademark sign-off. She had to admit she felt a little better after talking to her. That wasn't always the case, since her mother could be insensitive at times too. She meant well, but her delivery system wasn't always the best, despite her master's degree.

She walked over to the calendar hanging on the wall. The picture for the month was a set of colorful teacups perched on a bleached wooden shelf. She looked at her work schedule for the rest of April, prefilled because her shifts rarely changed. Time management. She needed to get some if she was going to work at Sunshine *and* open the café. While she had a large amount in savings, she couldn't afford to buy and renovate #3 outright. She'd have to get a loan, and she wouldn't be able to do that without an income stream coming in. She wasn't great with numbers, but she knew that much.

Eventually she'd have to leave Sunshine. The thought saddened her. She had worked there for such a long time, and George was a good boss, even though he hadn't been around much lately. She would miss chatting with the customers and working with Mabel and Fred.

And Tanner.

That thought launched another attack of nerves, but she resisted the chocolate this time. *I can do this. I will do this.* Not only opening the café but getting rid of her feelings for Tanner.

She was doing the right thing, for herself and for Maple Falls.

As long as she kept telling herself that, she would eventually believe it

Chapter 5

On Thursday Tanner arrived at the diner and walked into the office, ready to punch his time card. When he opened the door, he was surprised to see George sitting at his old desk. "Hey," he said, heading over to the time clock. "Long time no see."

George turned around in the squeaky office chair. "Hey, Tanner. Good job with the books this month. I see we've turned a little profit over the winter."

"The catering business helped." He inserted his card in the time clock, then stuck it in the nearby holder.

"Don't go to the kitchen yet. I need to talk to you." George squinted at him. "You look different today."

Tanner almost laughed. Leave it to George not to notice the obvious. "I got a haircut."

"That's it. Suits you. Close the door for me, will ya?"

Tanner closed the door, a little uneasy. George rarely wanted to talk to him privately.

"Yep. I gotta admit, the catering business was a good idea," George said.

His tense shoulders relaxed. He was more than

happy to talk about catering. "Even though I had to twist your arm?"

"You didn't have to twist it much." George frowned. "I should have thought of it a long time ago."

That was as close as he'd ever heard George come to admitting a mistake.

"You've got a good business head on your shoulders," his boss continued. "You're the best assistant manager I've ever had. I never have to worry about payroll, scheduling, making sure supplies are ordered and the bills paid on time. You've pretty much put me out of a job."

George ran his palms over his baggy jeans. "I gotta admit, my heart hasn't been in this place for a long while now. The other day I realized Sunshine is almost eighty years old. Did you know it started as a hot-dog cart on the corner here?"

Tanner nodded. He'd heard this story more than once, but not in a long while. The unease returned.

"Sunshine's had a few updates over the decades, and more than her fair share of turbulent times, but overall she's pretty much the same business she was back then. We were in our heyday in the fifties and sixties when I was still a young'un. I'd hoped to pass her down to my kids, but the good Lord didn't see fit to give us any."

Why was George taking this trip down memory lane? "Has something happened?"

George looked up at him, his expression

wistful. "The era of the Sewell family owning Sunshine Diner is coming to an end. I'm going to sell the place, Tanner."

He was too shocked to speak. There was no way George could know about his plans to talk to him about buying the diner. No one knew because he hadn't told a single soul. Not his mother, nor his brother, nor even his best friend, Hayden. Since his promotion to assistant manager, he'd wanted to buy Sunshine when the time was right. Truth was he'd always wanted to own a restaurant, ever since he started working as a busboy when he was in high school. He loved cooking and making people happy with his creations, enjoyed all the tasks required to run a successful business, and he was confident in his abilities. He'd worked hard and scrimped and saved for nearly a decade, waiting for the opportunity when he had enough money. Right now he had more than enough to make a fair offer. "Funny you should say that, George, because—"

"I got an offer yesterday afternoon."

Tanner's train of thought squealed to a halt. "What?"

"Out of the blue, some guy contacted me and said he was a lawyer representing a prospective buyer who wanted to remain anonymous. Caught me by surprise, but I didn't have to think too hard about it. I'm not ready to tell the rest of the crew, but I wanted you to know. I owe you that much."

His brain spun. All his plans for Sunshine and all those years of hard work were circling the drain. "How much did he offer?"

When George told him the amount, Tanner almost passed out.

"I know that's a lot for this place, but I'd be a fool not to take it. I'm ready to let go, Tanner. Have been for a while, but I guess I needed the kick in the pants to make me do it." George chuckled. "And that was a huge kick, let me tell you. I'll be set for life even if I live to be one hundred and twenty. Make that one hundred and twenty-five."

Tanner's mouth stretched into a tight smile. His hands and brow were already growing damp, but he didn't want George to see him sweat. The amount was ridiculously high. "Don't you want to know who the buyer is?"

George shrugged. "Don't need to. Not for that kind of money."

"But what if he tears it all down?"

George paused. "Hadn't thought about that."

"Wouldn't it be terrible if all the hard work your family put into Sunshine disappeared?"

His boss rubbed his chin. "Yep. That would be plumb awful, for sure."

Good, now Tanner had some breathing room.

"But I can't hang on to Sunshine forever," George said, sitting back in his chair. He folded his hands over his large belly. "I can't keep on waitin' for someone who loves this place the way I used to."

"You don't have to wait." Tanner grabbed the one spare chair in the room, an old fold-up, and sat in front of him. "I want to buy Sunshine, George. I promise I'll take care of this diner and honor what your family has done for Maple Falls over the years. I have a few ideas for some upgrades—"

"Upgrades?" George lifted a gray brow.

"A computerized cash register, replacing the old linoleum with tile, and . . ." He smiled for real this time. "Putting in a gourmet coffee bar."

George rubbed his chin again. "I can see updating the cash register and linoleum," he said, "but why waste money on fancy coffee?"

"The diner won't lose money. It will make money." He explained how coffee shops were not only popular but also a financial boon. "People take their coffee seriously nowadays. We don't have to turn Sunshine into a full café. We can keep the diner and add on a small coffee bar where the jukebox is. Customers can order from there, and we'll have the sugars and syrups and creamers available on the bar. All we need is a barista or two, and we're good to go."

"What's a barista?"

Tanner almost face palmed. George really was old school. "An employee who makes coffee."

"Like what our waitresses do now."

"No, that's different." He fought for patience. He didn't want to get sidetracked by details when his future hung in the balance. "What do you say, George? I can buy the diner from you right now."

"For the same amount as the other offer? In cash?"

"Cash?" he said faintly.

"The offer was cash."

Tanner wouldn't have pegged George as a greedy guy. Then again, he didn't know the man's financial situation. He also wasn't sure he would be able to resist an offer of financial security if he were in George's shoes, either. "Yes. I can match the offer."

George tapped his fingers against the tops of his knees and stared at the floor. Finally he looked at Tanner again. "I don't know, Tanner. I'd really like to take you up on this. It doesn't feel right to back out of the other deal, though. Maybe I just need to stick with the other guy's offer."

Not willing to be outbid, Tanner blurted, "I can offer you more."

One of George's gray eyebrows lifted. "How much more?"

After some quick, desperate calculations, Tanner said, "Ten percent."

"Are you sure? That's a lot of money. A *whole* lot of money."

Tanner swallowed. "I'm sure. In cash." His boss was going to bleed him dry.

George held out his hand. "Deal."

Tanner shook it, both elated and horrified. What had he just done? His formerly robust bank account would be down to almost zero once the deal went through.

It's worth it. "I'll talk to Harper about drawing up a contract," he said.

"Sounds good." George placed his hands on the desk and stood, his grin reaching both ears. "Thanks, Tanner. This is a load off my mind."

As Tanner nodded, a thought occurred to him. "Can we keep the news quiet for a little while?" He didn't want anyone to know he'd bought the diner until the deal had gone through and he had his business plan in place.

"I won't say a word until you tell me. Now I'll leave my diner in your capable hands. I have to call the lawyer back and tell him I changed my mind. Let me know when we can put our John Hancocks on the contract." He looked around the office. "I'm going to miss this place, but it's time to move on. I never thought I'd see the day Sunshine would leave the family."

He walked over to Tanner and clapped him on the back. "But you're the next best thing. I know you'll take good care of her." He left, closing the door behind him.

George's words almost took the sting out of the huge amount he'd have to pay. *Almost.*

Tanner stood in the office, trying to process

what had just happened. He was flustered and soon to be almost flat broke . . . but he would also own Sunshine.

Grinning like a fool, he pulled out his phone and sat down at the desk—no, *his* desk. He would have to get used to that. He did a quick search for Harper's business number. When he found it, he clicked on the hyperlink, and soon the phone was ringing.

"Wilson Realty, Harper Wilson speaking."

He'd expected her receptionist to answer, so he was caught off guard. "Uh, hey, Harper. It's me."

"Me who?"

"Tanner. Um, Castillo." Yep, he sounded like a confident businessman. More like an idiot.

"Hey, Tanner," she said as if she hadn't heard him fumbling his words and didn't already know his last name. "Everything ready for the party Saturday night?"

"Yes," he said, switching gears in his head. He still needed to pick up a few more ingredients for the tapas he'd chosen to serve, but otherwise everything was good to go. He was going to make the bandarillas and empanadas Anita had tried, along with some other recipes he had decided on beforehand. "I hope you like tapas."

"I adore tapas. I've got a lot of important clients coming that night, and I know they're going to love whatever you make."

No pressure. "Great. I didn't call about the party, though."

"Oh?"

"George agreed to sell me the diner." After a long pause, he added, "Harper? You still there?"

"Um, yeah. I'm here. When did this happen?"

"Just now." He explained his conversation with George, including the anonymous buyer and the amount Tanner had agreed to pay.

Silence. Then she ripped into him. "*Why* did you do that, Tanner? You should have called me. I could have negotiated on your behalf."

He gripped the receiver. She was right, of course. "There wasn't time. George was going to accept another offer."

"You couldn't have stalled him?"

Now it was his turn to pause. Could he have asked George to wait until he called Harper? Probably, but at the time he'd been desperate not to lose Sunshine, so desperate he would have done anything . . . and pretty much had. "No. He was set on taking the other offer."

"Just add that to my growing list of surprises," she mumbled.

"What?"

"Never mind. I had no idea George was selling the diner. Or that you wanted to buy it. Do you have any documentation from your conversation with him?"

Uhhh . . . While he had thought through his

desire to own Sunshine, he hadn't done the same when it came to the details of this last-minute deal. "Does shaking hands count?"

"A gentleman's agreement has some validity, but it doesn't replace a contract." She sighed. "Next time you want to buy real estate, call me first. I'll make sure you don't get ripped off again."

Tanner didn't think he was getting ripped off. Not completely, anyway. Buying Sunshine wasn't only a business decision for him. It was an investment in his future, and possibly in Maple Falls's. Once he was finished with his upgrades, which included a menu overhaul that he hadn't mentioned to George, the customers would be coming in droves. He'd make back more than he paid. And the cherry on top of the sundae? His mother could quit her job. Both of them. When the diner was making double or triple it was making now, he'd be able to support her and even help out Lonzo.

"Can you draw up a contract?" he asked, impatient to start everything rolling along.

"Of course." He heard her scribbling on something. "Do you want an inspection?"

"Don't need one. I know this place inside and out."

"Are you sure?"

"Positive. I just want to get this signed and official."

"All right. I should have the contract ready in

a few days. What's George's email? We can do a virtual document signing."

Tanner laughed. "This is George we're talking about. He doesn't own a computer. Or a cell phone. I'd be surprised if he had a TV that didn't have a tinfoil antenna on it."

"Whatever that is. All right, we'll do an in-person signing, then. Once all the paperwork is complete, I'll set up a meeting at the title company. But only on one condition."

"What?" he asked, wary. He didn't know if he could make another concession right now.

"As soon as you can, you have *got* to get rid of those hideous pink uniforms."

"Already planning to." He had never liked the Pepto-Bismol–colored uniforms, a call back to the sixties. Or fifties. Whatever, they looked awful on everyone. Only Anita managed to make them look presentable.

"Excellent. Text me George's home phone number. When I calculate the full amount you owe, I'll text you back."

"I know the amount."

"There are fees involved, even though I'm going to waive mine."

"Thanks, Harper." He grimaced. His account might truly be empty by the time this was over.

"Congratulations, Tanner. Honestly, I'm thrilled for you. When are you making the big announcement?"

"Soon. Until then I'd like to keep it between us. And George, obviously."

"My lips are sealed." Another pause. "Seems like I'm the designated keeper of secrets lately."

He had no idea what she was talking about, and he needed to get to work. "Thanks for taking care of this for me, and for the catering job."

"No problem on both counts. Talk to you soon."

He clicked off the call and fell back against the chair, which squealed loudly in protest. The ancient piece of furniture was going into the dumpster with the uniforms once everything was settled.

What he'd done was starting to sink in. Even though he had overpaid for the diner, he didn't have any regrets. He couldn't wait to implement some of his plans, and he was excited about his most ambitious one: the café. Almost all of the diner's younger customers had at one time or another asked for a greater variety of desserts and for a specialty coffee now and then. George had ignored those requests, saying the diner had always served the same dessert and coffee and no one had complained before. "All these young folks want the fancy stuff," he'd grumble as he'd throw yet another written suggestion for espresso into the trash. "We ain't a fancy diner."

Tanner didn't want to turn Sunshine into a fancy diner, either, but they could at least add some twenty-first-century flavor to counterbalance the fifties vibe. The café was still an idea floating in his head, but tonight after work he would flesh out his plans on paper. After doing some more calculations, he figured that as long as he carefully watched what he spent over the next six to eight months, he would have a few thousand to work with in addition to what the diner was already pulling in. Once Sunshine was legally his, he would start ordering the equipment he needed, along with the renovation supplies.

The door opened and Pamela rushed in. "I know, I'm late," she said, hurrying over to the time clock. She quickly punched her card. "I took a nap this afternoon and slept through my alarm."

He hadn't realized what time it was.

"Don't worry, I'll stay late tonight." She grabbed her apron and dashed out the door.

He slipped on his own apron, then grabbed one of the hairnets from the box on top of the time clock. Packages of them were all over the place in case someone forgot to put one on. He was putting it over his head as he passed by Fred and Bailey, who were on their way to clock out.

"Sorry I'm late," he apologized.

"Not a big deal. We've been slow as molasses," Fred said, slipping off his hairnet.

"Yeah," Bailey added. "I reorganized the silver-ware."

"Wow," he said. "You must have been desperate."

"I can't stand being bored."

Tanner told them goodbye, then walked into the kitchen. Pamela was stacking the clean dishes Kevin had taken out of the dishwasher. He watched as they worked, then turned to look at the empty dining room. He smiled. Even though he hadn't officially purchased the diner, he felt like he already owned Sunshine—and he was determined to make it the iconic success it had been in its heyday. Soon enough, it would be time to tell everyone.

Chapter 6

"You're buying #3?" Olivia gasped.

"Shh." Anita held a finger over her lips, even though they were alone in the library's break room. "No one knows yet except for Harper, and I've sworn her to secrecy."

Olivia crossed her arms and sat back in her chair. "You told her first?"

Were Olivia's feelings hurt? That wasn't like her. "I had to. She's the real estate agent brokering the deal for me."

Olivia's expression relaxed. "Oh. That makes sense, then." She stuck a short celery stick into the small cup of homemade hummus on the table in front of her. Posters about books and reading hung all over the walls of the small, tidy room, along with employee information. As often as they could, the two of them shared lunch together here or grabbed a quick cup of coffee when Anita was off work and Olivia had time for a break. Lately they hadn't gotten together much since Olivia was busy with work and school. Anita was glad she'd had time to meet today.

"But how in the world are you able to afford to buy #3 on a waitress's salary?" Olivia asked.

"I have savings, and I plan to get a loan too."

"You've saved up that much money?"

"Yes."

Olivia smiled. "I'm impressed. How did you accomplish that?"

Anita started ticking off her fingers. "My rent isn't that much, and I don't have any bills other than that and utilities. I buy only what I need, and I walk almost everywhere. I bought my car thirdhand, and I've saved a lot on gas and insurance because I rarely drive."

"Good thing, because I'm not sure that bucket of bolts is safe."

"Rusty said it was." At least it used to be, up until the other day.

"When did he say that?"

"Um, four years ago?" Or was it five?

Olivia smirked. "This is why one of us always offers to drive."

Anita chuckled as she picked at the crust of the peanut butter and jelly sandwich she'd slapped together before coming over here. She usually loved PB&J, mostly for the convenience. No cooking involved, and no matter the type of peanut butter or flavor of jelly, a person couldn't go wrong with the childhood favorite. But after her gorge-fest of brownies yesterday, her appetite was sparse.

"So what are you going to do with #3 once you buy it?"

The scent of fresh coffee filled the break room. Olivia always insisted on a fresh pot every two hours, even though she was a tea drinker. She paid for the extra coffee herself so she didn't strain the library's already tight budget. Anita smiled. Her friend was going to love her news. "I'm opening a café."

"Really?" Olivia's deep-brown eyes sparkled. "What a wonderful idea! What made you decide to start your own business?"

"I've been thinking about it for a while."

Olivia paused, the baby carrot she was holding poised above the hummus. "Uh-oh."

Anita's gaze snapped up. "What? What's wrong?"

"Nothing so far. But you don't sound excited."

"I am. It's just . . ."

Olivia set down her carrot. "You're doubting yourself, aren't you?"

"I'm trying not to."

Olivia nodded. "It's understandable. I'm sure your parents can help you if you need it."

But she wasn't planning on asking them for help. Even though she wasn't sure how much the building and café would cost, she was determined to do it all on her own. This was her business, and hers alone.

"You know, I've been hoping you would do something like this," Olivia said. "Not specifically a café but doing something other than waitressing."

"What's wrong with waitressing?"

"Nothing." Olivia took a sip of her bottled water. "But for a while now I've suspected you might not be satisfied with your job."

Anita had no idea her friend had picked up on her restlessness. "Why didn't you say anything?"

"How could I? I couldn't just come up to you and say, 'Oh, Anita, by the way—you hate your job, don't you?' "

"I don't hate it. There's a lot to like, actually. I enjoy visiting with the customers, and surprising them when I remember their drink orders or what they always pick for dessert. I like bringing Jasper his coffee. Do you know he gives me a little smile every time I put the cup in front of him at breakfast? I also like the hours. It's nice to have Sundays off and not have to work weekends."

"But you're not satisfied with waitressing any-more."

Anita stared at her sandwich. "I'm not unhappy with my job. I'm unhappy with my life."

"I didn't know that." Olivia frowned. "Although I should have. I hate that we don't spend time together like we did before. I've been so wrapped up with school, and summer is around the corner, and that's always a busy time. I'm sorry, Anita. I haven't been there for you."

"Don't be. I only realized recently that I need a change."

"And you think this will make you happy?"

She wasn't sure. "I hope so."

"I can't think of anyone who is more suited to run a café." Olivia beamed.

The doubts hit her again. "What if I'm not? What if I fail? I've never done anything like this before."

"You won't fail. You can learn everything you need to know."

"Ha. Right. My track record with learning isn't the greatest."

"I'll help you whenever you need me," Olivia said.

"What about school? Summer programs?"

"I can find time for my best friend."

Anita's heart warmed. Still, she didn't want Olivia to have to add anything else to her packed schedule, and Anita didn't want to depend on anyone else. "Thank you," she said, but decided she wouldn't take her friend up on the offer.

Tapping her short, plain nails against the table, Olivia thought for a minute. "You know, we have some books on accounting and business management. Even better, you could take a class in both of those subjects. You could audit the course and not worry about the grade."

"Really?" She hadn't known that was possible. If she didn't have the pressure of making a good grade, she might be able to relax and learn the material at her own pace.

"We have some catalogs near the front desk.

Take a couple and look through them." Olivia grinned. "Who knows, you might actually find the man of your dreams in Business 101."

"Like you found the man of your dreams in the hundreds of classes you've taken? You're working on your second master's. Why haven't you met anyone yet?"

"I'm happy being single, much to Aunt Bea's chagrin. She would have married me off before I got my bachelor's if she had her way. I keep telling her not everyone is meant to get married, but she won't listen. 'Any man would be over the moon to have you, sugar,' she's always telling me."

Anita laughed. Olivia did a great imitation of her very southern aunt.

Olivia started to pack up her empty containers into her insulated lunch bag. "I'm sorry to cut our conversation short, but I have to get back to work. We're developing the final touches for our summer reading programs this afternoon." She got up from her chair and grabbed her lunch bag. "Call me after work and we can talk more about your plans. And promise me you'll let me know if you need any help, okay?"

Anita nodded but didn't say anything.

Olivia smiled and put her hand on Anita's shoulder. "I can't wait to see what you come up with for the café. This is so exciting! I have dibs on the first Earl Grey."

"Done. Also, don't say anything, not until I've actually purchased #3. If I can't buy the building, I can't open the café."

"I won't say a word." She gestured to Anita's uneaten sandwich. "Take your time with lunch, and help yourself to coffee."

After Olivia left, Anita propped her chin up with the heel of her hand. Now two people knew about her plans, and she trusted both of them not to say anything. She wondered if she should tell Riley, but she was busy with wedding plans—so much so they had canceled the rest of their Tuesday meetings until after she and Hayden returned from their honeymoon. Riley would find out soon enough, along with the rest of Maple Falls.

She put her sandwich back into the washable plastic bag she liked to use instead of regular plastic and left the break room, heading for the section of the library where the business books were. She found two she might be able to handle: *Accounting for Dummies* and *Beginner Business.* Surely she would be able to read these without any help.

As she took the books over to Wendy, the librarian manning the front desk, she paused by the rack that held catalogs for Arkansas colleges, including vo-tech schools and community colleges. She picked up one for the local community college. Maybe she could take a class as long as she made sure plenty of tutoring was available. Reading a book was one thing. Taking a class was another thing altogether, even if she didn't have to worry about making a perfect grade.

After she checked out her books, she pushed on the glass door of the library and walked outside, the bright noonday sun hitting her eyes. What a beautiful day, and also her day off. Slipping on her sunglasses, she couldn't help but smile. She was scared and nervous but also enthusiastic about her new venture. She had a lot to learn, but this time, instead of endless school assignments, she would be learning on her own terms the information needed to open the café. *Anita Bedford, Owner*. She was starting to believe she could be.

Halfway home, she realized she hadn't given Tanner a single thought . . . until now. Maybe she was finally making a little progress.

Tanner arrived home dead tired after his shift. Sunshine had been a wasteland most of the day, but a sudden influx of customers, including a peewee soccer team passing through Maple Falls on their way home from a match in Rockport, had made his evening beyond hectic. But even though he was exhausted, he was happy. An uptick in business always put him in a good mood, and that mood was doubled by the knowledge that he was soon to be the proprietor of Sunshine.

He intended to go straight to the shower and then to bed when he saw the light on in the kitchen. Mom was still up? Work started for her at 5:00 a.m., so she usually turned in early for the night. As he entered the kitchen, he saw her preparing her evening tea—chamomile with lavender and peppermint. "I figured you'd be in bed by now," he said. "Is everything all right?"

She turned around and smiled. "Everything is fine. Do you want some tea?" she asked, gesturing to the kettle on their old gas stove.

"No, thanks." Despite his exhaustion, he sat at the kitchen table. It was rare he and his mother spent time together lately, much less twice in one week.

She stirred a little honey into the mug, then joined him. "How was your day?"

He paused, wondering if he should tell her about the diner. No, it was enough that George and Harper knew about it. If he told her and then the deal fell through—and he prayed it wouldn't—he'd have more explaining to do. Better to let her find out with everyone else. "Oh, the usual."

"You look tired." She peered at him, swirls of steam floating from her tea, filling the air with hints of the relaxing herbs.

"We were busy tonight." He told her about the twenty-four hamburger baskets followed by twenty-four hot-fudge sundaes, in addition to the rest of the customers' orders. "The little guys won their game, so they were celebrating."

"That's delightful." She lifted her mug. "I recall when Maple Falls had all the peewee teams. Soccer, football, baseball. Do you remember when you and Lonzo were in T-ball?"

"A little."

"You were both stars of your teams. According to your father, of course." She smiled, but it didn't reach her eyes. "I wish you could have done more fun things like that when you were young."

"I did a lot of fun things. And don't forget the year I played baseball in junior high."

"Oh, I haven't. I went to every game I could. You were really good at fieldstop."

"Shortstop." He chuckled.

"Right. Shortstop. The coach said you could have been one of the top players on the high school team."

"But I chose to work after school instead. I don't regret that decision."

Mom stared into her tea. "Maybe you could have been a professional like Hayden."

He shook his head. "Definitely not. First off, Hayden was in a class of his own. He also busted his tail to get to the pros. I like the game, but not that much. Being on the church team is satisfying enough." When she still looked doubtful, he added, "If I'd played on the high school team,

I wouldn't have worked at McDonald's or that restaurant in Hot Springs or any of the other food-service jobs I've had. I wouldn't have realized how much I enjoy cooking, and I wouldn't have gotten the assistant job at the diner." And he wouldn't have ended up owning the diner, fulfilling his dream. "Like I said, I don't have any regrets."

"But—"

"How was your day?" he asked, eager to move on to a different subject.

"Fine. Not much changes at the plant, and cleaning the offices has been easier lately."

Despite her assurances, he could hear the weariness in her voice and see the shadows underneath her eyes. The light in the kitchen also showed a few new threads of gray in her hair, something he hadn't noticed before. He didn't say anything about her obvious fatigue, even though he was concerned she seemed constantly tired. She would just deny everything, and he would just tell her to find a physically easier job or quit altogether and enjoy an early retirement. They were the flip sides of the same broken record.

"I'm so happy you cut your hair." His mom reached over and touched his ears. "Now when are you getting rid of these?"

Tanner touched his gauges. She'd been shocked, then angry, when he'd come home with them in high school, so much so she threatened to ground him. She'd changed her mind when she realized the pointlessness of punishing him for something he'd already done. Since then she would occasionally look at his ears and shake her head.

"Someday," he assured her, not admitting that he'd already been thinking about taking them out and repairing his earlobes. "I've got a full schedule right now."

"You always do." She took another sip of her tea, one eyebrow raised.

He wasn't taking the bait. "Do you know Harper Wilson?"

"Yes. I see her realty signs everywhere, and we've talked a bit at church. Friendly girl. Beautiful too." Her eyes widened with excitement. "Oh, Tanner! Are you *finally* dating someone?"

Oops. He hadn't thought she would jump to that conclusion. "I'm catering her cocktail party tomorrow night, that's all."

"Oh." Then she added, "Is she single?"

"I don't know. Never asked."

"Why not?"

Brother, how had he stepped into this? "She's not my type."

"Then who is your type?"

"I'm going to prepare some of Abuela Castillo's recipes for the party tomorrow."

Her eyes brightened. "That's wonderful. She

would be so pleased. What are you making?"

Tanner told her the specifics of the menu, glad to get off the topic of women. When he was finished, she was beaming.

"My son the businessman."

He tensed. Surely she had no idea about him buying Sunshine. "What do you mean?"

"You're the one who started the catering business, and from what you've told me, you're in charge of the whole thing. I'm so proud of you, Tanner. Your father would be too."

His heart warmed at seeing the pride in her eyes. "Thanks, Mom. I couldn't have done this without you."

"Of course you could have," she huffed. "You're the one who put in the hard work. All those hours at the diner and catering. That was you, not me. And don't think I didn't notice you fixed the broken pipe under the sink before you went to work today."

"It's just a patch. I'll repair it on my next day off."

"Or we could call a plumber."

"I know how to fix it." He'd learned lots of home maintenance growing up in order to save money, and after he bought the diner, he'd have to economize more than ever.

"All right." She smiled. "Now, back to Harper. If you're not interested in her, then what about Anita? She's such a sweetheart. Did you know her preschool Sunday school class made Valentine's Day cards for all the older single people in church? What a thoughtful gesture, and the cards were adorable."

"That's nice." And so like Anita. "But—"

"Is she single?"

"Yes." At least he was fairly sure she was. He'd never seen her with a date or a boyfriend and hadn't heard her talking about anyone special. Then again, he'd only recently been paying attention.

"Excellent," his mother said.

"What is all this about, Mom?"

She got up and took her mug to the sink, rinsing it out slowly. Had she heard his question, or was she avoiding answering? Finally she turned around and looked at him. "You're almost twenty-eight years old, Tanner, and you still live with your mother."

Talk about a shot out of nowhere. "I didn't know you had a problem with me living here."

She sat back down, this time next to him. "Like any mother, I love having my children close to me. But most people your age in Maple Falls are either married, getting married, or living on their own. As far as I know, you've never even had a girlfriend."

She was making him sound pathetic. He was also thankful he'd never introduced her to Heather. "I've gone on a few dates."

"Maybe you should go on some more. Like with Anita."

He ran his knuckles over the top of the table, not looking at her. "That's not a good idea."

"Why?"

Even if Anita were interested in him—and he was convinced she wasn't—a romance between them was out of the question. Soon he would be her boss, and he considered dating an employee unethical. "I don't have time," he said, deciding on the simplest, not to mention most truthful, answer.

"You can always make time for the things you care about." She patted his hand.

Right now he cared about keeping up with his business and making sure his mother wasn't overworking herself. "Do you really want me to move out?" he asked, a little hurt at the idea.

"If you're staying just for me, then yes, I want you to move out. When your father died, you took on his responsibility for the family. I didn't realize it at the time, but now I clearly see that you're putting your life on hold. I'm worried you sacrificed too much making up for your father's absence."

So that was it. She thought he might be staying here because of her. Which was true, but he had never minded living with her as an adult. And he'd never put his life on hold. Living here had allowed him to save money so he could purchase

Sunshine, even as he helped her out with the bills and kept trying to convince her to slow down. But he couldn't tell her those things right now. Once the deal was complete, though, she would understand.

"Mom, I never feel obligated when it comes to you, and I haven't sacrificed anything." A thought occurred to him. "Are you thinking about selling the house?"

She put her hand on her chest. "Heavens, no. I would never sell. I love living here."

"Even with all the bad memories?" A lump formed in his throat.

Her eyes grew soft. "The good ones outweigh the bad ones."

That might be so, but he was starting to warm up to the idea. "This is a big house, and it will be a lot for you to take care of by yourself when I do move out."

"So you are planning to get a place of your own?"

"Yes, eventually." But he wasn't ready to leave her, not when she continued to work so hard. He wondered if they should have had this talk a long time ago, but he'd been too busy to think about it before now. "Maybe you should consider downsizing."

Her lips flattened into a line, and he could see her mentally digging in her heels. "Maybe you should consider going out with Anita."

Well played, but not an option. "Mom, I'm not opposed to getting married someday, but I'm also not going to start dating anyone right now. So don't go matchmaking for me, okay?"

"Oh, all right." She got up from the table. "I won't bring up the subject again."

"Thank you."

"I'm still proud of you, Tanner, even though you're a late bloomer in the dating department."

"Does that mean you're not kicking me out?" he asked, only half joking.

"I would never kick you out. But you should focus on moving on with your life instead of worrying about mine." She cupped his cheek with her work-roughened hand. "I love you for it, but I'm fine, and I will be fine on my own, in my own house. In *this* house." She removed her hand. "Sleep well, son."

After she left, he thought about what she had said . . . and what she didn't know. His throat tightened again as he remembered the last words his father had said to him. *"Take care of your mother and brother."* Tanner had only been eight, but he had taken those words to heart, and over the years he had done everything he could to fulfill his father's request. And he'd done it without sacrificing anything, or at least not much. Maybe he hadn't spent all his time partying like his friends had in high school and had missed out on going to college when he had several scholarships for his excellent grades. So what if he'd stayed behind in Maple Falls while a lot of his classmates moved to larger cities or even out of state? And did it matter that he hadn't dated a lot? He had spared himself a lot of unnecessary heartache.

Still, one thing his mother had said stuck with him. He was twenty-seven, still living at home, and had no relationship prospects. From the outside looking in, he probably did seem like a loser. Was he missing out on something? And why did Anita suddenly come to mind when he thought about the possibility of a relationship?

Because Mom brought her up, that's why.

As he walked upstairs, though, he knew his mother's comments weren't the only reason he was thinking about Anita, enough that he had to remind himself of his own ethics. Even with all the distractions this week, he kept remembering how much he'd enjoyed sharing tapas with her—and he couldn't get that sexy sigh out of his mind.

He undressed and got in the shower, letting the hot water soothe his tired body. How ironic. He'd known Anita all these years, and worked with her for three, but for some reason it had taken being alone with her and some Spanish appetizers to get his attention.

If only things were different . . .

But they weren't, and he couldn't afford for them to be. Anita was the best waitress he'd ever worked with, and he would have to depend on her to make his plans for Sunshine a reality. He'd even thought about putting her in charge of scheduling staff while he focused on the coffee bar and new menu. He trusted her completely, and he refused to mess up their professional relationship because his timing was terrible. Business came first, and he didn't see that changing for a long while.

Rosa eased down on her bed, the aches and pains from a long day's work making themselves known in her joints. Normally she was in bed and conked out by now, but the past few nights she'd had trouble sleeping. Her nightly tea wasn't helping her relax the way it usually did, even though she was feeling more fatigued than normal. And after her talk with Tanner, she knew sleep wouldn't come easily tonight either.

Her eldest had been uppermost in her thoughts the past few months. She didn't have to worry about Lonzo, who was doing well in school and made sure to call her once a week to give her updates about his life in Tulsa. He'd started dating someone and said that he might bring her home to meet the family on his next break. Meanwhile, she'd never seen Tanner go out on even one date.

Oh, Tanner . . . what am I going to do with you? Her handsome, hardworking son. Of course she was biased about him, and she was puzzled that he was still single and seemingly content living with her at his age. Tonight was the first night she'd voiced those thoughts, and she was relieved they had finally talked about the subject.

While she didn't quite believe him when he said he didn't feel obligated to her, now he was aware he didn't have to stay here with her. She would miss him, but he needed to cut the cord he'd mistakenly believed tied him to her and Lonzo. Losing his father so young had been hard on him, although Tanner had rarely shown his grief. Almost from the moment of Alonzo's death he'd slipped into the role of head of the family, and she'd been too bereft and filled with worry about raising two young sons on her own to stop him from carrying a burden that wasn't his. She wished she would have seen it sooner.

She picked up the picture on her nightstand and touched Alonzo's face, eternally handsome in his wedding tuxedo. He wasn't as tall as Tanner, but they had the same athletic build, light-brown hair, and sage-green eyes. Alonzo also had a thick mustache, the height of style back in the day.

She looked at this photo every evening and every morning. Their time together had been brief—far too brief. And yet . . . Her husband might not be physically here with her, but he was forever in her heart.

Rarely did she look at herself in the photo, but

tonight she gazed at the young woman standing close and smiling up at her new husband, young and pretty in the size 4 dress her mother had made. She had become pregnant with Tanner not long after their honeymoon, and she hadn't seen size 4 since. Alonzo had never minded her weight gain, often telling her he liked her "pretty and plump," as he used to say.

"You would be proud of our boys," she whispered to his image, her voice thick. "Tanner has his own catering business. He's an excellent cook and a loyal son—a little too loyal for his own good, I think. And Lonzo is doing so well in school. He's dating a girl named Molly, and he's considering attending graduate school for his master's in chemical engineering." She ran the back of her hand over her eyes. "I wish you were here to see what fine men they've grown into."

She lifted her gaze and glanced around her bedroom, memories washing over her. How could Tanner even think she'd consider selling her house? She and Alonzo had papered this bedroom when she was six months pregnant with him. They had searched for weeks before finding the perfect dresser at a thrift store, the only place they could afford to shop at the time. That dresser hadn't moved from its spot against the wall on the opposite side of the room. The carpet was old, her mattress was lumpy, and she had worn the same Easter dress to church twelve years in a row.

She wouldn't change anything about her house. Or her life. She was tired, but she was also happy, and she wanted her sons to be happy too.

After a few moments she set the frame back in its place. Next to their picture, she noticed the card she'd put on the nightstand yesterday. She had an appointment with Dr. Bedford on Monday. He was her new cardiologist and also happened to be Anita's father. Her general practitioner had recommended him after some of her blood work had come back abnormal. "You should get your heart checked out," Dr. Earley, her family doctor, had said. "Walter has an excellent reputation, and he'll take care of you."

Rosa stared at the card. She had known Walter Bedford when he and the rest of Anita's family used to live in Maple Falls, and she didn't doubt he was an excellent cardiologist. But she didn't have time to see a doctor—not next week, anyway. She'd had abnormal blood work before, although this was the first time she had been referred to a heart doctor. Whatever was going on, it could wait another week or two. She felt fine, other than being tired, and she couldn't remember a time when she wasn't tired.

I'll reschedule tomorrow.

She readied herself for bed and said her evening prayers, adding an extra one for Tanner and his future. As an afterthought she said another quick one—for him to be more open-minded about dating Anita. The more she thought about the two of them together, the more she realized they were perfect for each other. Tanner needed a sweet, kind, supportive woman in his life, someone who was as loyal to him as he would be to her. Anita had that kind of loyalty and had shown it by not leaving Maple Falls when her parents and siblings had, in addition to staying at the same job for many years. Rosa couldn't imagine her doing anything to hurt Tanner or anyone else.

When she climbed into bed, she flipped off the light and sighed. Ultimately Tanner would have to decide whom he should date. She would have to be patient. But hopefully he would realize that work wasn't everything. Family was, and she wanted him to start his own—before a prime opportunity passed him by.

Chapter 7

On Saturday morning, Anita and Peanut had a showdown. Or more accurately, a stare-down. She glared at her cat, who was meowing at her from the roof again. Was there such a thing as counseling for cats?

"You need a therapist," she yelled, shielding her eyes from the sun. "The tree you climbed up is right there." She pointed to the weeping willow next to the house, having determined he was using it to get onto the roof. "All you have to do is climb *down*."

He responded by turning around, his tail up in the air.

"Rude." She went to the shed and retrieved the ladder. Usually she was at work by now, but Pamela had taken her shift so she could be off today for Harper's party. Anita leaned the ladder against the roof and climbed up. Peanut, apparently in a forgiving mood now, was purring as he rubbed his cheek against her forehead. "Crazy cat." But she smiled as she cuddled him against her and made her way down the ladder again.

Her phone buzzed in her jeans pocket. She'd finally remembered to put it on vibrate the other day. When she had more time, she'd pick out another ringtone that didn't make her break out in hives every time she heard it. She gave Peanut a pat on the head and set him down, then answered her phone. "Hey, Harper."

"Ready for tonight?"

"Sure."

"Well, aren't you a ball of excitement."

She opened the sliding back door and walked into the kitchen. "I am excited." And nervous, but she didn't need to tell Harper that. "I've never been to a cocktail party before."

"You haven't?"

"No. Mom goes to them all the time, but this will be my first one."

"Then I'm happy it's mine. I'll pick you up around one thirty."

"Thanks." She still hadn't called Rusty about her car, although Harper wouldn't have agreed to ride in it even if it was running. "I feel bad that you have to take me home after the party," she said. "I still can't find anyone to take over my Sunday school class."

"I don't mind. The party starts early, so it will end early, one of the perks of serving only cocktails and finger foods rather than a meal. Cleanup won't be hard, and I don't like missing church anyway. Lake Hamilton is less than an hour's drive, so it's not a big deal."

"I can't wait to see your parents' vacation house."

"And I can't wait to show it to you. I was hoping they would come tonight, but you know Madge and Don. Always on the go."

Anita didn't miss the note of disappointment in Harper's flippant tone. She and her parents had a strained relationship, one that Harper never talked about. "I'm glad they're letting you borrow the lake house."

"Yeah. That's the *least* they could do. Anyway, you're going to love what I picked out for you to wear."

"Huh?"

"I'm giving you a makeover. Didn't I mention that?"

"No." She'd spent all day yesterday trying to figure out what to wear, and when she'd finished her shift she'd gone to Hot Springs and shopped until her feet ached, finally settling on a plain white shirt and slim black pants. Harper would think her choices were boring, and they probably were, but they were comfortable. "Can't I just bring my own outfit?"

"No, you cannot. Half the fun tonight will be getting you gussied up to meet Dylan."

"Wait, what? Who's Dylan?"

"Didn't I mention Dylan?"

She sat down on the chair near the back door, not buying Harper's innocent act. "You definitely did not."

"My bad. He's a friend of mine, and he'll be

tending bar. I guess I also didn't mention he's in medical school."

Anita didn't like where this was going. "Are you fixing me up?"

"Mayyyybe." Harper laughed. "Look, if you two hit it off, fine. If not, that's fine too. He's nice, you're nice, and I think together you would both be *very nice.*"

"Then why don't you date him?"

"Please. That would be like dating my brother—if I had a brother. I've known Dylan since junior high."

About as long as Anita had known Tanner. Why couldn't she see him like a brother the way Harper saw Dylan? "I don't know about this."

"I won't push you and Dylan together, I promise."

She trusted Harper, but no one had ever given her a makeover before or set her up with a possible date. And yet, if she was going to move on from Tanner, she needed to ignite her social life. "All right. I'll meet Dylan."

"Yay! This is so exciting. Once I've worked my magic, you're going to be a knockout. Dylan won't know what hit him. Remember what happened to the last person I made over?"

"Riley?"

"Yep. For her first date with Hayden. I'm not saying that you and Dylan will get married, but . . . you *never* know."

Anita gulped.

"Oh, before I forget, I'm still working on tracking down the owner of #3. For some reason, this guy—or gal—doesn't want to be found."

"Is that a problem?" Anita asked.

"This is just a hiccup. I'll use every detective skill I have to track him down." Harper paused. "You're still sure about this, right?"

Anita frowned. "Yes. Why?"

"Running your own business is hard work, especially in the beginning."

"I know." In fact, she knew quite a bit now, having made it through two chapters of *Beginner Business*. She had struggled with the reading, but not as much as she'd anticipated.

"You can still change your mind, you know," Harper added.

Where was this coming from? When she'd first told Harper about her idea, her friend had been as supportive as Olivia. Now it seemed like she was trying to talk her out of opening the café. "You don't think I can do this?"

"That's not what I said. I *know* you can do this. But I wouldn't be a good friend if I didn't point out that there will be some bumps in the road. That happens with every business, including mine."

Relieved, Anita nodded. "I appreciate you looking out for me, but I'm not changing my mind. I'm buying #3, and I'm opening a café."

"Even if someone gets mad at you for it?"

Who would be upset about her opening a café? She thought for a minute. She'd been so convinced that a new business, especially one that was so popular everywhere else, would be welcome. "George, maybe?"

"George is a possibility. Or someone else," Harper added, her last words barely audible.

But Anita was convinced that George would be fine with her decision once she explained her reasons for opening the coffee shop. Her business reasons, that is. "If George has a problem with me, I'll deal with it."

"Well, I declare. Look who's being Ms. Tough Guy."

Anita chuckled at Harper's exaggerated southern drawl. The giggle disappeared, though, when she said, "I should have toughened up a long time ago."

"You're not allowed to be jaded, Anita. We need your optimistic sweetness in our group. You balance out the rest of us. I'll see you in an hour or so."

"Bye." Anita set down her phone, trying to ignore the sudden worry swirling in her stomach. Would George really be angry with her for opening the café? She'd worked for him for a long time, and even though he hadn't been around the diner much since Tanner took over as assistant manager, he was a reasonable man.

No, she didn't need to be concerned. She could handle George. What she wasn't sure she could handle was tonight's party. A new outfit? Makeup? Dylan?

She drew in a deep breath and tried to relax. If Harper said Dylan was a nice guy and someone Anita would like, then she needed to give him a chance.

But what if she liked him and he wasn't interested in her? What if it was the Tanner situation all over again? She couldn't handle another one-sided relationship.

Great, she was working herself into a tizzy over a guy she'd never met and a guy she was trying to forget. *I'm the one who needs a therapist.*

Enough of that.

She got up from the chair and headed to the bathroom to take a shower before Harper picked her up. She'd never been a knockout before in her life.

Maybe it's time I became one.

Meow . . .

Anita stopped in front of the bathroom door and shot a glare at the ceiling. "Peanut!"

"You're looking handsome today."

Tanner tucked the back of his white shirt into his black pants and smiled at his mother. "You're biased."

"Yes, but I'm also honest." She walked over to

him, wearing her bottling-plant uniform. When he'd found out she had picked up a shift tonight, he'd tried to get her to call in. Of course she balked. Now he was getting ready for Harper's party and she was leaving to work her second shift. "I still think you should call in," he said, pulling at the cuffs of his dress shirt.

"I refuse to lie to my employer."

"Then tell him you need a rest. You won't be lying about that."

She shook her head. "You're stubborn."

"Wonder where I got that from." He grinned.

"I have no idea." She smiled back and picked up her purse off the kitchen table. "Don't wait up for me."

"Don't wait up for me either."

"I can't make any promises." She waved to him and left.

Tanner heard her car start up and sighed, wishing she would listen to him for once. He picked up the black belt he'd draped over one of the kitchen chairs and put it on. This wasn't his typical catering uniform. Usually he wore a red polo shirt with the diner logo on the left front, but last night when he'd called Harper to finalize everything for the party, she had insisted he dress up. "Just make sure whatever you wear is white, black, or both. I don't want anyone clashing with my theme."

He didn't think red clashed with black and

white, but she was the client, and for the next few hours she was his boss.

He stuck his wallet into the back pocket of his pants and grabbed his keys and phone. Before heading for Lake Hamilton, he would stop by the diner and pick up the food he'd prepared and packed last night, making sure to grab his black apron while he was there.

Buzz . . . buzz . . .

The cell vibrated in his hand, and he slid his thumb over the screen. "Hey, Bailey. You ready for tonight?"

"Tanner, I'm so sorry. I can't help you with the party."

He stilled, hearing fear in her voice. "Are you okay?"

"My sister just called. One of my nephews fell off the playground equipment at the park, and she needs me to watch her other two kids while she's at the ER with him."

"Is he all right?"

"I don't know."

"Don't worry about it. Text me later and let me know how your nephew is."

"Will do," she said, sounding a tiny bit calmer. "Thanks."

He hung up, unsure what to do. He hoped Bailey's nephew would be okay, but now he was in a jam. He couldn't cater the party by himself, not unless he wanted to come off as incompetent—the last thing he needed when he was trying to attract new clientele.

Mabel. Maybe she could help him out. He had every diner employee's number in his contacts, and he quickly found hers and pressed Call. She hadn't catered with him before, but he could get her up to speed.

"I'm sorry, Tanner," she said after he explained his predicament. "It's bingo and brats at the VFW tonight. I'm calling the numbers."

"Can you find someone to take your place? I wouldn't ask if it wasn't an emergency."

"Nope. I'm the only decent caller we got. Wish I could help you out, but I don't want to let down the veterans."

He rubbed his forehead. "I understand. Have a good time."

Who else could he call? Then he remembered Anita had asked for the day off. He quickly called her number and prayed she would answer.

Anita looked in the mirror, shocked at what she saw. The reflection staring back at her was her, yet not her. How confusing.

Harper moved to stand beside her. "Was I right? You're a knockout."

Anita regarded both of their images in the full-length mirror in Harper's bedroom. Harper was the true knockout, wearing a sleeveless black dress and sparkling gold heels. Anita was also wearing a dress, but hers was white with black spaghetti straps and had a flared skirt that was shorter than she was used to, although still modest. The neckline plunged a little lower than she preferred, but she was nowhere near Heather territory.

Actually, Heather would probably rock this dress.

Ugh. Why did she have to think about Heather now?

Harper clasped her hands together, her long white nails clicking against each other. "What do you think?"

The dress was beautiful, and because it was a gift from Harper, she loved it. "It's very pretty," she said, pulling the skirt away from her a little bit to admire the chiffon overlay.

"*You* are very pretty." Harper turned Anita so they were facing each other. With her sky-high heels, Harper stood several inches taller. "That pixie cut is so cute on you, but it needs a little pizazz." She walked over to her dresser and fished through a small case of sparkly accessories. "Ah, perfect."

She went back to Anita, smoothed her bangs, and slid a jeweled barrette into her hair. "Now you're flawless."

Anita gazed at the mirror again. The barrette was adorable, but Harper was overstating things. She fidgeted with the neckline, then looked at the sheer hose she'd put on a few minutes ago. When was the last time she'd worn hose?

Near the mirror sat a pair of black pumps with heels higher than she usually wore but still more sensible than Harper's. "This all had to be expensive," she said, frowning.

"It wasn't, trust me. I know how to shop. Now turn that frown upside down and relax. You're supposed to be having fun." Harper chuckled. "I know I am."

Anita managed a small smile. The longer she looked at her ensemble in the mirror, the more her apprehension eased. "I do look nice," she murmured. "I especially like the barrette."

Harper grinned, then dragged her over to her vanity. "Time for makeup. And before you say anything else, I already know you don't wear makeup."

"I wear a little on Sunday mornings," Anita protested.

"Lip gloss doesn't count." She pulled out the chair for Anita, then put both hands on her shoulders and gave her a gentle but firm push onto the seat before picking up a compact that held six shades of foundation.

Anita had no idea how long she sat still while Harper applied foundation, powder, eyebrow pencil, eyeshadow, highlighter, eyeliner, and blush. But when her friend held up a pair of tweezers gripping a spidery-looking row of false eyelashes, Anita knew she'd reached her limit. "No."

"You only have to wear them for a few hours. They'll look stunning, I promise." Harper batted her eyes. "See? You don't have to worry about them falling off."

While the lashes were attractive on Harper, Anita was resolute. "I'm not wearing those."

"How about some mascara, at least?" Harper said, setting the lashes down on the vanity with a pout.

"I can definitely do mascara."

When Harper was done, Anita opened her eyes and turned to face the mirror. "That's me?" she asked, amazed.

"Yes, it's you. Don't you love it?"

She turned her face from one side to the other. Considering all the makeup Harper had applied, she'd feared looking clownish. Not even close. Her complexion softly glowed, making her a sophisticated version of herself. She touched her cheek with her fingers. "Harper, you're a genius."

"I know." Harper picked up a tube of lipstick, bent down, and looked in the mirror as she applied a fresh coat of matte dark pink to her own lips. "See how fun makeup is?"

She could never replicate Harper's expertise, but being gussied up would be fun for a night.

"I'm going to get a bottle of water," Harper said, grimacing as she slipped out of her heels.

"I love these shoes, but they kill my feet. Do you want anything?"

Anita shook her head, surprised Harper was complaining about wearing heels since she wore them all the time. "No, thanks."

"Be right back."

As soon as Harper walked out the door, Anita's phone sounded.

She groaned and picked up the cell. There was definitely something wrong with this thing. As she'd waited for Harper to pick her up, she'd turned the ringtone back on and tried to change it, but it kept defaulting to this one.

Looking at the screen, she didn't recognize the number. "Hello?"

"Hey, Anita. It's Tanner."

Stunned, she gripped the phone. He'd never called her before. "Hi," was all she could manage to say.

"I'm sorry this is last minute, but is there any way you could help me cater Harper's party tonight? Bailey has a family emergency."

"Sure," she said quickly. Too quickly. She should have given his request a second or two of thought since this was her day off. But this was also Tanner, and she couldn't think of a time she'd ever told him no when he asked her to do something.

"Awesome," he said, sounding relieved. "I'll pick you up after I get the food from Sunshine."

"Actually, I'm already at Harper's."

"Oh? Are you helping her get ready for the party?"

"No. I'm a guest."

"I didn't know that. I'm sorry." He paused. "Really. If everyone else wasn't working or busy, I'd say never mind."

Her spirits sank. Not only did he automatically assume she would be Harper's assistant instead of attending the party, but she was also his last resort. "It's okay."

"I knew I could count on you. See you there."

She shut off her phone and tossed it onto the vanity. *Good old dependable Anita.* He hadn't said that, but he might as well have. She shouldn't be surprised or disappointed, but she was both.

Harper entered the room, holding a bottle of sparkling water. She stopped when she saw Anita's face. "What's wrong?" she said, hurrying over to her.

"Nothing." Anita stared at her lap.

"Right, and I'm Martha Stewart's long-lost twin." Harper set the bottle on the vanity and sat on the edge of her large bed. "I was only gone for a few minutes. What happened?"

"Tanner called. He wants me to help him cater tonight."

Harper's brow shot up. "And you told him no, right?"

"There wasn't anyone else available." She

explained the phone call, hoping Harper didn't catch on that he'd called Anita last. Then she got up from the chair. "I brought my original outfit with me," she said.

"In case you didn't like what I picked out for you?"

"Yeah. But I should have known you would find something beautiful. If real estate doesn't work out, you should be a personal shopper."

"I actually thought about that at one time. But I like real estate a tad bit more. There isn't much of a market for personal shopping in Maple Falls, anyway."

Anita was glad her friend wasn't offended. "I'll change and then wait in the kitchen for Tanner."

Harper stepped in front of her, blocking her way. "You can wait for Tanner, but you're not changing out of this dress."

"But I have to work."

"You can serve appetizers wearing this." Harper adjusted one of the thin black straps. "In fact, this is ideal. My party will have the sweetest and sexiest server in town. No, scratch that. In the state. Maybe even the country."

Anita giggled. "You're laying it on a little thick."

"Am I? I'm not wrong, though." Harper stepped back and grinned. "I'm still amazed at your transformation. Dylan won't be able to keep his eyes off you."

Dylan. She'd forgotten all about him. "I guess I'll have to meet him another time."

"Are you kidding? You're not hanging out in the kitchen all night. You have my permission to mix and mingle as much as you want, and that includes mingling with Dylan, if you so choose. Remember, I'm your boss for the next"—she glanced at the thin gold watch on her wrist—"four or five hours." She picked up her water and took a sip as though the decision was final.

Anita nodded. She didn't want to upset Harper. She also realized she didn't want to change out of the dress now that she had worn it for a while. She felt feminine, pretty, and more than a little special.

"I'm glad that's settled." Harper sat down at the vanity and glanced in the mirror, then fluffed her long blond waves. "Are you sure Tanner couldn't find anyone else?"

"That's what he said."

"Hmm." Her friend moved a lock of her hair behind her ear.

Anita sat on the edge of the bed, making sure she didn't wrinkle the dress. "What do you mean by 'hmm'?"

"Oh, I'm not saying he's lying or anything." Harper frowned at her reflection, then moved her hair back to its original position. "But . . ."

"But what?"

Harper faced her. "I've always wondered about

you two. You've worked together for a long time. Olivia mentioned that he used to tutor you back in high school. And you both attend the same church and have played on the same softball team."

Anita squirmed, averting her gaze. "What are you getting at?"

"In all that time, there's never been anything between you?"

Her cheeks heated. This was embarrassing. There was plenty of spark on her side, just not on his. How could she admit that out loud, even to one of her best friends?

She stood and turned to the small suitcase she'd brought that was open on top of the bed. The T-shirt she'd worn when Harper picked her up was laying on top of her other clothes, and she stared at the hand-painted *Maple Falls, Y'all* she'd painted on the front when she was a volunteer at church camp years ago. "No," she said, fiddling with the shirt. Suddenly she'd forgotten how to fold clothing.

"Not even a little sizzle? Or a spark?"

She tossed the shirt back into the suitcase. "Nothing."

Harper pursed her lips. "Then Tanner is an idiot."

Anita tried to smile, but she couldn't. He wasn't an idiot. She was, for pining after him for so long.

131

The doorbell rang, and Harper stood. "That must be the florist. I'll take care of the flowers, and you can finish getting ready."

"I am ready."

"Your lips need a touch-up. The lipstick is on the vanity." Harper slipped into her heels and grimaced. "The things I do for fashion." She walked out of the room, not showing a single hint that her feet ached.

Sighing, Anita stood and went to the table. She searched for the lipstick and sat down, staring at her reflection again. How did a simple cocktail party get so complicated? Then again, she hadn't had much luck with parties. At least she didn't have to worry about ending up in a closet with Tanner tonight. Or kissing Tanner. Or doing anything with Tanner except being good old dependable Anita, always ready to help him out.

She stared at her reflection, then sat up straight. She wasn't a person to wallow in self-pity, and she wasn't going to let her personal feelings get in the way of making sure she did her job to the best of her ability. She applied the lipstick—*Brick Red,* the sticker said on the bottom of the tube—with a light hand, then slipped her feet into the shoes Harper had given her, not surprised at the perfect fit.

Before she went downstairs to wait for Tanner, she walked to the large bedroom window that overlooked Lake Hamilton. The sun was still shining, and a few late-afternoon boaters drifted on the shimmering water. She gazed at the peaceful scene in front of her, growing more confident by the second. Tonight was just another part of this new chapter in her life, and she was determined from now on to enjoy every minute of it.

Chapter 8

Tanner had been looking forward to Harper's party, even though he had the usual nerves that came along with each catering gig. He figured he'd eventually lose his apprehension as he gained more experience and more clients. But right now he wasn't only amped up for the catering aspect or even the opportunity to expand his business. He grinned. He was working with Anita tonight.

He tried telling himself his anticipation was because she was more experienced than Bailey, although Bailey had always been an excellent assistant and server. Who was he kidding? He was excited about spending more time with Anita, even though they would be busy working. And there were always downtimes during a small catering event. While he still intended to keep things on a professional level, with Anita helping him things would go extra smoothly.

A little more than an hour after he'd talked to her, he pulled his Jeep into the curved driveway in front of Harper's vacation house, an A-frame that boasted a spectacular view of the lake. He wished he had time to admire the scenery, but he had work to do.

He put his Jeep into Park and pushed the button

on the dash that opened the trunk. His load was less than usual since Harper was providing chafing dishes, serving platters, utensils, plates, and glasses. All he had to do was unload the food.

"Hey, Tanner."

He turned to see Harper heading toward him, dressed to the nines even more than usual. "Hey. Nice place you have here."

"Thanks, but it's hardly mine," she mumbled as he opened the trunk. When the scent of his cooking labor escaped, she nodded her approval. "Everything smells amazing."

He grinned. He'd warmed up the hot dishes at the diner before loading them into his Jeep. If she thought the food smelled good now, she was going to be even more pleased once the tapas were ready to serve.

"Do you need any help bringing things in?" she asked.

Tanner looked at her, noted her *very* high heels, and shook his head. "Anita can help. Is she around?"

"She should be out in a minute." She looked at him for a long moment.

"Something wrong?"

"No. Nothing." Harper smiled again. "You can take the food to the kitchen, and you should find everything you need. If not, let me know." She pointed to a back-door entrance on the left side of the house. "When you're finished unloading, do you mind parking your car down the street? Parking is going to be tight tonight."

"No problem."

She headed back to the house, and he grabbed a tray of bandarillas. As he brought them into the kitchen, he surveyed the house's open concept. The kitchen led straight to the living room, although there was a six-seater dining table made of a light wood, possibly oak, that gave the illusion of sectioning off the two rooms. He had brought a fold-up table and tablecloth from the diner, but this table would work just as well and would allow for a nicer setup. He then did a quick investigation of the kitchen, noting the updated but rustic décor that fit the atmosphere of a lake house. Nice, very nice.

He started to leave to get another tray when he saw Harper talking to a woman near a small built-in bar in the back corner of the living room. The woman had the same short hairstyle and willowy build as Anita, and she was wearing a white dress that revealed endless, shapely legs. The woman might resemble Anita, but he couldn't see her wearing a dress like that . . . until she turned around.

He did a double take, almost tripping over himself.

Anita?

His eyes suddenly gained a life of their own as his gaze traveled upward from her gorgeous legs to the fitted top portion of the dress. The spaghetti straps showed off her smooth shoulders, and the curved neckline revealed a sexy sneak peek but still left plenty to the imagination.

His imagination was on fire right now.

"Hey, Tanner." Harper waved from across the room. "Everything okay?"

"Uh . . ." His voice, along with his senses, evaporated.

"I'll be right there," Anita said, then turned back to finish talking to Harper, who was grinning like a cat in charge of a dairy farm.

"Uh . . ." He'd intended to say okay, but he was still thunderstruck. Now Harper was outright laughing. That broke his trance. "I'll get the rest of the food," he said, his announcement sounding lame since they weren't listening to him anymore.

He hurried out the door and skidded to a stop in front of his car. He tried to think of Anita wearing her hideous waitress uniform instead of the dress she had on now, but when he started thinking that she always looked hot in that horrendous outfit, too, he gave up. When he ran the back of his hand over his forehead, it felt slick. Beads of sweat? Seriously? Over Anita?

Oh yeah. Over Anita.

Scowling, he tried to get himself together. So what if she was dressed up? He'd seen her in braces, in Pepto-pink, and in casual outfits at church. He'd even seen her covered in dirt when they played on the softball team.

Great, now he was thinking about how well she filled out the church softball uniform, which consisted of shorts and a T-shirt. "Get a grip, Castillo," he muttered.

"What?"

He stilled at the sound of Anita's voice, then turned around. His breath caught again. The lake glistened behind her, and the setting sun bathed her in its glow. "Hey," he said, his voice sounding like a bullfrog burping in a cave.

"Were you talking to yourself?"

"Me?" He turned and grabbed a box of . . . of . . . What was in this box, anyway? "No. That would be crazy. And I'm not crazy." He didn't sound convincing.

She lifted her brow, drawing his attention to her eyes. Stunning, even more so than the dress. "What are you doing with that?" she said, pointing to the box in his arms.

Catering. Focus on the catering. "Taking it to the kitchen." He headed in that direction.

"Why would you bring a giant box of straws to a cocktail party?"

He looked down and frowned. Instead of grabbing the box that held his apron, knives, and seasonings, he had grabbed the one filled with boxes of straws he'd picked up last week from the restaurant supply store in North Little Rock.

He'd kept forgetting to put it in the diner supply closet. He shoved it back into his Jeep and took the cooler instead, pretending he hadn't just outed himself as a little crazy after all.

"What can I carry?" she asked.

Tanner glanced at her dress again, trying to shift his mind to business gear. It would be a shame to ruin that dress while she was catering. "Are you wearing that tonight?"

She glanced down at her outfit, then back at him. "What's wrong with it?"

Not a single thing. He cleared his throat. "You should change into something else. I can bring everything inside."

Hurt flashed in her eyes, and her lips, luscious and red, flattened into a line. "I'm not changing," she said.

He was about to point out the obvious fact that she could spill something on the dress when Harper came outside. "Dylan's here," she said, walking toward them. "You don't mind if I borrow Anita for a minute, do you, Tanner?" Without waiting for an answer, she slipped her arm through Anita's and led her back to the house.

Dylan?

Unable to help himself, he watched Anita walk away, enjoying the view. When she disappeared into the house, he muttered a curse and turned, accidentally clipping the trunk lift of his Jeep. Pain shot straight to his funny bone.

Setting the cooler on the edge of the trunk, he rubbed his elbow, scrambling to regain his bearings. He couldn't afford to blow it tonight, and so far, he was on course to do exactly that. If Anita didn't want to change into something more suited for catering, that was her business. His business was making sure he didn't tank his business.

Leaving the cooler for now, Tanner grabbed another covered tray of tapas and headed for the kitchen. When he didn't see Anita there, he glanced at the living room. She was standing by a small bar in the corner with Harper, talking to a clean-cut guy in a white shirt and black bow tie standing behind the counter. That had to be Dylan.

Something twisted inside him, and when he set down the tapas tray on the quartz countertop, the clatter echoed in the room. The three of them looked at him. "Sorry," he mumbled. Harper nodded and headed for the stairs while Anita and Dylan went back to talking—and Tanner could tell he wasn't the only one who appreciated Anita's new look.

After he'd gone outside and brought the last tray to the kitchen, she was still talking to Dylan. Irritated, he went to her. "You're on the clock," he said, barely giving Dylan a glance.

She flicked her gaze at him, then turned back to Dylan. "I'm sorry, I have to get to work."

"Come by later if you get the chance," he said. Then he held out his hand to Tanner. "Dylan Sears," he said.

Tanner shook, but his focus remained on Anita. "Pour the dips into the dipping cups," he said, sounding bossier than he ever had when they worked together at Sunshine. "Got it?"

"Got it," she muttered and went to the kitchen.

He followed her, making sure to keep his eyes on the stone floor and not on her. He and Anita had never been at odds before. He'd also never seen her show interest in another guy before.

He went back outside to get the cooler, which held the mini apple cheesecakes, stopping in between the house and his Jeep and inhaling the fresh lake air. Tonight was going to be a disaster if they didn't get back on their usual footing. There was still some time left before the guests arrived, and he hoped they could talk for a few minutes and get their focus back on the job.

But when he returned, she wasn't in the kitchen. She wasn't talking with Dylan, either. "Anita?"

"In the pantry."

The pantry was located next to the fridge and out of sight from the living room. When he got to the door, he saw how small it was, with barely enough room for one person. "What are you doing in here?" he said, stepping inside.

"Harper asked me to get the box of margarita

salt from the top shelf. She forgot to put it at the bar, and one of the guests is already here." She pointed to the box at the back of the pantry. "Do you see a step stool somewhere? I can't reach it."

"I'll get it." He walked up behind her and grabbed the box. "Here."

As Anita started to turn around, his hand knocked against a row of metal canisters sitting on the shelf with the salt. Before he could catch it, one of them fell over with a clatter. Anita jumped, and he instinctively put his arms around her. The box of salt hit the floor. "Are you okay?"

Anita nodded, tilting her face up to look at him. "Just startled, that's all."

His heart hammered in his chest. He hadn't been this close to her since his high school party, and at the time they had been in the dark. Here he could clearly see her topaz eyes, the gold color enhanced with shimmery eye shadow. His eyes dropped to her mouth, and he vaguely felt himself pulling her close to him, his hands tightening at her waist. She was tempting. Oh, so tempting.

They needed to talk, and now was the prime time to do that. But talking was the last thing on his mind.

Anita was stunned, confused, and, God help her, loving every second she was in Tanner's arms even though he was just comforting her from a scare. She'd been fighting her attraction from the moment he first arrived tonight, when she and Harper had been talking by the bar. When she'd caught him bending over the trunk of his Jeep . . . He made black pants look very, *very* good. Then he'd turned around and she almost lost her senses. His short hair was slicked back, the light-brown locks mingling with golden highlights only nature could create. He was also freshly shaved, and whatever cologne he was wearing, he needed to wear it more often. It smelled that delicious.

Wait, scratch that. He didn't need anything extra to make him attractive. He was perfect. And now she was in his arms, a near imitation of being in the closet together at his house so long ago. She'd been crazy about him then, and despite all her vows to see him only as a coworker, she was fast losing her resolve.

Why, why, *why* was she still so attracted to him? She couldn't pull her gaze away from his eyes. Were they changing color? They seemed darker, more intense.

"Tanner?"

He immediately let her go. "Uh, glad you're okay."

Whatever had her spellbound vanished. "What's your problem?"

"My problem?" He stepped back, almost knocking a box of Rice-A-Roni off the shelf. His eyes dropped to her dress, then back to her face. "You're the one wearing a white dress while catering."

"You make that sound like a crime."

"It's dumb, don't you think?"

She stilled, the word *dumb* going straight to her core. Even though she knew he wasn't talking about her intelligence, she'd been called dumb and stupid so many times during her childhood that the insult always left her raw. "I can't believe you just said that."

He scrubbed his hand over his face. "I'm sorry, Anita. You're right, I shouldn't have."

But his apology rang hollow. "You never cared what I wore before."

This time his eyes never left her face. "You've never worn *this* before."

For a split second she started to fall into self-pity again. Even Harper's magic couldn't make her attractive to him. But she'd had enough. "I like *this,*" she said, gesturing to the dress with her arms. "I think I look pretty. In fact, I'm a knockout."

Harper threw open the door. Fortunately, the door opened outward, or it would have smacked Tanner. Now that Anita thought about it, that wasn't a bad idea.

"What are you two doing?" Harper said, flashing both of them an irate glare. "The guests are here, and there's nothing ready to eat!"

Anita gasped. "Oh, Harper, I'm so sorry. I was just getting the salt for Dylan—"

"We'll get right on it," Tanner said and walked out of the pantry.

When Anita grabbed the box of salt off the floor, Harper held out her hand. "I'll take that to Dylan," she said. "You help Tanner."

Anita nodded and hurried to the kitchen island where Tanner was already busy setting out the appetizers. She set aside her personal issues with him and followed his directions without question. They got everything ready in record time, and soon she started circulating with the opening appetizer, something Tanner called *Pintxo Gilda*, along with the bandarillas. The Pintxo Gilda were smaller skewers that held manzanillo olives, pepperoncini, and a tiny bite of goat cheese. They looked scrumptious, and according to the guests who tried them, they were.

As the party went on, Anita continued to serve a variety of Tanner's creations, some she hadn't tried before. Near the end of the evening and after several guests had already left, Harper came into the kitchen. "Everyone's pretty much helping themselves now," she said. "Where's Tanner?"

"He went to get some dip cups from his car. We ran out."

She leaned over and whispered, "What were the two of you doing in the pantry?"

"Getting the box of salt, like I said."

Harper arched a doubtful brow. "It took both of you to do that?"

"I couldn't reach the box." She shifted on her feet. As nice as the shoes were, her feet were starting to hurt. "The shelf was too high."

"And you two just happened to be standing *really* close together."

Anita held out her hands. "It's a small pantry."

"Not that small. He's been watching you all night, by the way."

"Who?"

"Tanner." Harper smirked.

"No, he hasn't."

"Yes, he has," Harper said in a singsong voice. "You've been too busy to notice."

"And you're seeing things."

Harper laughed. "I know what I see. Anyway, the party has been fantastic. A lot of these people are business contacts, and they've been raving about the food and the service. You two make a good team."

"But—"

"Oh, there's Robert Kasey. He's always unfashionably late. I'm off to schmooze. Take a break and let Dylan make you a cosmo. He's famous for them."

"A what?" she asked, but Harper was heading over to a short, balding man with thick black glasses wearing a tweed jacket and a white scarf tucked into his red shirt.

Anita hesitated. It didn't feel right to take a break while there were still guests to attend to. But she was thirsty, and she wouldn't mind sitting down for a minute. She walked over to the bar. Dylan was alone and straightening up the liquor bottles on the shelves behind him.

"Hi," she said, feeling the same shyness she had when Harper had introduced her to him. She wasn't used to going up to guys and talking to them out of the blue. When he turned around, she said, "I'm, uh, Anita."

"I know. We met earlier, remember?"

"Oh, right." Way to make a good impression. He probably thought she was an idiot.

"I'm glad you came back." He grinned. "Can I get you a drink?"

Water or a soft drink would be the wisest choice, since she couldn't recall the last time she'd had alcohol. "Um, Harper said that your cosmos are good."

"I try my best. One cosmopolitan for the pretty lady coming right up."

Now it was her turn to smile. At least someone other than Harper thought she looked nice tonight. Then she frowned, thinking about Tanner criticizing her outfit. He hadn't said anything else to her tonight, but his words still stung.

Stop thinking about Tanner. Focus on Dylan.

"Here you go." Dylan set down a martini glass in front of her.

"Thank you." She picked it up and examined the pinkish-orange drink. "What's in it?"

"Vodka, triple sec, lime juice, and cranberry juice. I added a splash of peach schnapps to finish."

That sounded yummy. She took a sip and made a face.

"Is it too tart? I can make you another one."

She saw his concerned expression and shook her head. She didn't want to insult his drink, even though it was tart and the vodka had a kick. "Perfect," she said, taking a big swig.

Dylan chuckled. "I guess you do like it." He leaned on the bar and smiled.

He really was a handsome man. Brown hair cut short in the back but long in the front and thick, straight eyebrows that hovered above heavy-lidded dark-brown eyes. He wore a long-sleeved white shirt and black bow tie. Strange that she wasn't feeling any spark from him, though. "Do you live in Hot Springs?" she asked. Maybe if they talked a little more she'd start feeling something.

"I'm from there, but I live in Little Rock right now. I met Harper in high school. We managed to stay good friends despite going our separate ways after graduation, but lately I've been so busy with school we haven't had time to hang out. I tended bar in college, so she called me earlier in the week and asked if I could work her party. I jumped at the chance, not only to see her but to make a few bucks." He grinned, his teeth as straight and white as Harper's. "But enough about me. I want to hear about you."

"Oh, there's not much to tell." She was a waitress, lived in Maple Falls, and had brunch every month with her family. *Boring.* There was her possible café business, but she wasn't going to say anything about that. "Harper said you're a resident."

"I'm a *poor* resident."

"My brother is a pediatrician."

"That's a tough job. One pediatrics rotation was enough for me."

"I love kids." She picked up her drink and sipped. Wow, this was good. Now that she was used to the vodka and tart lime and cranberry juices, she was enjoying the taste. She started to take another swallow.

"Can I ask you something?"

"Sure." She smiled. She still wasn't feeling anything for Dylan, but she was becoming more relaxed.

"Are you dating the caterer?"

Anita choked. When she started coughing, Dylan leaned over and patted her on the back.

"You okay?"

"Yes," she scratched out, her eyes watering. She accepted the napkin he held out to her. Carefully she wiped the corners of her eyes, not wanting to smudge her makeup. She glanced down at her dress, worried she might have spilled the drink on the pristine fabric, and sighed with relief when she saw she hadn't.

"You shouldn't drink those so fast."

He was probably right, but that didn't stop her from draining her glass. He thought she and Tanner were dating? To quote her favorite movie line, *"Inconceivable."* If she wasn't sure of that before, she was positive now after their encounter in the pantry.

"I need another drink."

He paused, then quickly made it for her. "Take this one slow, okay?"

Anita tried, but the drink was so good, she couldn't help but take a big gulp. "FYI, Tanner's *not* my boyfriend," she said, finally remembering Dylan's question. "We are *not* dating."

"I'm glad to hear that."

She gazed at him. Even tilted her head as she met his eyes. Nope. Nothing. That was disappointing. He was handsome, nice, and a doctor—what else could she ask for? But there were no rough edges to Dylan. There were plenty of delicious ones to Tanner.

Stop thinking about him!

"I guess I figured you two were together because you seem so in sync," Dylan said.

"What do you mean?"

He shrugged. "It's hard to explain. You both

anticipated each other's needs when you were putting out the food and taking care of guests."

"We've worked together for a long time." She finished off her drink.

"Yeah, but there's something else." He took the empty glass from her hand. "Mr. Not-Your-Boyfriend has kept his eye on you all night."

She laughed, and for some reason it sounded both muffled and too loud. "Ha! Harper said the same thing. But I'm here to tell you, you're both wrong."

"Good." He leaned over the bar until their faces were close. "Want to grab some coffee after the party? I'm staying with my parents over the weekend, so I don't have to drive back to Little Rock tonight."

"Would that be like a date?"

"Yeah. Like a date."

Her thoughts swirled. Should she say yes? No? Maybe so? "Can I have another cosmo?"

The drink miraculously appeared in front of her. "So, about our date," he said, leaning forward again.

Anita picked up the martini glass. It had been so long since she'd had a date. She couldn't even remember the last time she'd been on one. Wait, it had been Gary what's his face, her sister's fiancé's best friend. She couldn't remember anything about him except that the date was awful.

She finished the cosmo in one gulp.

"Anita?"

She fixed her gaze on him, although it took a little while for him to stay still. Coffee would be nice. And Dylan would help her forget about Tanner, wouldn't he?

Just say yes.

Chapter 9

Tanner's jaw clenched as he washed the dishes, acutely aware that Anita and Dylan were flirting with each other at the bar. Harper had told him to take five, and he had meant to. He'd even headed to the back kitchen door to get some fresh air, only to stop when he saw Dylan pour Anita a drink. His mood had slid downhill from there.

He was also kicking himself about their conversation in the pantry. He'd been so close to kissing her, and he would have—until she said his name, bringing him back to reality and reminding him about the true nature of their relationship. They were coworkers. The end.

Then he'd said she was dumb, and even though he'd been referring to her choice of work clothing, the damage had been done. He knew how sensitive she was about her learning disabilities. How she'd been teased through school, and how that affected her self-confidence. Worse, his insensitivity had come out because he was trying to cover up the fact he'd been teetering on crossing the line with her.

More than anything he wanted to go over there and find out what was going on between the two of them. No, what he really wanted was to whisk her away from that bartender.

Something he didn't have the right to do.

He grabbed a sponge from the sink and scrubbed the tray until his forearm hurt.

Harper walked into the kitchen. "I thought I told you to take a break." She reached over and turned off the water. "Don't worry about the dishes. The company will pick them up tomorrow. They don't have to be clean."

"I don't need a break." He turned the water back on. When she shut it off again, he looked at her. "Don't you have guests to attend to?"

"There's only two left, and they're relaxing in the four-season room." She frowned. "I don't know why you're being so snippy. Everyone raved about the food tonight. You really have talent."

She didn't have to tell him that everyone enjoyed the food. Five of the guests had asked for his card, and one had said she was going to call him next week and book him for her twins' high school graduation. He should be ecstatic about the new business contacts, but all he could think about was Anita with Mr. Perfect.

Powerless to stop himself, he glanced over his shoulder and saw Anita pounding back a full drink. Was that the same one, or was she already on her next?

Harper handed him a dish towel. "Just go over there and talk to her already." She leaned closer to him. "You know you want to."

He didn't look at her as he dried one of the trays. "Why would I do that?"

"Because you're jealous of her and Dylan."

"Anita can talk to any guy she wants to."

"Does that go for dating too?"

The tray slipped out of his hands and clattered to the floor.

Harper leaned down and picked it up. "You two are going to drive me nuts." She handed him the tray and left.

Tanner turned on the tap and finished washing and drying the trays. After stacking them, he walked over to the table, intending to put away what little food was left. Then he saw Anita swaying against the bar and Dylan putting his hand on her shoulder to steady her.

Without hesitating, he hurried to Anita to see if she was okay. When he got to her, Dylan was still touching her shoulder, even though she'd stopped swaying.

"No more cosmos for you," Dylan said. He looked at Tanner and jerked his hand back.

"Don't be a party pooper," she half slurred, flipping her gaze up at him. "Wow, two Dylans."

Obviously, she was drunk. Not plastered, but silly drunk, and that wasn't much better. "Anita—"

"I hate these shoes." She spun around and kicked one off—hitting Tanner square in the chest.

"Oops!" She put her hand over her mouth and laughed.

He rubbed the center of his sternum. Man, that hurt. He glared at Dylan.

To his credit, Dylan had stepped away from her. "She doesn't drink much, does she?"

"I sure don't." She faced Dylan again and leaned forward. "You're cute," she said, booping his nose. "But you're no Tanner."

Tanner's eyes widened. He would have enjoyed that compliment except she was a sheet and a half to the wind and had no idea what she was saying. He moved close behind her in case she became unsteady again.

"I didn't know she was such a lightweight," Dylan said. "She seemed fine a minute ago."

"How much has she had?"

"Three cosmos. That's it." Dylan shoveled his hand through his perfect hair. "I put half of the vodka I usually do in the third one."

"Where's my cosmo? I want my cosmo." Anita started to waver again.

Tanner looked around the room. The guests were gone and so was Harper. Good. Anita would be mortified if she knew she was acting this way in front of the partygoers. He put his arm around her shoulders and said to Dylan, "I've got it from here."

"I'm sorry. I really am."

Since he appeared genuinely sorry, Tanner tempered his anger.

"I'm gonna get my check from Harper now,"

Dylan said. "You've got the situation under control."

"Tanner, Tanner, Tanner." Anita leaned against him and sighed.

"Let's go outside for a minute." But as soon as she took a step, she stumbled. He moved his hand to her waist and looked down at her feet. He'd forgotten she only had one shoe. She fumbled trying to slip it off. He bent down and took it off for her.

She gazed down at him, a dreamy, tipsy look in her eyes. Then she winced. "I ruined Harper's party, didn't I?"

"You didn't ruin anything," he said, standing up. Then he opened the back sliding door and nudged her outside. "The party's over anyway."

"It is?" She stepped out onto the stone patio. Then she halted. "Wait, I'm supposed to go out with Dylan after the party."

His chest squeezed. Harper was right. He was outright jealous, something he'd never experienced before.

"But I'm not going to." She snuggled against him. "I'd rather be here with you."

Relieved, he smiled. Whether she was drunk or not, he liked what she was saying.

"You're my knight in shining armor, you know that?" She put her arms around his waist, leaning her cheek against his chest.

He was no knight, that was for sure. If he were

a better person, he'd take Anita back inside and make her a cup of strong black coffee. And he *would* do exactly that . . . after he rested his chin on her soft hair for a minute. Or two. He closed his eyes and put his arms around her.

Heaven.

"Hmmm hm-hm hm hmmm."

His eyes flew open. Was she humming?

"By the dawn's early light . . ."

Tanner fought back a laugh. Tough to do when she was hum-singing "The Star-Spangled Banner" in a key unknown to man.

Anita stopped humming and lifted her head. "I wanna go sit by the lake."

"I don't think that's a good—"

She shoved away from him, and he had no option but to let her go. She swayed a little as she walked on the grass, heading toward a gravel path he assumed led to the lake. He hurried after her.

When she stepped onto the stones, she looked at her feet. "Ow. Where are my shoes?" She turned to him. "Did I lose my shoes?"

"They're back at the house."

"Then I guess you'll have to carry me!" She jumped into his arms and clung to him.

This was too much. He held her, not wanting her to fall. But having her in his arms like this was dangerous for both of them. "You need coffee," he said, sounding breathless. "Let's go back inside, and I'll fix you some."

"What if I don't want to? You can't tell me what to do." She moved her hands from his shoulders to his neck, her fingertips brushing the ends of his hair. "I like your haircut," she said, sounding almost sober. "Did I ever tell you that?"

Had she? Right now he couldn't think straight. Her touch sent a shiver down his back, and her mouth was so close to his he could kiss her without moving more than an inch or two.

"Tanner?" she whispered. "Is this real?"

Never had his name sounded so sweet. Never had he wanted something to be more real than this moment with her. It wasn't. He set her on her feet. "Coffee. Now." She had reduced him to one-word sentences.

She plopped down on the grass and then lay down on her side. "I don't feel so good."

Uh-oh. He crouched beside her. "Are you nauseous?"

Her eyes were closed. "No. Just tired. Tired of hoping . . . wishing . . . *pining* . . ." Her eyes opened and she met his gaze.

Up until tonight, the only time he'd ever seen Anita defeated was when they'd met for tutoring after they kissed at his party. She had that same look in her eyes now. Eyes that were clear, not cloudy with drink.

"There y'all are."

Tanner looked up and saw Harper heading toward them. Like Anita, she had taken off her shoes, but she stayed on the grass. "Dylan told me what happened," she said. "Is she okay?"

He shifted his gaze to Anita. Her eyes were closed again, and she leaned against him. "She's drunk, but I think she's ready to sleep it off."

"Oh boy." Harper shook her head. "I already started the coffee. Let's get her back inside."

Instead of helping her to her feet, he knelt down and gently picked her up, then followed Harper inside. The scent of coffee hit him as soon as they walked in.

"Put her on the couch," Harper said. "I'll get the coffee and some water."

Tanner nodded and laid Anita down on a large, tan leather sofa that looked more masculine than Harper's flashy feminine style. She sank against the cushions, already asleep, her body small against the oversized piece of furniture. He tucked a soft throw pillow under her head. She stirred a little, and he was thankful she hadn't full-on passed out. He grabbed a furry white throw off the back of the couch and covered her with it.

Harper came back with a steaming mug and a bottle of water. "Should we wake her up to drink these?"

Tanner shook his head. "Let her sleep a bit."

Harper set the coffee and water on the black acrylic coffee table in front of the couch. "She's going to have a killer hangover tomorrow."

"How is she getting home?" he asked.

"I'm taking her after I clean up from the party." Harper moved her gaze to the couch. "She's teaching Sunday school in the morning. She'll have to double up on the aspirin. Although I don't know how she manages to teach those kids when she's sober."

Tanner half grinned. He wasn't sure either. "Don't worry about giving her a ride. I'll take her home."

"Thanks. That will give me more time to clean up. Actually, I think I'll just spend the night here." Harper yawned. "I'm getting too old for parties."

"I doubt that. I'll come back for her once I load everything up."

It didn't take him long to put everything into his Jeep, and when he returned to the living room, Anita was still asleep. Harper was sitting in a club chair that matched the couch, her feet up on the coffee table, her eyes closed. "I'm ready to go," he said, walking over to her. When she started to get up, he motioned for her to stay seated. "I know my way out."

"Thanks, Tanner. I meant what I said before. You're an amazing chef." She glanced at Anita and lowered her voice. "I'm sure you could work at any fancy restaurant you wanted."

"Been there, done that. I'm more suited to Sunshine."

She paused, then nodded. "All right. Then I just have one question." She gestured between him and Anita. "What's going on with you two?"

Not this again. "Nothing. We're coworkers, that's all."

"And that's what she said about you. But methinks you both protest too much."

Tanner shook his head. Harper wasn't the only one who was tired, and he wasn't in the mood for pointless discussion. "Methinks this isn't any of your business."

"You would be correct, and normally I have a policy about not getting involved with people's love lives."

"You should stick to that."

"Did I hit a nerve?" She got up from the chair, and now that she was barefoot, he had to look down instead of them being eye level like before. "Anita is one of my dearest friends, and I'm very protective of my friends. Be careful with her feelings, Tanner. She's special."

Tanner frowned as Harper went to the couch and sat next to Anita.

"Wake up, sleepyhead. Time to go home."

Anita moaned but didn't wake up. When Harper started to nudge her, he stopped her. "I'll carry her. That way she can keep sleeping."

Harper nodded and moved away as he gathered Anita in his arms. She hung Anita's purse around his neck. "If she wakes up on the way home, tell her I'll bring her other bag to church tomorrow morning."

"Will do."

Harper smiled. "Thanks, Tanner."

He went to the Jeep and carefully put Anita into the passenger seat. He'd already opened the door and tilted the seat back a bit before he brought her out here, expecting that he might have to carry her again. He gazed at her, then lightly brushed her bangs off her forehead.

I know she's special. I should have realized it long before now.

Harper didn't have to worry. He would never hurt Anita. He cared about her too much.

Chapter 10

"Anita! Open up!"

Anita tried to force her eyes open. Ugh, her head was pounding, and her mouth felt like someone had crammed a whole bag of cotton puffs inside. She squinted and licked her dry lips, looking around her bedroom. Wait. What was she doing here? The last thing she remembered was being at Harper's party.

"Anita!"

Kingston? She slapped her hand on the nightstand near her bed, searching for her phone. Panic set in. She always kept her phone on her nightstand when she went to sleep.

Shoving off the covers, she started to sit up. Pain battered her head, and she pressed the heel of her hand against her forehead. What was wrong with her?

She pulled off the covers and glanced down. What in the world? She was wearing the same dress she'd had on last night. How had she gotten home last night?

Why can't I remember getting into bed?

"Anita!"

Now her brother sounded frantic, which wasn't like him. "Just a minute," she hollered, although that made her head pound even more. She stood up, got her balance, staggered to the front door, and threw it open. "What?" she said as she slumped against the doorjamb.

"Thank God you're okay." He looked her up and down. "I think. Geez, sis, you look like hell."

"Thanks a lot," she mumbled, turning around and finding her way to the kitchen.

"What happened to you?" Kingston shut the door behind him. "When you didn't show up for church this morning, I got worried."

"Church!" She whirled around—a mistake because the room spun with her. She gripped the edge of the countertop. "It's Sunday? I have class! What time is it?"

"Relax. Tanner is taking care of your class."

She squinted at him. Then she tapped her aching head. "There must be something really wrong with me, because I thought you just said Tanner is teaching my Sunday school class."

"You heard me right. At this very moment he's educating ten preschoolers about Noah's ark." He walked over to her. "As far as something being wrong with you, my professional guess is yes."

"Very funny." She filled a glass with water and drank every drop. Ah, that felt good. Now she had to do something about the jackhammer in her head.

He took the glass from her hand and began filling it with water again. "That must have been some party last night."

"How did you know about that?"

He handed her the water. "When you weren't in church, I talked to Harper, and she told me what happened."

Anita thought she might have to ask Harper what happened too. "What did she say?"

"That you had too many cosmos."

Right. The cosmos. Her stomach lurched. "I don't feel so well."

"That's called a hangover."

"I don't ever want one again."

"Go sit down, and I'll bring you some aspirin."

She sat down on the couch and leaned back, closing her eyes. A few minutes later the scent of strong coffee filled the air. Kingston tapped her on the shoulder.

"Here's your aspirin and more water. Drink as much as you can today. Alcohol dehydrates you. The coffee will be ready in a minute."

"Thanks, but I don't want coffee," she muttered, taking the aspirin and water.

"Doctor's orders."

Anita looked up at him and scowled. "I'm too old to be your patient."

He laughed her off and went back into the kitchen. She swallowed the aspirin and drank half the water. She had to admit the water made her feel a little better.

After he'd handed her a mug of black coffee, Kingston opened the front window curtains.

Sunlight streamed straight into her eyes. "Is that part of the prescription, or are you torturing me now?" she said, squinting against the bright light.

"A little of both." He sat down next to her. "Remember this next time you drink too much."

"I'm never drinking again." She looked at the coffee, her stomach turning again.

"Good. Hangovers are no fun, as you can see."

"How do you know?"

He cleared his throat. "We're talking about you, remember?"

She sipped the coffee, burning her tongue in the process.

I wish I'd never gotten out of bed.

"Anything else happen last night?"

The note of concern in his voice surprised her. She turned to him. "Last thing I remember was Dylan making me a second cosmo."

"Who's Dylan?"

"Harper's friend. He tended bar for the party."

"That must have been some fancy party." He settled back on the couch and crossed his ankle over his knee. Even his blue jeans were neatly pressed, along with the olive-green T-shirt he was wearing under a long-sleeved teal shirt.

"Not too fancy, but very nice. Anyway, I drank the cosmos and—" *Oh no.* Something about last night came back to her. Not clearly, but enough that she started to cringe. "Oh no," she repeated, this time out loud.

"What?"

"Never mind. I drank too much and got a hang-over. End of story."

"Um, no, Anita. You're not getting off the hook that easily."

She gulped down the coffee, ignoring the heat scorching her mouth. "Like I said, I don't remember anything else." A blatant lie because fuzzy images of last night were circling her brain. Something about calling someone a knight in shining armor. Had she really said that to Dylan? Or worse, to Tanner?

"Are you sure?" he asked.

"Why are you being so nosy?"

"Because things happen sometimes when you get drunk."

"And how do you know *that?*"

"Never mind." His voice was tight. "Who brought you home?"

"Harper." She looked down at her clothes again. Weird that her friend hadn't helped her get undressed. Then again, Harper was probably annoyed about having to take care of her. She cringed. This was awful. As soon as her head stopped pounding and she showered and dressed, she was going to call Harper and apologize.

A relieved expression crossed Kingston's face. "She's a good friend."

"She definitely is."

"Are you going to be all right now?" He

uncrossed his legs and looked into her eyes.

The aspirin was working, and so was the coffee, despite her burned tongue and queasy stomach. "I'm okay. You don't have to babysit me."

"I wouldn't call it babysitting. But I'd like to get back to church before the service is over."

Guilt flooded her. "I'm sorry you had to check on me."

"It's okay." He smiled and got up from the couch. "Call me if you need anything, and I'll be right over."

She nodded. "Thanks, Kingston."

"By the way, did you get a cat?"

Oh no. "Please tell me he's not on the roof."

Kingston shook his head. "No, he was perched in the willow tree on the other side of your house."

Oh, thank goodness. Hopefully he would stay there.

"Love you," he said, walking out the door.

"Love you too."

Once her brother had left, she stared at the blank TV in front of her. The sun wasn't bothering her anymore, but her conscience was. She had caused problems for both her friend and her brother, and she'd let her Sunday school class down. Thank God Tanner had taken over the class, something she never would have guessed he'd do. She'd never even seen him interact with a child before. She hoped her lively students weren't scaring him off of children forever. They were sweet, but they could be rambunctious.

She got up from the couch, went to the bathroom, and made the mistake of looking in the mirror before she took a shower. *Horrific* was the word that came to mind. No wonder Kingston had been so worried. The makeup Harper had expertly applied yesterday was smeared all over, and black streaks ran from her eyes down her cheeks. Her dress was rumpled, her hose were torn, and the barrette was dangling by a thin lock of hair. How embarrassing. Was this how she'd looked when Harper brought her home?

Another unclear memory shot through her mind. Her eyes widened and her stomach twisted, and not because of the hangover. Harper hadn't brought her home last night . . .

Tanner had.

Tanner dipped a paper towel underneath the running water in his sink and tried to rub the purple paint stain off the hem of his blue shirt. Part of today's Noah's ark lesson had involved finger-paint handprints, and somehow his blue-and-red-striped polo shirt had ended up with paint on it. He hadn't noticed it until he arrived home. Fortunately, the spot was small, which could be the reason no one had pointed it out.

He turned off the water and started to go upstairs to change clothes when he heard a dripping sound. He looked at the faucet, hoping that was the problem. Nothing there. He opened the cabinet and groaned. The drain trap was leaking through the patch he'd put on earlier in the week. He'd hoped it would hold out longer.

Figuring he had to fix it now, he walked out to the garage and looked for his toolbox. But his mind wasn't on plumbing. It was on Anita. Teaching the kids this morning had helped distract him from thinking about what had happened last night—not just at Harper's party but when he'd brought her home.

She'd slept all the way from Harper's. Although he could have woken her up, he didn't. Instead he found her key in her purse and carried her inside to her bedroom, telling himself the entire time he was being noble when deep down he simply wanted to hold her again.

He had set her on top of her pale-pink comforter, then noticed a book on her nightstand, *Beginner Business*. Huh. He had no idea she was interested in business. Excellent, though. Forget about asking her to help with scheduling once he owned the diner. She was going to be his assistant manager.

"Tanner?"

"Hey," he'd said, sitting down next to her, all thoughts of business flying out of his head. "How do you feel?"

She had laid her head back on the pillow, her

heavy-lidded eyes holding his. "Why are you here?"

That was an easy question. "I'm taking care of you."

She smiled. "Thank you."

He stood and helped her move under the covers. When he thought she was settled in, he said, "Good night, Anita."

She grabbed his hand. "Don't go."

"I'm not leaving yet. I'll be in the living room." But when he tried to move away, she held on tight.

"Stay." She pulled back the comforter. "Stay with me."

At that point he had frozen. Logically he knew she was still too out of it to know what she was asking him to do. But *he* knew, and for a minute he was tempted. A *long* minute. He was a man, not a saint.

"Go back to sleep." He'd pulled his hand from hers, turned off the light, and shut the door, keeping it cracked open. He stayed at her place for the next hour, pacing back and forth, trying to burn off energy. When he was sure she was okay, he had gone to the diner and unloaded the leftover food, then dragged himself home, exhausted and still frustrated but knowing he'd done the right thing.

He pressed the heel of his hand against his forehead. He had to get his feelings for her under control, especially if he was going to promote her to assistant manager. If she accepted, they would be working closely together, and he couldn't allow himself to be distracted.

But even now he was hoping her hangover wasn't too bad and wondering if he should stop by her house and check on her. No, he needed to stay put. Kingston had already gone over there this morning, and Tanner had seen him come back before the service was over. If something were wrong with Anita, he would have taken care of it.

He grabbed his toolbox, along with a new pipe connector he'd picked up from Price Hardware before his shift on Thursday, and went back inside. He took a wrench from the toolbox, slid underneath the cabinet, and removed the patch, then gave the washer a quick turn.

Water spewed everywhere.

He shouted a curse and turned the shutoff valves, something he should have done in the first place. Soaked, he crawled out from underneath the sink. This was what he got for not paying attention to the task.

"Tanner, what is going on in here?" His mother hurried into the kitchen, still wearing the pink-and-purple-flowered dress she'd worn to church. She looked at him and gasped, her hand covering her cheek. "Oh my word," she said, starting to laugh.

"I'm glad you think this is funny." He stripped

off his shirt and tossed it onto the counter.

Her laughter disappeared. "You're right. That's not funny. I'll call the plumber."

"I can fix it," he said, catching himself almost snapping at her. They didn't need a plumber, especially on Sunday when rates doubled. What he needed was to stop thinking about Anita.

Fat chance of that happening. He crawled back under the sink and examined the pipe.

The doorbell rang. "I'll see who that is," his mother said.

Tanner picked up the wrench and set to work. After replacing the connector, which took all of two minutes, he tightened everything up. He held his breath and turned on the cold-water valve. Good, no leaks. Then he turned on the hot water and backed out of the cabinet. When he turned on the faucet, he looked at the pipe again, then grinned. Fixed.

He put the wrench back into his toolbox on the counter, turned around . . . and almost jumped out of his skin.

"Hi." Anita gave him a little wave. "Sorry, I didn't mean to scare you." She peered around him to the sink, then looked at him again. "Everything okay?"

"Uh, sure." He leaned against the counter, trying to act casual and as if he hadn't soaked himself right before she arrived. "Just a leaky pipe. No big deal."

"That must have been some leak."

Was she blushing? Her cheeks were the color of fresh-picked apples, and he had no idea why they would be. "Not really. I forgot to turn off the shutoff valves." He picked up his wet shirt and tried to find the armholes.

"I wanted to thank you for taking my class today," she said, moving away a few steps until she was standing behind one of the kitchen chairs. She stared at the table in front of her. "I hope they weren't too much trouble."

"They weren't. That Hunter is a pistol, though."

She laughed. "That he is. His older brother was too. He was in my class two years ago."

"They're all pretty cute, though." Unable to make heads or tails of his shirt, he rolled it up into a ball.

His mother entered the kitchen with a bright smile on her face. *Uh-oh.* He liked seeing his mother happy, but not *this* happy. "We were just about to have lunch, Anita."

Riiiight. On Sundays he and his mother usually grabbed a sandwich and went their separate ways—her to nap in the recliner and him to tend to a few neglected chores around the house.

"We'd *love* for you to join us," Mom said, sounding as subtle as a moose crashing a ballet.

Anita hesitated, and for a second he thought she would refuse. Then she said, "Thank you for inviting me."

His mother turned to him, barely able to contain her giddiness. "Go change your clothes," she said out of the corner of her mouth, then smiled back at Anita.

"Be right back." He hurried out of the kitchen and ran upstairs, stripped off his pants, and searched for clean clothes in the disaster that was his bedroom. He finally found a gray T-shirt and black shorts, jamming them on and hoping his mother and Anita weren't talking about him. Or worse, about last night.

He ran back downstairs in his bare feet and rushed into the kitchen, almost sliding into the table where his mother and Anita were sitting. Geez, now he was breathless. "What do you two want for lunch?" Smoothing down his damp hair so he didn't look like he'd electrocuted himself, he started for the pantry. "Sandwiches? Soup? I can whip up some tuna or chicken salad—"

"I'm making lunch today." Mom rose from the table and walked over to him. "You cook all week. Have a seat and relax."

He opened his mouth to protest, then clamped it shut. No point in arguing with her, as usual. He sat down across from Anita. "Yeah, I was glad to take over your class today," he said, making sure Mom knew that Anita was here to thank him and not for any other reason. "The kids and I had a good time."

"Tanner's always been wonderful with children," Mom said, her smile spreading from ear to ear.

When had his mother seen him with children? Unless she was talking about Lonzo when he was little. Otherwise he'd never been around kids.

"Do you like sweet tea, Anita?" Mom asked.

"Yes, ma'am. Can I help you with anything?"

Mom poured two glasses of tea from the pitcher she'd made when they arrived home from church. "That's lovely of you to offer, but no thank you." She walked to the table and handed each of them a glass. "Why don't you two go into the living room and visit while I finish up lunch? I'll let you know when it's ready."

Anita faced him, a questioning look in her eyes.

He didn't like the tension between them, and he definitely didn't want her to feel uncomfortable in his home. "Sure, Mom, thanks." He got up from the chair and motioned for Anita to follow him to the living room.

"I didn't expect to stay for lunch," she said as soon as she sat on the couch. "I hope I'm not imposing."

"Believe me, you're not." He parked himself on the chair opposite the sofa and set the tea glass on the coffee table. "Mom likes company. We don't have people over too often because she works so much." Hard to admit, but it was true. He couldn't remember the last time they'd had a guest over.

She nodded, then stared at her tea glass, showing no signs of having a hangover. She was wearing an outfit more typical of her style—slim jeans, an apricot-colored sweater, and gray slip-on tennis shoes. "She's not the only one, is she?" she said.

If Anita was noticing his overloaded work schedule, that wasn't good. "Things will slow down soon." Not all that soon, but eventually, and then he could chill. "How are you feeling?"

"Better now. Kingston came over this morning."

"I heard he went to check on you during Sunday school."

She glanced up. "I still can't believe you took my class."

He couldn't believe it himself, but it seemed the right thing to do when he'd overheard the head of the Sunday school ministry say that Anita hadn't shown up. "Like I said, it was fun. Who knows, I might volunteer to teach again."

"We can always use substitutes." She smiled.

His pulse jumped. Dressed up or dressed down, she was beautiful inside and out, and he had to have been blind all these years not to notice how much.

"I have to thank you for something else, Tanner."

She spoke the words so quietly he had to strain to hear everything she said. "What's that?"

"Last night."

He stilled. "What about it?"

"I remember what happened." She gulped, her cheeks turning red again. "I remember everything."

Chapter 11

As soon as the words were out of her mouth, Anita wanted to disappear. *What am I doing?*

She sank farther into the purple and gray cushions on the Castillos' old but comfy couch. She should have just thanked Tanner for taking her home last night and left it at that. But no, she had to confess that she remembered everything from last night—and she remembered *every* single thing now, including asking him to spend the night with her. Why, why, *why* hadn't she pretended not to remember? He hadn't even asked her about it.

Stupid, stupid.

She was staring at her tea glass again, and he had to think she was a complete lunatic. She sure felt like one. But it was hard to look at him and not remember seeing him without a shirt in the kitchen. Or how hard it had been to pull her gaze away. He was so hard to resist. Obviously, since she'd basically asked him to sleep with her last night.

How humiliating.

"The cosmos did a number on you, didn't they?"

His gentle tone was irresistible, allowing her to finally look at him. There was no judgment in his eyes, only kindness. "I'm never drinking those again," she said. "Or anything else. Tanner, I'm so sorry for the things I said . . . and did."

"Don't worry about it." He rested his ankle on his knee.

Of course he had great legs, too, and this wasn't the first time she'd seen them. She'd played behind him in the outfield last summer on the church softball team while he played short-stop . . . and she had noticed a lot more than just his legs.

"You're not the only one who's lost their senses when they're drunk," he continued. "I've worked in a lot of restaurants, and most of them sold alcohol. Have I got some stories."

His words, while kind, didn't ease her shame much. "Thanks for understanding."

His gaze held hers. "You don't have to thank me, Anita. I'm glad I was able to be there for you."

Despite everything, she was glad he had been. "Me too."

He hesitated, then got up from his chair and came to sit next to her. "You're not the only one who needs to apologize. I acted like a jerk yesterday."

She'd been so mortified about last night she'd forgotten about their fight in the pantry. "I still don't understand why you had a problem with my dress." Or why he'd said she was dumb for wearing it. *Ouch.* Her feelings were getting hurt all over again.

"I was concerned it would get stained."

Her brow lifted. "Really? That was it?"

Tanner rubbed the back of his neck. "Yeah. That was it."

She set the tea glass down on the end table beside the couch. "Then why didn't you just say that?"

"I should have, I know. I've been stressed lately, about the party, about the— Anyway, that's not a good excuse." He paused, then spoke again. "Remember back in high school?"

A warm shiver ran down her back. "Um, what specifically about high school?"

"After the party when we met up in the library for tutoring." He angled his body until he was facing her. "I asked you then if we were friends. We're still friends now, right?"

The *F* word again. Truth be told, he was a friend. He'd taken care of her when she was drunk and hadn't taken advantage of her. He wasn't judging her now, and he'd apologized for what he'd said to her. He wasn't only a friend, but a good friend. And she realized in that moment that she wanted his friendship. Her attraction to him was still present, but it would eventually fade. Again. Having him in her life as a friend was better than not having him in her life at all.

He was looking at her expectantly, waiting for an answer. "Yes," she said, surprisingly content. "We're friends."

"Good." He sat back against the couch, the tension in his face disappearing.

And because everything was going right between them, she had to ask, "How's Heather?" *Ugh. I can't leave well enough alone, can I?*

He shrugged. "I don't know. I haven't talked to her since she came to the diner."

"Didn't you go out with her after work?"

"I checked her car engine after work," he said. "Then I told her . . ."

"Told her what?"

"That I wasn't interested in her," he said quickly. "And then I blocked her on my phone."

That was a surprise. "Really?"

"Really. I followed your advice and told her the truth." He glanced away, then looked at her again. "When she and I were dating, she wasn't so, um, so—"

"Misguided?"

"That's a good way to put it. I'm kind of glad she showed up, though, because it reminded me why we didn't work out in the first place."

"Why didn't you?" she asked.

"She's totally *not* my type."

Anita grinned.

"Lunch is ready." His mother burst into the room, her grin still on her face. "I hope you like egg salad."

"I do."

"Good. There's also some fresh veggies, dip,

and fruit. And Tanner made some brownies the other day that are to die for."

"That's no surprise." Anita turned to him, catching his smile and smiling back, the exchange feeling natural instead of awkward.

Half an hour later, after finishing a tasty lunch, Anita dug into a thick, chewy brownie. Little Debbie had nothing on Tanner's baking skills. "You're right, Mrs. Castillo," she said, resisting the urge to shove the whole thing in her mouth. "These are incredible."

"Call me Rosa." Tanner's mother took a large bite of her own brownie.

Anita was in the habit of calling elders by their surnames, not only because southern manners had been driven into her and her siblings by their mother but because she liked to show respect. But their lunch had been so comfortable now that she and Tanner were on an even keel that she didn't hesitate to agree. "I will, Rosa."

Rosa beamed. At first glance, Anita hadn't thought Tanner resembled his mother, but now she could see that he had her wonderful smile.

"Do you need anything else?" Rosa got up and started to clear the dishes.

"I'll take care of them, Mom." Tanner put his hand on her forearm. "It's your turn to relax."

"But—"

"He's right, Rosa," Anita said. She had noticed earlier that the Castillos didn't have a dishwasher.

Between her and Tanner it wouldn't take any time to wash the dishes. They both had more than enough experience in that department. "I'll help him clean up."

Rosa glanced at her, then at Tanner. A wry smile appeared. "You know, that is a *good* idea," she said, getting up from the table. "You kids have fun." She hurried out of the kitchen.

"Oh boy." Tanner rolled his eyes. "Sorry about that."

"About what?" She picked up several brownie crumbs from her plate and popped them into her mouth, unwilling to waste a single bite.

"Mom." He stood and grabbed the dirty lunch plates. "She's been after me to move out and get married."

Hold up. "She has?"

"Yep. I guess twenty-seven is hovering over old-maid age. Or is it old-man?" He chuckled and put the dishes in the sink and turned to her. "Do you think it's weird I still live with my mother?"

Well, the conversation had taken a strange turn. "No," she said. "You and your mother have a good relationship. If you're both happy living here, why not?"

"I think so too." His expression sobered. "I guess I'd better give you a heads-up. She had this crazy idea the other night that you and I should go out."

Anita stilled, gaping at the platter containing

leftover veggies. "Oh," was all she managed to say.

"Yeah. Nuts, right?" He turned on the tap and squirted dish soap into the sink. "Even though I told her that wasn't going to happen, when you showed up today, I'm sure she got the wrong idea. Don't worry. I'll set her straight later."

Her heart squeezed, but not as much as it had in the past. Today had been nice. Comfortable. For the first time in years she'd been able to set aside her nerves and gawkiness around Tanner and enjoy lunch with him and his mother. Now that there wasn't a shred of doubt she was firmly in the friend zone, she was discovering that wasn't a bad place to be.

She finished clearing the table while he washed and dried the dishes. He was rinsing off one of the tea glasses as she dipped the large mixing bowl that had held the egg salad into the soapy water. At the same time Tanner reached into the bubbles.

They touched hands. "Sorry," she said, ready to pull away. But when his fingers curled around hers, she froze in place.

What am I doing?

If he were a smart man—and lately he hadn't been acting that smart—he would apologize and release her hand and continue washing dishes as if he hadn't touched her. But his IQ must be hovering in the negative range because he couldn't think, only feel the spark pulsing through him from when their hands had brushed together, and he couldn't help imagining himself reaching for her and gazing into her eyes like one of those melodramatic actors in the telenovelas. Everything had been going so well between them up until this point. And that was the problem. While he was insisting that they were only friends, he wanted so much more.

Not only was he a hypocrite, he was also hurling mixed signals at her. An abhorrent combination he needed to stop.

"Sorry," he said, yanking his hand from hers. "Thought I'd grabbed a fork." He inwardly cringed. Her soft skin felt nothing like a metal eating utensil.

From somewhere behind them erupted the strains of Gloria Gaynor's "I Will Survive."

Anita's brow shot up and she yanked her hand out of the water. "That's my phone."

The iconic disco tune continued.

"Interesting ringtone." He pulled his own hand out of the water and grabbed the dishcloth.

"I finally figured out how to change it this morning. Now where did I put that thing?" She was digging through her purse with the fervency of a dog burrowing under a fence.

The catchy chorus sounded from somewhere inside.

Tanner muttered the next line, scrubbing the egg salad bowl.

"Found it!" She yanked the cell out of her purse and stared at the screen. "Oh, that was Harper. Do you mind if I go into the living room and call her back?"

"Go for it." He rinsed off the bowl.

After she left, he shut off the water and leaned against the sink. *We're friends. Only friends. Get that through your thick head, Castillo.*

During their talk in the living room he'd brought up their relationship in high school to reinforce that, but that hadn't been the smartest decision either. Sure, she'd agreed that they were friends, and he was pleased that they were. But bringing up the past had brought up the kiss, and that memory hadn't been far from his mind all through lunch. Fortunately, his mother and Anita spent most of the meal talking. They really did get along well. No doubt his mother was planning their wedding right now.

He blew out a long breath. The two of them were going to have a long talk after Anita left.

"I'm sorry," Anita said as she came back into the kitchen. "Harper wants to get together this afternoon."

"You can invite her over here." He grabbed a dish towel and turned around, wiping his hands. Harper would be a good buffer between the two

188

of them. That, and Anita could hang around a little longer. *As a friend. As a friend.*

"No, I have to, uh, talk to her about something." She grinned and grabbed her purse. "Thanks again for lunch. See ya at work."

"See ya—"

She rushed out of the kitchen.

He turned and tossed the dish towel onto the counter, hearing her thank his mother for lunch and tell her goodbye. He caught the excitement in her voice. Now that he thought about it, there had been a sparkle in her eyes as she left.

Wait. She wasn't meeting Dylan, was she? Last night she'd said she turned him down for a date. Then again, she'd also sung a janky version of the national anthem too. A cosmo-filled Anita wasn't exactly a reliable narrator.

"Oh, I love that girl," Mom said, breezing into the kitchen. "She's a sweetheart, isn't she?"

She was, and so much more. But she was only his friend. He turned to his mother, prepared to convince her of that fact—and convince himself.

Chapter 12

On Monday evening, Rosa pulled into the parking lot of the one-story office building she cleaned each week, still floating on air about Tanner and Anita. While she'd listened to her son as he explained that he and Anita were only friends and coworkers and admonished her not to get any ideas beyond that, she'd known he was full of baloney. Friends. What a load of poppycock. She'd seen how the two of them kept giving each other tender glances when they thought the other one wasn't looking.

She had no idea why the two of them were in denial about their feelings for each other, but she had promised not to interfere . . . and that was turning out to be harder than anticipated.

Her phone buzzed, and she pulled it out of the pocket of her apron. "Hello?"

"Hello, Mrs. Castillo. This is Dr. Bedford's office. I'm reminding you of your appointment tomorrow."

She winced. She'd forgotten to call and reschedule. "I'm sorry, I can't make it tomorrow. Do you have any appointments open next month?"

"I'm sorry to hear that, but when your general practitioner referred you, she asked us to schedule your appointment with Dr. Bedford as soon as possible. Is there any way you can come in sooner?"

She grabbed her calendar out of her purse and flipped through it. Other than Sundays she was booked solid with her day and night jobs. "I'm sorry, I can't."

"Then I'll put you down for May 6 at 3:00 p.m."

She checked the date, and it was clear. "That will work. I'm sorry for the inconvenience."

"No problem. We'll send you a reminder before the appointment day."

"Thank you." Rosa hung up the phone and wrote the appointment on her calendar and circled it four times. If she forgot this one, she would have to reschedule again, and she didn't want to burn up any more goodwill with Dr. Bedford's office.

She got out of the car and opened the trunk, grabbed her cleaning supplies, and headed to the building. The janitorial closet at the end of the hallway housed plenty of supplies, but she liked using her own tried-and-true ones. Just as she opened the glass door, her phone buzzed again. To have two calls in such a short time was unusual. Alarmed, she found her phone again, relieved to see Erma McAllister's name on the screen.

"Hello?" she said, balancing the phone between her shoulder and ear as she lifted the buckets again.

"Hello, Rosa. This is your monthly invitation to

join us on Thursday nights at Knots and Tangles."

For the past seven months without fail, Erma had called and invited her to join their group, the Bosom Buddies, for knitting or crocheting, snacks, and, as she called it, news dissemination, which really meant plain old-fashioned gossip. Rosa appreciated the invites, and she meant to attend one of their meetings, but so far she hadn't been able to. "I'm sorry—"

"Rosa Castillo, I'm not taking no for an answer this time."

"But—"

"Honey, you need some sweet tea and a few laughs with good friends," Erma said, her tone more tempered. "Playing with yarn is a bonus."

Rosa entered the first office and set down the buckets by the door, then cradled the phone. "I will come, Erma. Next month."

"You said that last month. We're a little worried about you, Rosa. You looked a bit peaked yesterday. Is everything all right?"

"Yes, it's fine. I'm just . . ."

"Busy. I know." Erma sighed again. "I'll give you a call next month, then. But please, let us BBs know if we can help you out in any way. That's what friends are for."

"I will. Thanks, Erma."

"Anytime."

Rosa slipped the phone into her pocket. There was a time when she had hung out with the

BBs, but that was long ago, and only on a few occasions. Over the years she hadn't had time to indulge in knitting, something she'd learned from her mother. "Maybe one day," she said, settling her earbuds into her ears and connecting the plug to her cell phone. She turned on the audio book she'd been listening to for the past week and started to dust.

She was halfway through with the offices when a sharp pain stabbed her chest. Slapping her hand over her heart, she froze. Other than that one burst of pain, she didn't feel anything else. Her heartbeat was steady, and her pulse wasn't racing. After a few minutes, she relaxed. Probably a little attack of gas. That happened sometimes, especially when she ate her meals too fast, like she had with the dinner she'd picked up from a local fast-food place before she arrived at the office building.

Rosa waited few more seconds to see if the pain returned. When it didn't, she went back to work. She'd learned her lesson—next time she wouldn't eat while she was driving in between jobs.

"Congratulations, son. I know you'll do this place proud."

Son. A lump formed in Tanner's throat as George added a flourish to his signature on the Sunshine Diner sale documents. For a plain-Jane kind of guy, he had quite the fancy autograph.

Tanner sat back in the chair in the small but comfortable conference room at the county title office. It hadn't taken long for Harper to get the documents ready, and since the diner sale was cash, the process had been easy. She was pointing to the last line George had to sign on the final document while Wanda, the title company's manager, organized the other documents they had already signed.

Tanner tried to focus on the signing process instead of the unexpected emotion inside him. He couldn't remember the last time anyone other than his mother had called him "son," and he hadn't heard a man say it since he and his father's last conversation. "Thanks, George," he somehow managed to utter. "Thanks for everything."

"No, thank you. I have peace of mind knowing my life's work is in good hands."

"I'll be right back." Wanda left the room.

"I'm sorry I can't stick around, fellas, but I've got another appointment." Harper picked up her enormous handbag off the floor and stood. "Congratulations to both of you. This is a momentous occasion." She looked at Tanner and grinned. "You should celebrate." She exited the room, leaving him and George alone.

"Welp, I'm glad that's done," George said.

But Tanner could tell by the way he tugged at

his thick fingers that the process wasn't as easy as he was letting on. "Don't worry, I'll make sure Sunshine is taken care of."

"Oh, I know."

Tanner thought for a moment. "Come to think of it, I'm sure I'll need some help settling in, though."

George lifted a bushy gray brow. "You? You've been basically running the place over the past year."

"But I've never owned a business before. I'll need some advice from time to time."

"Well, I guess you could give me a call if you run into trouble." George stuck his thumbs underneath his black suspenders, the strain easing from his face. "When you're in a pinch, that is."

"But only in a pinch," Tanner added.

"Right. Only in a pinch." George smiled.

"Thanks for your patience," Wanda said, hurrying back into the room. She handed a neat stack of papers to each of them. "Here's your paperwork. Congratulations."

George and Tanner thanked her, then left for the parking lot. They stopped in front of their cars, which were parked next to each other.

"Oh," George said. "I forgot to tell you—the first Tuesday of every month there's a business owners association meeting at the town hall."

Tanner knew about the meetings thanks to Hayden, who'd made sure to attend every one of them since he'd bought Price Hardware from his parents last year. "I didn't know you went to those meetings."

"I don't."

"Why not?"

George gave him an enigmatic grin. "They start at 6:30 p.m. Don't be late. Quickel is a stickler for punctuality."

Tanner didn't know Mayor Quickel very well, other than the man always ordered extra rolls and peppermill gravy with every meal he ate at the diner, even a hamburger and fries. "Got it."

George looked around the almost empty lot. "Guess that's it. On to a new chapter in my life." He clapped Tanner on the shoulder and got into his car, an old jalopy he'd had for almost as long as he'd owned the diner.

Tanner waved goodbye but didn't get into his Jeep right away, letting what had just happened sink in. He was officially the owner of Sunshine Diner. He could hardly believe it, but he had the paperwork in his hand to prove it.

Harper was right. He did need to celebrate. He glanced at his watch. It was only eight thirty. In his excitement over finalizing the diner purchase he'd skipped breakfast, and now his stomach was growling. Then he grinned. Today was Wednesday, and both he and Anita worked second shift tonight. There was a good chance she was home right now, and he couldn't think of a better person to celebrate with. Of course, he wasn't ready to tell her, or the staff, just yet. Mabel wasn't coming back from her white-water rafting trip until next Wednesday, and he didn't want to make an announcement until the entire Sunshine crew was available.

So what if Anita asked why he wanted to have breakfast with her? Easy answer: there was nothing wrong with two friends sharing a meal together. After talking with his mother Sunday afternoon, he'd made a convincing case for his and Anita's friendship, enough that he believed what he was saying . . . almost. The important thing was that his mother had believed him. Since then she hadn't said a peep about Anita.

He got into his Jeep and headed for her house. It wouldn't be easy to keep this news to himself, but he only had to for a little bit longer.

Meow . . . meow . . .

Anita shoved a pillow over her face. For the past hour— at least it felt that long—Peanut had caterwauled nonstop. She grabbed her phone from the nightstand and checked the time. Seven thirty. Not all that early, but she'd had a tough time sleeping last night, and Wednesdays were her one opportunity to sleep in. Peanut apparently had other ideas—and he had interrupted a wonderful dream she was having about Tanner.

She crammed her pillow back behind her head,

trying to reason with herself. She couldn't shut off her feelings right away. That would take time. And so what if she'd had a dream about him? Dreams didn't mean anything.

Better she concentrated on the news Harper had given her when she called on Sunday, asking to meet in front of the building. She had finally gotten in touch with the owner, and he was willing to set up a walk-through for them. "He didn't say when exactly, but in the next few days."

"Who is he?" Anita asked.

"He goes by Bob, no last name, which makes me wonder if he's really named Bob. Anyway, he is interested in discussing a sale with the right owner. I figured we could at least do an outside inspection of #3 this afternoon, since there's never anyone around downtown on a Sunday."

That's what they did, both of them making copious notes about the outward appearance of the building, including the crumbling asphalt right outside the back entrance. "We can ask him to fix all this up for you, or to lower the price so you can do the repairs yourself," Harper had said when they were finished. "I'll let you know when he's ready to do the walk-through."

Meow . . . meow . . .

She threw off her covers and marched out the door, still in the tank top and matching pajama shorts she'd thrown on last night. She didn't bother to put on a jacket. She didn't bother to scold Peanut either. He would ignore her anyway. A chill went through her, and she hurried.

Get the ladder. Climb the ladder. Get the cat. Put the ladder back. She knew the drill.

But when she got to the top rung, he was still in the center of the roof. "Don't do this to me." She was tired and cold and in no mood to deal with a fussy feline. When he didn't move, she used a tried-and-true method: bribery. "Come on, Peanut," she said in the baby voice she used on the rare occasions he decided to be cooperative. "Let's get down from here and get a treat."

He backed farther away.

"Darn, darn, darn." After a second's hesitation, she climbed up the rest of the rungs and gingerly maneuvered herself onto the roof. Lying on her stomach with her feet dangling over the edge, she yelled, "Get over here, you dumb cat!"

He dashed off into the weeping willow.

"Argh!" That was it. She was buying a set of earplugs. That way he could stay up here and meow himself hoarse.

She scooted back a few inches, then wagged her foot, feeling for the ladder behind her—

Crash!

No, no, no, no! She glanced over her shoulder. No ladder.

Anita scrambled to a sitting position and peered over the edge of the roof. There was the ladder, lying on her concrete patio, Peanut sitting next to it and looking up at her.

Meow.

Closing her eyes, she fought for calm, but instead she became dizzy. Her eyes flew open. She looked at the weeping willow. It had held Peanut's weight, but it wouldn't hold hers. Then her eyes darted to the opposite side where Mabel and her husband, Porter, lived. They were gone on their annual trip to Colorado and Wyoming and wouldn't be back until next week.

"Help!" she called out. "Help!" But it was pointless. Her neighbors had already left for work, and during the day only two or three cars traveled on her street.

Wind shot through her thin tank top. She shivered, not just from the chill but with fright. She couldn't spend eight hours up here waiting for a neighbor to get home. But how was she going to get down?

Chapter 13

When Tanner pulled into Anita's driveway, he slammed on the brakes. A small calico cat sat in the middle of the drive, its tail curled around its body, staring directly at Tanner. He waited for the cat to move, and when it didn't, he honked his horn. The cat dashed off, and Tanner pulled closer to the house and got out of the car. As soon as he stepped onto the concrete, he heard someone yelling.

"Help!"

Anita! He spun around, searching for her. "Where are you?"

"Look up!"

He did and saw one lone hand waving at him from the roof. What in the world was she doing up there? He dashed to the backyard, then froze. Anita was sitting in a tight ball, her arms around her knees. Even from here he could see she was shivering.

"The ladder." She pointed to the ground.

Tanner saw the ladder, the same calico cat that thought he owned the driveway sitting beside it, watching the proceedings with bland interest. When he grabbed the ladder, the cat didn't move. Tanner quickly leaned it against the house.

"Stay still until I get up there." He scrambled

up, stopping at the second-to-top rung. "Give me your hand," he said, holding out his own.

She shook her head. "I don't want you to fall."

"I'm not going to fall."

Anita started to reach for him, then pulled back and hugged her knees again.

He saw the fear in her wide eyes, her short hair wild as if the wind had wreaked havoc with it. How long had she been up here? "Anita?"

"Yeah," she answered in a shaky voice, still not moving toward him.

"Do you trust me?"

She paused, and for a minute he thought she wasn't going to answer him. Then she nodded and grabbed his hand.

He helped her turn around so she could climb down the ladder. Once her foot touched the top rung, he let go of her hand and put his arm around her waist. "I'm right behind you."

Slowly they made their way down the ladder, and he could see not just her voice was shaking but her entire body. No wonder—she was scantily dressed and obviously terrified.

Afraid she would lose her footing and fall, when he stepped on the next-to-last rung he jumped down and grabbed her by the waist, pulling her off the ladder and into his arms.

She leaned against him. "Thank God you showed up," she gasped.

"You're shivering. Let's get you inside." He

opened the back door and led her into her small efficiency kitchen. The décor was all Anita—white, with a splash of pale color here and there. The kitchen and living room were one large area, and he spied a fuzzy lavender blanket draped over the back of a small sofa. Quickly he grabbed it and wrapped it around her. "You should sit down," he said, guiding her to the couch. She complied without a word.

Once she was huddled on the couch, he sat next to her. "How long were you on the roof? Better question: *Why* were you on the roof?"

She snuggled into the blanket and her body stopped quivering slightly. "I was trying to rescue Peanut."

"Peanut?"

"He's my cat. He was the one sitting next to the ladder."

Tanner listened as she told him how she had tried to get Peanut off the roof. "Of course he jumped off as soon as I got up there. Then the ladder fell, and I was stuck."

"Why didn't you call the fire department to get the cat down?"

"I didn't want to bother them."

He wasn't surprised she would be that considerate and compassionate, but she shouldn't have taken such a risk.

"This isn't the first time he's been up there," she added, "just the first time the ladder fell."

"Next time Peanut gets on the roof, call them." The impact of what she'd said hit him square in the gut. Each time she'd climbed that ladder, she could have had an accident. He couldn't bring himself to think about her getting hurt. "Let the fire department do their job," he said sternly.

"I will."

She started to sniff. Was she cold or still tearing up over a cat dumb enough to get stuck on the roof? On second thought, Peanut wasn't all that dumb since he'd managed to get down by himself. "You okay?" he asked, moving closer to her.

"A little. Not as cold." She looked at him, her golden-topaz eyes round and thankful. "I don't know what I would have done if you hadn't come along."

They were inches away from each other, his leg nearly touching hers. "I'm glad I did."

A moment of silence passed as they looked at each other, and he fought the urge to pull her closer. Although the blanket fully covered her, he knew what little she had on under it. "You should put something warmer on," he said as he stood. *For both our sakes*.

"Oh. Yes, that would be a good idea." She rose from the couch, clutching the blanket to her. "Are you hungry? I can make you some breakfast if you want."

He raised an eyebrow. "You mean a bowl of cereal?"

She laughed. "Everyone knows my cereal skills are top notch. That, and I can't cook. Wait, I'm not keeping you from anything, am I?"

"No. I was up early this morning, and I was stopping by to see if you wanted to get breakfast anyway. Why don't I make some for us? Do pancakes sound good?"

Her eyes brightened. "That would be great. I have some pancake mix in the cupboard. I don't think it's expired yet. And there are exactly two eggs in the fridge."

"That's all I need."

While she changed clothes, Tanner searched the kitchen, not only looking for a bowl and a pan but also inspecting her small, very sparse pantry in case she had the ingredients for scratch pancakes. She didn't, but he did find some vanilla and cinnamon. He grabbed those and the pancake mix and set to preparing breakfast—after he'd checked the expiration date on the box.

Anita finally returned, wearing jeans and an old-looking red sweatshirt that had faded to dark pink. "Have a seat," he said, flipping over the last two pancakes. He'd made so many of them over the years he could prepare them in his sleep. "They're almost done."

"I'll get the syrup."

"Already on the table." He grabbed the butter dish and placed it next to the bottle, then went back to finishing the pancakes.

"These look yummy," Anita said when he set the stack in front of her and sat down. She took three before reaching for the syrup, glancing at his plate as he put only one pancake on it. "Is that all you're having?"

"I can't eat a lot of pancakes anymore. I've made too many of them."

"I'm like that with hot dogs. Blech." She dug into the food. "Wow, these are so good. They never taste like this when I make them."

"It's the vanilla and cinnamon."

She looked at him. "First you save me, then you make me pancakes. I don't know how I'm going to pay you back."

"I didn't save you," he said, looking down at his lone pancake.

"Yes, you did." Unexpectedly, she set down her fork, her hand beginning to shake again. "What if no one had noticed me on the roof?"

"One of your neighbors would have."

"They're all at work." Fear entered her eyes. "I was so scared," she whispered.

"Hey," he said. "I would have been scared too."

Anita scoffed. "I doubt it. You probably would have scrambled down somehow."

"Why didn't you climb down the tree?"

"I was afraid I'd fall. I could have broken my arm, my neck, my back—"

He took her hand. "But you didn't."

"Because of you. How can I repay you, Tanner?"

He glanced down at their hands clasped together. Holding her fingers felt so natural. So right. But it was also wrong. He was her boss now, even though she didn't know it. "You don't have to repay me, Anita," he said, slipping his hand out of hers.

"Oh, I'll figure something out." She went back to finishing off the pancakes. When she was done, she asked, "Are you going to eat that?"

Her escapade on the roof—and the reminder that he shouldn't have held her hand—had killed his appetite. "You can have it." He speared the pancake with his fork and put it on her plate.

She started to cut into it, then stopped. "Oh boy." She set down her fork.

"What?"

"I hope my parents don't find out about this. I'll never hear the end of it, especially from Mom." She grimaced. "She'd probably use it as an excuse for me to move back home."

"After living by yourself all this time?" he said. "That seems extreme."

"Never underestimate my mother's ability to underestimate me." She sighed, picking up the fork again. But instead of eating she pushed the pancake around on her plate. "The thing is she's almost always right. Compared to my siblings, I'm the problem child."

Tanner leaned forward. "I don't believe that."

"I do. Not as much as I used to, but the feeling

is still there. I just took a different path than they did, but sometimes I can't shake the thought that I failed them."

"There's nothing wrong with that—finding your own path, I mean. If you're happy with your work and your life, what does it matter?"

"Your brother isn't a lawyer or a pediatrician. Your father isn't a well-known cardiologist . . ." Her eyes widened. "Oh, Tanner, I'm so sorry. I shouldn't have said that."

"It's okay."

"No, it's not. Here I am complaining about my family when your father . . . See, I'm doing it again. Not thinking before I speak."

He met her gaze. "Anita, it's okay to talk about Dad. He's gone and has been for a long time."

"But . . . you rarely ever mention him. At least around me."

Tanner paused, unsure if he could adequately explain how he felt. But he needed to reassure her that she hadn't committed a cardinal sin by bringing up Dad. "That's because talking about him makes other people feel uncomfortable. I remember right after he passed away, even though I was young, everyone around me avoided mentioning him. My mom, teachers, other family, and friends. They resisted talking too much about him when I was around." An unexpected stab of grief hit him, but he pressed on. "Later, my mom was able to talk about Dad more often, and that helped me process the grief. That and half a year of visits to the school counselor." He glanced at his lap. "I guess I'm still in the habit of keeping him to myself."

She nodded, and when he looked up he saw the compassion in her eyes. "Anytime you want to talk about him, I'm here."

A lump blocked his throat. He could tell her offer was genuine. "Thanks," he finally managed to say. "The hardest thing about him being gone, other than missing him, is making sure I live up to the promise to take care of Mom and Lonzo."

She smiled. "You've definitely done that."

He grinned, amazed not only that he'd admitted his fear of failing his family but that it felt right to share it with her. He never expected they had that in common: trying to live up to their parents' expectations.

But he also didn't want to dwell on the past right now. His emotions were too close to the surface for comfort. "Your pancake is getting cold," he said, pointing to her plate.

"That's okay." She picked up her fork. "I don't mind cold pancakes. Or cold pizza. But I draw the line at cold tacos."

"Yuck. Same here."

As he sat back in his chair and watched her eat, his phone vibrated. He pulled it out of his pocket and saw Sunshine's number on the screen, then flashed it at Anita. "Tanner here," he answered.

"Hey, it's Fred. We've got a problem."

Concerned, he popped up from his chair. Unbelievable. He'd owned Sunshine for little more than an hour before a problem happened. "What's wrong?"

"Your buddy Hayden, that's what's wrong. Did you know he was doing a 'Buy two tools, get one free' special today?"

"No. I haven't talked to him in a while. He's been busy with wedding plans." *And I've been busy with my own plans.* "What does that have to do with the diner?"

"He's been sending his customers over here after they finish shopping. Tanner, I'm not kidding you, there is a line down the block. Almost all the way to Knots and Tangles. We're swamped, and we need help. I couldn't get a hold of George, so you were next on the list."

"Hold tight. I'm on my way." He hung up and nearly fist pumped, stopping himself just in time so Anita didn't get suspicious. Still, when he told her what Hayden had done, he couldn't stop grinning. He owed him dinner or a cigar or probably both for sending so much business his way.

Anita got up from the table. "I'll go with you."

He shook his head. "That means almost a double shift for you today. I don't mind working one."

"I don't either. I just need to change."

Tanner shook his head, halfway to the front door already. "Don't worry about it. You can wear that."

She frowned. "George won't like it."

He grinned. "I promise he won't mind."

Chapter 14

It was nearly four thirty by the time Anita was able to take a break. Fred had been right about the number of customers waiting to get into the diner, and with Mabel gone, she and Tanner were sorely needed to handle the crowd. This was the busiest she'd ever seen Sunshine; she and Bailey had practically worn a path in the floor between the dining area and the kitchen.

But while the rest of the crew was frantic, Tanner remained calm. He was also whistling, as if making a dozen hamburgers at a time was no big deal. And it probably wasn't, considering how skilled he was as a cook. No, make that chef. He'd managed to make boxed pancake mix taste gourmet.

Bailey and Fred had clocked out a few minutes ago, leaving the diner empty . . . and her alone with Tanner. The past few hectic hours had distracted her from what happened this morning. She'd been so afraid and upset from her experience on the roof that it had barely registered when he told her he hadn't coincidentally been in her neighborhood like she'd initially thought.

He wanted to have breakfast with me.

That not-so-little fact was sinking in now, and it made her smile. Just as friends, of course, and she was fine with that, even though when he'd held her hand to comfort her, she hadn't wanted to let go. But there was no angst, and most of all no pining.

There was a connection between them, though. Admitting to her fear that she'd failed her parents was something she had never brought up with anyone before, and there had been no judgment from him, only encouragement. That reminded her of their tutoring sessions in high school. He'd never made her feel dumb, and he'd always boosted her confidence.

But it wasn't only his response to her admission about her parents that made her feel closer to him. She was glad he had trusted her enough to discuss his father, and she hoped that if he needed to talk about his dad again, she would be there for him.

She would have to find a way to pay him back for helping her off the roof, though. That would take some thinking, because whatever she decided to do, it would have to be special.

She was standing at the counter, folding napkins around silverware still warm from the dishwasher, when Tanner appeared. His apron was covered with fresh food stains, proof of how busy they'd been. His continual smile was contagious, and she smiled back. "What a day," she said, placing the wrapped silverware on a small pile in front of her.

"Definitely." He started helping her. "I owe Hayden big time for today."

That was an odd thing to say. "More like George owes him."

"Ah. Right. George." He ineptly wrapped the fork and knife and put it on the pile.

Anita picked it up with a smirk. "Leave this to me," she said.

"Gladly." He turned to leave. Suddenly he uttered a curse.

She stilled. She'd only heard him cuss a handful of times, and only when he was angry. She looked up from the silverware bundles. "What's wrong—" Oh.

Heather was looking through the window.

Tanner grabbed Anita's elbow and dragged her to the kitchen, out of sight of the serving window. "This isn't good," he said, starting to pace. The doorbell rang above the diner door, signaling that she had come inside. "This is *not* good."

"I thought you blocked her," Anita said, confused.

"I did."

"Then why is she here?"

He whirled around. "Will you be my girlfriend?"

"What?"

"I'll explain everything after she leaves, but right now we need to be dating." His expression was frantic. "Please, Anita . . . be my girlfriend."

Had she heard him right? All these years of

wishing he wanted to date her, and now that she was over him—almost—he changed his mind?

"Tanner," Heather yelled from the dining room. "I know you're back there. I saw you through the window."

Okay, that sounded weird. Like, stalker weird. Coupled with Tanner's panicked expression, she could see he needed help. "What do you want me to do?"

"Pretend you like me."

Easiest request he'd ever made. "Done."

He stared at her a second, then scrubbed his hand over his face. "Never mind. This isn't fair to you."

"Hey," she said, moving close to him. "Friends help each other out, right?"

He nodded, still looking off kilter—and Tanner Castillo never looked off kilter.

"I'll go talk to her," she said.

"No." He shook his head. "I won't let you solve my problems for me."

"Helloooo!" Heather's shrill, annoyed voice pierced the air.

"We'll talk to her together, then," she said.

After a last pained look, he nodded and they left the kitchen. When Anita saw Heather looking at Tanner like he was a snack, she automatically slipped her hand into his. He gently squeezed her fingers and didn't let go.

"Hey, Heather." Tanner led Anita over to the far

side of the counter. When they stood in front of the other woman, he dropped Anita's hand and moved it to the other side of her waist.

She almost gasped at the pleasant shiver traveling down her spine. Even though they were pretending, she could enjoy the fringe benefits.

Heather's gaze zipped to Tanner's hand, then back to his face. She smiled and leaned forward, ignoring Anita. "I wanted to let you know my Jeep is A-okay. You were right about the oil. The mechanic changed it, and now she purrs like a kitten. I tried calling to tell you about it, but there must be something wrong with your phone."

Did this woman own anything other than low-cut shirts? Anita's face turned red as she averted her gaze from Heather's revealing top. This was so embarrassing. The woman didn't have to be so overtly sexual.

Tanner's hand tightened on Anita's waist. "Glad it's fixed."

Somehow he was managing to keep a straight face. She glanced at him. This close up she could see the tension at the corners of his mouth. He was struggling, and that made her want to help him more.

"When do you get off work?" Heather asked. "There's a great little bar in Hot Springs I just discovered. Small. Intimate. We could get a drink and talk about old times."

How dare this woman hit on Tanner right in

front of her? "He's working late tonight," she snapped.

Heather turned to her, rolled her eyes, then focused on Tanner again. "Or we could skip the drinks, go back to my place, and . . . talk."

Anita narrowed her eyes. "Why, you—"

"Heather," Tanner said, his voice as calm as a waveless sea. "This is my girlfriend, Anita. The one I told you about, remember?"

Anita jerked her head toward him. He'd told Heather they were together?

"Riiiight." Heather sat back and crossed her arms over her chest. "I'm not an idiot, Tanner. You two act more like brother and sister than a couple."

Stunned, Anita blurted out, "That's not true. We *are* dating."

"This?" Heather pointed at them, arm in arm together, then rolled her index finger back and forth. "Screams awkward. I don't believe you're dating at all."

"It's true." Tanner turned to Anita. "She means everything to me."

Anita glanced up, expecting to see desperation in his eyes again. Instead she saw passion. Longing. Wow, he should give up cooking and become an actor, because she was feeling the heat from his gaze straight to her toes. Her pulse went into overdrive.

Now that's a spark.

"Um, yeah. Sure," Heather said in a bored tone then limply waved her hand at Anita. "Why don't you do your job and get me a cup of coffee, m'kay? Tanner and I need to talk."

Something exploded inside Anita. She didn't know if it was the intense attraction to Tanner she was experiencing or the anger boiling inside her, but it didn't matter. There was only one way to shut Heather up. She slipped her arms around Tanner's neck—and kissed him.

Her intention had been to give him a soft peck on the lips, but when he circled his arms around her waist and drew her against him, she forgot about Heather, the diner, and pretending. The feelings coursing through her were real. Oh, so real. As real as the feeling of his mouth on hers.

After a delicious, sensual moment of exploration, Tanner drew away. He gazed at her, their breath mingling before he surprised her by gently kissing her again. A quick, sexy nip. Then he turned to Heather, his arms still around Anita. "I'll be busy tonight, as you can see."

Heather's mouth had dropped open. She closed it quickly, glowering at Tanner. Then she grabbed her purse, shot them both a sharp glare, and stomped off.

Anita couldn't breathe. She wasn't even sure if Heather had actually left the diner, and she didn't care. All the romantic clichés she'd read about over the years were happening to her—trembling legs, curling toes, tingling lips. Her senses were pleasantly confused. She felt the pressure of Tanner's hands on her lower back but couldn't remember where the two of them were standing. All she could focus on was Tanner still holding her . . . still looking at her with those dreamy eyes—

"That was some kiss."

She let out a yelp as Tanner instantly released her, causing her to lose her footing and almost fall to the floor. When she regained her balance, she looked up. *Oh no. No, no, no.*

Jasper Mathis stood in front of them grinning his gray head off.

Tanner willed his pulse to slow, but he was losing the battle. Jasper had scared half the life out of him—although that wasn't the entire reason his heart felt like it had just finished a marathon. No, two marathons, thanks to Anita and that incredible kiss.

The first time they had kissed back in high school had been sweet, but this time— No, he wasn't going to relive it right now. As it was, he was glad he was standing behind the counter. "Uh, hey, Jasper," he said, leaning forward. "How's things?"

Jasper grinned. "From where I'm standing things look pretty doggone good. For you two, that is."

Tanner's face heated. "We were . . . uh, were—"

"I'll get your tea," Anita squeaked. "Mr. . . . Mr. . . ."

"Mathis," Jasper supplied.

"Right." She disappeared into the kitchen as if she'd grown jackrabbit feet.

Reality cut through Tanner's hazy mind. Oh man. He had kissed Anita Bedford in front of Jasper, one of the biggest mouths in Maple Falls. The man lived to chew the fat with almost anyone willing to have a conversation with him. Except for Erma McAllister. For some reason they rubbed each other wrong, although Erma liked to rile him up regardless. In any case, if a person wanted to hop on the Maple Falls grapevine, Jasper was the starting point.

"I didn't know you two are a thing," Jasper said.

"We're not a thing." Tanner grasped for an excuse. "See, there's this girl, Heather—"

"The hussy." Jasper nodded.

He frowned. "What?"

"You don't have to explain your relationship to me. I'm not surprised one bit that you and Anita are knocking boots."

"We're not knocking boots, whatever that is."

"That's not what it looked like to me."

Tanner groaned. He was knee deep right now and had hauled Anita in with him. He should have talked to Heather himself, like he'd planned

220

to if she ever showed back up. But like last time, he'd panicked, and now he'd embarrassed Anita in front of Jasper. "Forget you saw what you saw. Please?"

The old man's eyes widened a bit. "Are you saying you and Anita are a secret?"

"No. I mean yes." There was no point in trying to convince Jasper that he and Anita weren't together.

Jasper grinned. "Well then, your secret's safe with me."

Tanner wanted insurance. "Swear to me you won't tell a soul."

"Boy," Jasper said, his eyes narrowing, every trace of humor instantly gone. "I don't swear on anything or to anyone. My word is as good as gold."

"Yes, sir." Tanner stood straight. "Understood."

"I'm hungry." Jasper ambled to his usual table. "Make sure you give me extra taters today."

"Yes, sir," he repeated.

He headed to the kitchen to check on Anita. She was standing in front of the tea dispenser, but she hadn't poured any. He walked over to her, filled with remorse. "Are you okay?"

She nodded but didn't look at him as she filled Jasper's tea glass. Her cheeks were the color of Red Delicious apples. No, she wasn't okay.

"I'm sorry," he said, feeling worse than a jerk.

When she glanced at him, her eyes were filled

with confusion . . . and her lips were parted in a way that made him want to kiss her again. What was wrong with him? She had shocked him when she initiated the kiss. But that was just for Heather's benefit, no matter how much he wished differently.

She turned to him, composed now. "Don't apologize. We got rid of Heather, didn't we?"

Her calm words helped him relax. "Yes. Thank you."

"You're welcome." She swallowed. "That's what friends are for."

Friends. That kiss had been miles away from friendly— to him anyway.

"Don't worry about Jasper," he said. "I talked to him, and he won't tell anyone what happened. The last thing we need is for the whole town to get the wrong idea."

Anita paused, her brows furrowing the tiniest bit. Then she said, "He's probably wondering what's taking me so long. Jasper's not the most patient man." She left the kitchen, and he heard her say, "Sorry this took so long, Mr. Mathis. We were so busy earlier that I had to make some more tea. Are you having a good day today?"

He had to hand it to her, she was talking with Jasper like nothing had happened. Like the kiss didn't mean anything to her. He touched his mouth. He couldn't say the same for himself.

The diner was busy for the rest of the evening.

Not an overwhelming crowd, but enough that there was no time to talk to Anita alone. Even though she had absolved him, he felt the urge to apologize again.

"Can I give you a ride home?" he asked as soon as Pamela was out the door.

"I can walk." She continued mopping the dining room floor.

"I'll finish that up." He walked over to her.

She dunked the mop into the bucket of soapy water. "I'll do it."

"Anita." He grabbed the mop handle, but he didn't try to take it away from her. "I really am sorry."

Finally she looked up at him with a strained smile. "It's no big deal."

"You seem upset."

"I'm just tired."

"Then let me take you home—"

Her ringtone erupted.

"Go ahead and get that," he said. "I'll finish the floor."

She let go of the mop and walked over to the counter as she pulled out her phone. "Hey." She paused. "Right now? We can't do it another time?" She sighed. "All right, I'll be there." She slipped her phone back into her apron. "I've got to go," she said. "Is it all right if I clock out early?"

"Sure." He was the boss, wasn't he?

"Thanks."

He went back to mopping the floor, flinching when he heard the back door shut as she left. He leaned on the handle and blew out a breath. She was obviously out of sorts. Or maybe he was reading more into her mood than was there. He was tired, too, and they'd both had a long, eventful day. She'd said the kiss was no big deal.

It was a big deal to me.

Tanner finished cleaning up and shut everything off for the night. He left the diner and headed to his Jeep, then stopped when he saw the lights on in #3. Weird, because he could have sworn there wasn't any power hooked up to the building.

Then he saw Harper's red Mercedes in the parking lot. Had someone finally bought the abandoned place? He hoped so. A new business downtown would be good for Maple Falls, and as Hayden had shown, cross-promotion worked. He made a mental note to call Hayden tomorrow, not only to thank him for sending so much business to Sunshine but to see if he knew what was going on with #3.

Whoever the new owner was, he wished him good luck and a lot of success.

Chapter 15

On Sunday morning Anita settled against the supple leather of Kingston's Audi SUV. He had picked her up from her house a few minutes ago, and she was looking out the window as they left Maple Falls and headed for Hot Springs. Her mind had been whirring since Wednesday, and it hadn't slowed down. Even work hadn't given her enough of a distraction, and when she had spilled coffee on Olivia's Aunt Bea's flowery— and very bright—top, she'd known she had to get it together.

So many things had happened this week. Harper had called Wednesday night saying Bob's Realtor was ready to show the building—right that minute. She'd been glad for the interruption, because things between her and Tanner were awkward again. And it was her fault. She never should have kissed him in front of Heather like that. But she'd been so angry, and he was so hot—

"You're quiet this morning," Kingston said as he merged onto the highway. "Is something on your mind?"

"Nope. Nothing."

"How's work been?" he asked.

She should have known he wouldn't let up. He wasn't exactly nosy, but he did like to know what was going on with her. An annoying trait that came from the heart. "Good."

"Just good?"

She didn't look at him. "Yes."

"Huh."

That made her turn. As usual, Kingston looked like he'd stepped out of a fashion magazine—a conservative one, of course. He was dressed in khaki pants, a pale-green-and-white-checked short-sleeved shirt, and tan loafers, every stitch of clothing pressed and shined, along with his short blond hair. He always dressed like this when they went to brunch because this style pleased their mother. Anita doubted Mom was aware that her clean-cut son had an impressive collection of classic-rock concert shirts stashed away in his condo.

"What do you mean, 'huh'?" she asked.

"Normally you have a story or two about the diner customers, or you talk about something funny or interesting that happened in the kitchen—"

"Nothing happening at the diner," she blurted. "Or in the kitchen. Especially not behind the bar."

Kingston glanced at her. "When was the last time you had a vacation?"

"I don't know. Why?"

"Because you're acting weird. First the drinking—"

"That was one time, and one time only."

"—and now you're dodging my question about work. Which makes me think something has happened."

Not wanting her brother to worry, she said, "Something has happened. But I want to tell you and Mom and Dad at the same time."

"Now I'm curious. You're not going to give me a little hint?"

"Not one. If the inquisition is over, what about you? How's your life going?"

"Busy." He stared straight ahead at the road.

"You're not seeing anyone?"

He shook his head. "No."

Anita frowned. "You sound disappointed."

"I am. A little. I'm so busy I can barely find time to go to brunch anymore. As it is, I'm on call right now." Kingston glanced at her. "You know, I'm a little envious of you."

The perfect son, doctor, and brother was envious of her? "Why?"

"You have a life outside of your job. You spend time with friends and teach kids at church. You're not glued to your work."

Not yet, anyway.

"Do you regret becoming a doctor?" she asked.

"No. There isn't anything I'd rather do than take care of my patients and help their families. But it can be all consuming."

She wasn't surprised to hear that. She couldn't remember a time her brother's life hadn't been hectic, even when they were kids. If he wasn't working hard in his advanced classes in school, then he was at the top of all the extracurricular activities their mother had insisted her children do. Now he operated two pediatric practices in addition to the time he spent at the hospital, and all at the age of thirty-one. No wonder he was too busy to have a social life.

"Why don't *you* take a vacation?" she suggested.

"My scheduler keeps telling me I should. And I will, once things slow down." He looked at her again, a sly grin crossing his face. "So what's the deal with you and Tanner?"

She stared out the window. How was she supposed to answer *that* question? "I don't know what you're talking about," she finally responded, hoping he bought her innocent routine. When he laughed, she knew he hadn't.

"I knew there was something going on with you two," he said, still grinning. "A guy doesn't offer to teach little kids for fun."

"You see little kids all the time."

"That's different because it's my job. And I see them one at a time, or maybe two if there are twins. I have several of those. But I'm not herding a whole group of them at once. Besides, Harper told me Tanner took you home from the party."

"Because he's a nice guy."

"And because he likes you."

"Ugh!" She shifted in her seat and faced the front, her arms still crossed. Of course Kingston would tease her about Tanner—although part of her knew the reason he did was because he didn't want to talk about himself anymore. "There is nothing between me and Tanner. Not a thing. Zero. Zip."

"Ah, so you like him too."

"I'm not talking to you anymore."

He laughed and clicked on the turn signal as they approached the off-ramp. "All right, I'll stop teasing. For now."

Anita rolled her eyes. She loved her brother, but right now she was tempted to punch him in the arm. She was surprised he had so much insight about her and Tanner, considering he didn't know Tanner that well—just from church and the infrequent times Kingston visited the diner when he managed to get a decent lunch break. Or maybe this was all just about getting her goat, something he'd loved doing when they were kids. Paisley was almost ten years younger than him, and he'd always handled her differently, more like a parent than a brother.

As they approached their parents' house, her nerves went on alert. Maybe she shouldn't say anything to them about the café until the paperwork was signed, which would be sometime next week. Harper had negotiated a phenomenal deal for her, one even Anita in her extremely limited experience recognized, and she had enough savings to buy out the building for cash. She would have to take out a loan to renovate and turn the space into a café, though, and planned to talk to the bank after everything was official.

Even better, she could just send her parents an email or a note:

BTW, I'm opening a café on Main Street. Ta-ta for now.

But that would cause more problems than telling them face-to-face. She had to tell them, and there was no getting out of it.

Kingston pulled into the driveway and cut off the engine. "I guess I can't just stay in the car, can I?"

"No," she said, his comment making her smile. While it was nice to see her parents, her mother could be overwhelming, a trait that seemed to be getting worse as she aged. "We're in this together."

He nodded and they both got out of the car, her parents' custom-built home looming large in front of them—Mediterranean style with an arched doorway, fat white brick, and small arched windows on every side of the luxurious house. The circular driveway was made of light-pink concrete several shades lighter than the salmon-colored roof. But as beautiful as the house was, Anita never felt at home here. The five of them had grown up in a modest home in Maple Falls until Paisley graduated from high school. She missed that old house but knew her mother didn't. They had started building this one midway through Paisley's senior year. The day after graduation her parents had moved in.

"Ready?" Kingston looked at her.

She nodded. "Ready." They walked toward the dark-stained door, the glass inserts glistening in the sunlight.

Kingston had barely knocked when the door flew open to reveal their mother standing there with a huge smile on her face. "Hello and welcome!" She held out her cheek for Kingston to kiss, and he dutifully did. "You look wonderful as always, dear," she said. "As soon as I'm finished with Paisley's wedding, we're going to work on finding you a bride."

"Can't wait," Kingston said, rolling his eyes as she turned to Anita.

"Hi, Mom," Anita said, giving her a hug.

"Don't you look . . . nice." Mom looked her up and down as if she were taking inventory of Anita's outfit, then leaned forward. "Those jeans are a tad tight, sweetie," she whispered. "You should stay away from formfitting outfits. Flowy fabrics suit your shape better."

She stepped back and opened the door wider to let them in. "I've got fresh coffee and mimosas ready! Your father is in the den. Hopefully he's relaxing and not on the phone again. This is his weekend off. But I know how busy you doctors are, Kingston." She laughed and threaded her arm through his. "*Very* busy and *very* important."

"Do you need help with anything?" Kingston said as Mom led him away.

"Oh, I'd love for you to help me finish setting the table," she said. "I want to know everything you've been doing since the last time we spoke."

"Which was two days ago."

"And I want you to catch me up on those two days." She glanced at Anita, still hanging on to her son's arm. "Please let your father know brunch will be ready shortly."

While her mother and brother made their way to the kitchen, Mom peppering Kingston with questions, Anita fought the temptation to look down at her jeans. She didn't think they were too tight, and in fact they were her most comfortable pair. But her mother never failed to give Anita fashion advice, and Anita never failed to ignore it.

Feeling a little sorry for Kingston and glad she wasn't the one fielding her mother's questions, she went to her father's study, knocking on the door before walking in. Like everything else in the house, the room was bright, white, and airy, with caramel-colored inbuilt bookshelves lined with books, a fireplace with an expensive painting above the mantel, and a TV in a custom-built entertainment center that was the size of one of the walls in her cottage. The Golf Channel was on, and her father was dozing in his white leather recliner.

She looked at him for a minute, not wanting to wake him up. Like Kingston, her father worked hard, sometimes too hard, and he had missed some important milestones in Anita and her siblings' lives. She had never begrudged him that. To the contrary, she was proud of him. His patients loved his bedside manner, and he was an excellent physician, which meant he kept a full schedule. Despite that, he tried to be there for her and her brother and sister when he could.

How often did he get to nap like this? Not as much as he should, she suspected. She started to quietly leave the room so he could continue to rest, only to hear him say her name.

"Anita." Her father was wide awake now. He had learned to wake up instantaneously during his internship in med school. Once he was up, he was always clearheaded. "I didn't realize I had dozed off."

"I'm sorry I woke you up. Mom said it's time for brunch."

"Good, I'm starving." He pushed a button on the side of the recliner, and the footstool went down. He stood and slid his feet into his comfortable tan leather slippers. He was a tall man, an inch shorter than Kingston, and as a cardiologist he was mindful of his weight and fitness, the only exception being Mom's brunches. "Today we're having my favorites," he said, making sure his emerald-green polo shirt was still tucked into his khaki pants that looked similar to his son's. "Smoked salmon pâté with capers, olive salad, and liverwurst."

Her stomach lurched. "That, uh, sounds great." It sounded like a gastronomical nightmare. She hoped her mother had made something more appetizing for the rest of them.

Dad put his arm around her shoulders and gave her a squeeze. "It's good to see you, Anita. You should drop by the hospital and visit sometime. We can have lunch in the cafeteria. The food is surprisingly good."

"Do they serve liverwurst?"

He sighed. "Fortunately, no, or else I'd eat it every day and ruin my heart and waistline." He led her out of the den and into the grand dining room.

As with everything her mother did, attention to detail was on display. Even though today it was just the four family members, all Mom's brunches were fancy enough to serve to the highest of society. Even her mother's outfit screamed sophistication—a gray-and-baby-blue-paisley maxi dress, a gray cashmere sweater, and the pearl necklace her father had given Mom for their twenty-fifth wedding anniversary. Baby-blue low-heeled mules completed the ensemble, and her chin-length hair was dyed platinum blond, even though her natural hair was the same shade of auburn as Anita's.

"You've outdone yourself as usual, Karen." Dad sat down and reached for the mug of coffee in front of him. "Everything looks great."

Mom's gaze darted over the table, as if she were searching for any flaws in her presentation.

Anita sat across from Kingston, noticing his harried expression. She picked up her cup of coffee and hid her smile as she took a sip. At least her mother wasn't harassing her about getting married, although she was sure her time would come.

Mom picked up a salad fork and polished it with a napkin.

"Karen, don't fuss." Dad gestured to the empty seat at the opposite end of the table. "Brunch is perfect as always."

Mom's sterling-silver bracelets jangled against each other as she repositioned an egg cup and took her seat.

After Dad said grace, he picked up the small platter of sliced liverwurst that Mom had put within his reach. Anita scanned the array of food displayed on the long cherrywood table that seated up to twelve people but, with the leaves taken out, provided for four with plenty of room.

In addition to her father's favorites, there was a large bowl of oven-roasted peanuts in the shell, crabmeat-stuffed mushrooms, orange cornbread muffins, a barbecued pork tenderloin garnished with thin slices of radish and cucumber, a lemony green-bean-and-tomato salad, farm-fresh boiled eggs, and pineapple and kiwifruit slices. Her mouth started to water.

"It all looks delicious, Mom." Kingston nodded his approval. He put two of the cornbread muffins on his bone-china plate and passed the basket to Anita.

She took one muffin then was hit with another attack of nerves. This was ridiculous. She wasn't going to be able to eat any of this amazing—except for liverwurst, *blech*—food if she couldn't get her seesawing anxiety under control.

Now or never.

"I have some news," she said, staring at the muffin in front of her as if the little mound of baked cornmeal could give her courage.

"Oh?" Mom placed half a muffin on her plate next to two mushrooms and a thin slice of tenderloin.

"You do?" Kingston quirked an eyebrow. "Is it about Tan—"

"I'm opening a café," she blurted out.

Chapter 16

Silence. Everyone was looking at her now, various levels of surprise on their faces. *Dang it.* That wasn't how she'd wanted to tell them. She had planned to give a bit of explanation before hitting them with the news. She scowled at Kingston. If she hadn't had to shut him up, she could have been more subtle about it.

"You're opening a café?" Mom repeated, tilting her head as if she were having trouble hearing. "You?"

Dad held a large serving spoon over the bowl of olive salad. "Where?"

"You know the building next to Sunshine?"

"The old Trimble Building?" Dad said. "It's been vacant for years."

"Not anymore." She was finally able to smile. "I bought it."

"With what?" Mom said. "You don't have any money."

She ignored her mother's thoughtless barb. "I've been saving up for a long time. Not to buy the building but for a rainy day."

"You saved that much on a *waitress's* salary?" Mom's mouth dropped open.

"Yes, although I'll have to take out a loan for the renovations," she said, disliking how her parents were reacting. Kingston hadn't said anything, but he hadn't dug into his liverwurst either.

"How much do you need?" Dad shoved the serving spoon back into the salad.

"We can write a check for you today." Mom started to get up. "I'll get my checkbook."

"Don't. Please." Now they were thinking she had come here to ask them for money. "I want to do this myself."

Mom shook her head. "No, you don't, sweetie. You don't understand how loans work. They charge you interest."

"I know. I learned about that in math class. And in *Beginner Business*."

"What's that?" Mom asked.

"A book I'm reading."

Her mother's left eyebrow lifted ever so slightly, as if she doubted Anita truly comprehended the situation, much less a book. "You wouldn't have to worry about paying that interest if we gave you the money."

Dad turned to her. "It's no problem for us to help you, Anita."

"I'll be right back." Mom hurried out of the dining room.

Anita winced. She didn't want their money, just their moral support.

"I think it's a great idea," Kingston said. "Maple Falls can use a café. The one near my office in Malvern is always full of people."

"So is the one by the hospital," her Dad pointed out. "I'm proud of you, honey." As her mother came back into the kitchen with a ledger-type checkbook, he added, "We're both proud, right, Karen?"

"Absolutely." Her mother's eyes were bright with excitement as she sat. "You're finally doing something important with your life! Now, how much do you need?" Her pen was poised above the checkbook.

"I don't need any money, Mom. I'm going to do this myself."

"Don't be foolish." While her expression remained optimistic, a tiny bit of irritation laced her tone. "A *smart* businessperson would take free-and-clear money without hesitation."

There it was, the elephant in her life. She wasn't smart; everyone in this room knew that. But her parents were, and so was Kingston. Was she being an idiot for not taking their money?

"Anita," Dad said, his tone gentle. "We paid for Kingston and Paisley to go to school. We want to do the same for you."

When he put it that way, she understood their insistence on giving her the money. And for a brief moment she considered accepting it. But she didn't want to depend on them, or anyone else, to make her business a success. This was something she wanted to do on her own. "Thank you," she said, looking at both of them. "But no."

"For goodness' sake." Her mother tossed the pen onto the checkbook. "Why do you always insist on doing things the hard way, Anita? Do you know how many people would love for someone to give them money?"

Her father's brow furrowed. "Karen, she's made her decision. We have to respect it."

Her mother's mouth pressed into a thin line, her pale-pink lipstick almost disappearing. She picked up the pen, closed the checkbook, and stood. "I'll be right back, then." She left the dining room again.

Anita closed her eyes, her stomach churning. Now her mother was upset, and she could tell her father was too. When she opened her eyes, Kingston's expression was blank. Was he mad at her too?

"There's a good golf match on today," Dad said to Kingston, picking up the olive salad spoon again and plopping a glob on his plate. "They should still be playing after we're finished eating, if you want to watch with me."

"Sure. Sounds good." Kingston cut into his liverwurst with the side of his fork.

Kingston hated golf, even though he had been the second-best player on the golf team when he was in high school, a sport her mother had wanted him to play.

Mom returned, her typical overly hospitable expression back on her face. She sat down and started eating the small piece of tenderloin on her plate, which had to be cold by now.

As her brother and father discussed golf and her mother focused on her tiny meal, Anita tried to choke down the cornbread muffin. She should have just taken the check, and everyone would have been happy.

Except for me.

After they finished eating and Dad and Kingston had gone to the study, Anita silently helped her mother clean up. She brought the dishes from the dining room while her mother loaded the dishwasher, a task she never allowed anyone else to do, even when Anita and her siblings were growing up. Her mother had a particular way of arranging the dirty dishes, and no one had been able to meet that standard.

Anita busied herself with wiping off the table, wondering if her mother wasn't going to speak to her for the rest of the day. When she went back into the kitchen to rinse off the dishcloth, Mom was standing at the butcher-block island packing up the leftovers in glass containers.

"I'm sorry," Anita said, setting the dishcloth by the sink. "I didn't mean to upset you."

"Who's upset?" Mom picked up the leftover muffins and liverwurst and walked to the professional-sized stainless steel refrigerator. "I'm certainly not. It's not my problem if you choose to go into debt when you don't have to."

"Mom . . ." Anita pinched the bridge of her nose then lifted her head. "You're right. It's not your problem."

Her mother slammed the refrigerator door shut and spun around. "I don't understand you, Anita. You live in a tiny old house that you can barely move around in, you have secondhand furniture, you work as a waitress, and don't get me started on your wardrobe—"

"Stop! Just stop." She drew in a deep breath. "Mom, can't you just support me?"

Her mother threw up her hands. "That's what I'm trying to do!"

"I don't mean with money. Or friendly advice or helpful hints or *simple suggestions*." She put the last one in air quotes.

"Then what am I supposed to do? I'm your mother. This is how I mother." Mom dropped onto one of the gold-colored barstools surrounding the island. "Your brother and sister were so much—"

"Easier?" Anita supplied, holding back tears.

Mom shook her head, her own eyes filling. "More like me." She gave Anita a watery smile. "I guess they were easier too. They did everything I suggested they do, and they never fought back."

Anita slipped onto the stool next to her. "Who am I like?"

"*My* mother, believe it or not. Maybe that's why we butt heads so much."

"Grandma had learning disabilities?"

242

"Not that I know of. But back then she didn't have the educational opportunities I had, and you and your siblings had. She also never understood why I wanted to go to college. She believed the highest calling was to be a wife and mother." Mom touched Anita's hand. "She wasn't wrong about that, even though I thought so at the time. I had to prove to her that I could do it all—get married, have children, and have a career. No, scratch that. I had to prove it to myself."

"You did," Anita said. This was the first time she and her mother had talked like this, and she was savoring every second of their conversation. "You succeeded with everything . . . except for me."

"That's not true." Mom sighed. "All that education in psychology, and I didn't apply it to my own parenting." She turned on the stool until she was facing Anita. "I've always been proud of you. How you persevered in school even though it was so difficult. You might not have the academic prowess of your siblings, but you are smart. I should have told you this much sooner. That's a failure on my part."

"No, it's not."

"Don't let me off the hook, even though it's your nature to do so. Don't tell your father this, but Paisley and I have been having arguments too."

"You have?" That was a surprise. She'd never

seen either of them raise their voice to the other.

"She tells me I'm micromanaging her wedding," her mom huffed. "Imagine that—me micromanaging." She shrugged. "I suppose she's right. I did get upset when she said she wanted ecru napkins instead of the cream ones at her bridal shower in August. I told her ecru looked old fashioned, but she insisted."

Anita wasn't surprised that her mother would be nitpicky about shades of off-white, but she was stunned that Paisley had held her ground.

"I'm starting to realize that you three have to live your own lives. It's hard for me to let go of being your mother." Mom gave Anita a sad smile. "Your father and I want to help you, so you really don't have to go into debt. But if you're determined to make this café happen your way, then tell us how we can be supportive."

Anita smiled. "I could use some interior decorating advice. You know I'm not good at that kind of stuff."

"Done! I have just the style in mind too." Her mother's hands moved in an arc. "Think minimalist meets small town."

"Sounds good." She had no idea what that meant, and right now she didn't care. They would undoubtedly have some differences of opinion over décor. And most other things. But right now she felt closer to her mother than she had since she was a little girl.

Mom got up from the chair and hugged Anita. "I love you," she said. "And I'll try to respect your boundaries more."

"That sounds like psychology," Anita said as she wrapped her arms around her mother's waist.

"It is, but it's also good parenting."

"Dad already wants to know if there's any liverwurst left," Kingston said, walking into the kitchen. He stopped and looked at the two of them embracing before he broke out into a grin. "Looks like everything is settled, then?"

Mom looked at Anita. "Is it?"

Anita nodded. *For now.*

"Group hug!" Mom waved Kingston over.

"Anything to get me out of watching golf."

But as her brother embraced them both, Anita knew she was loved.

Chapter 17

"You didn't have to bring me lunch, Tanner." Hayden looked at the gigantic serving of liver and onions in the carryout container in front of him.

"This is kind of an IOU. When we both have some time freed up, I'm taking you out for a steak." They were sitting in Hayden's office at Price Hardware, Tanner balancing his burger and fries on his knee. He handed Hayden the plastic knife and spork he'd brought. "I can't thank you enough for Wednesday. That was a record-setting day for us at the diner."

"You're welcome." Hayden rubbed his hands together. "I haven't had liver and onions in forever."

"It's the iconic Sunshine Monday special."

Hayden used the plastic knife to cut the liver, and it was so tender the serrated blade broke through with ease. "I'll let you know if I plan another buy-two-get-one sale. It was successful for us too. And even better, it brought customers from other cities here. Many of them didn't know we existed."

"How did they find out?"

Hayden took a bite of liver, humming his approval before he swallowed. "I put ads in every paper I could find within a fifty-mile radius. It was expensive, but I think it will be worth it in the long run. Maybe George will want to go in with me on some advertising next time we have a sale."

"Uh . . ."

"What? You don't think he'd be interested?"

Tanner hesitated. He'd scheduled a meeting for Wednesday morning to announce that he'd bought the diner. That was only two days away. Hayden was his best friend, and he knew he could trust him to keep a confidence. "George doesn't own the diner anymore. I do."

Hayden dropped his spork. "Seriously? You bought Sunshine?"

"Yep." While they ate, he explained everything to Hayden, asking him not to say a word to anyone. "That includes Jasper," he said. The old man was currently manning the front of the hardware store while Hayden took his lunch break.

"You got it." His friend grinned, looking like the all-American baseball player he used to be before blowing out his arm pitching in his one and only pro game. "Congratulations, man. This is fantastic news." He paused. "You're not changing the name, are you?"

"Absolutely not. I do have some changes in mind, though. I'm just working out the details."

"Cool." Hayden went back to eating. "Don't

get rid of the liver and onions. This is fantastic."

"I won't. Every senior citizen in Maple Falls would have my head."

"Except Erma. She hates liver and onions, but Riley's threatening to add it to the reception menu."

Hayden's wedding. How could he have forgotten about that? "I'm afraid to ask this, but why?"

"Because Erma is still insisting on wearing her prom dress, even though Harper has taken her shopping twice to find something from this decade."

"How bad can it be? It's just a dress."

"I've seen the dress. It's hideous, two sizes too small, and feels like drapery fabric. I'm on Riley's side with this. Although it's put me in the doghouse with Erma. What is it about weddings that make normally sane women lose their minds? I'm glad we're only doing this once."

"Has Harrison decided when he's throwing you a bachelor party?" Tanner asked, referring to Hayden's eldest brother who lived in Missouri.

"I didn't want one. Henry and Harrison have a hard enough time getting off work. I didn't want them to have to figure out how to throw a party too. That reminds me." He picked up a napkin and wiped his mouth before he grabbed a business card off his desk. "Riley wanted me to give you this the next time I saw you."

Tanner set down his cheeseburger and took

the card. *Sam and Rick's Formal Attire*. A date was written on the bottom, along with a time. "Tuxedo fitting?"

"Yep. A week before the wedding."

"And a month from now." Tanner put the card in his shorts' pocket. "Riley's organized, isn't she?"

"Very. Right now she's working on pairing up the bridesmaids and groomsmen." Hayden scooped up the last of the mashed potatoes and brown gravy. "She has you and Anita together, by the way."

"Oh."

Hayden looked at him, frowning a little. "That's all right, isn't it?"

"Sure. Why wouldn't it be?" Tanner crammed the rest of the burger in his mouth and immediately regretted it as he fought to chew the too-large piece.

"You seem uneasy." Hayden closed the takeout container's lid and threw it into the trash can next to his desk.

Tanner swallowed. "Well, I'm not. I'm fine, and being paired with Anita is fine." More than fine, but she wouldn't think so.

"Good. Riley has this plan for the reception too. She wants all the bridesmaids and groomsmen to be announced in pairs right before Riley and I have our first dance. Each pair will dance with each other, and then once we dance the guests will be invited to join in."

"Just how involved are you in these preparations?"

"Too involved. Mostly I'm there to keep Riley and Erma from killing each other." At Tanner's surprised look, he added, "Not really, but things have been tense. Harper's going to take Erma shopping again. Hopefully they'll find something close to appropriate. At this point Riley will settle for a bathrobe."

Tanner laughed but sobered when Hayden didn't join in. "I guess that's not as funny as I thought."

"It's funny. I'm just too fed up to laugh."

"Are you saying weddings aren't worth it?"

"Oh, they are." Now Hayden was smiling again. "I'd do anything for Riley, and I know she'd do the same. Being supportive while she goes crazy for another month isn't a big deal. Besides, she said she's going to make it up to me, and I'm holding her to that."

An odd sense of envy appeared in Tanner's gut. He wasn't jealous of Hayden marrying Riley, and he was glad his friend was happy—or at least would be once the wedding was over. But for the first time in his life, he wondered what it would be like to love a woman that much. And not for the first time, he wondered if he was missing out on something.

Hayden stood. "I'd better go relieve Jasper. Thanks again for lunch, and I'm down for that steak after Riley and I get back from Montana."

Rising from his chair, Tanner nodded. "That's where you're going to honeymoon?"

"Yep. Neither one of us has been there, and there's lots of hiking, bike riding, and sights to see."

"Right. Because you'll being doing *so* much of that," Tanner quipped.

Hayden simply grinned.

"Speaking of Jasper," Tanner said, putting his takeout container into the trash, "he hasn't said anything, uh, weird lately, has he?"

"He's Jasper. Of course he has."

Tanner stilled. "Like what?"

Hayden rubbed his chin. "Well, this morning he was asking why we didn't carry neon signs."

"Why would you carry neon signs?"

"That's what I asked him. He said they would look nice all lit up in the window."

Tanner laughed. "Okay, that's a little weird."

"Not for Jasper."

Relieved, he agreed. "True." Jasper had said he would keep his word, and as far as Tanner knew, he had. "I'll see you around," he said, heading for the front of the shop.

"See ya. Tanner?"

He turned around. "Yeah?"

"Thanks for being in the wedding. It means a lot to me and Riley."

"Wouldn't miss it for anything." He walked to the front door, past Jasper, who was sitting at the front desk. Jasper gave him a quick nod. Tanner returned it, then went outside and headed back to the diner.

He was due to clock in soon, but he stopped and walked across the street to check out #3. He'd forgotten to ask Hayden if he'd heard someone was going to purchase it. He could call Harper, but she wouldn't reveal any details, and no doubt she would tell him to mind his own business.

He stopped in front of the building. Sure enough, the *For Sale* sign that had been there for years was gone. What kind of business was going in there?

He shrugged. He'd find out soon enough.

When he arrived at Sunshine, the crowd was light enough for Bailey and Fred to handle, so he went back to the office—his office—and sat down in the chair. George always kept a large desk calendar, and Tanner didn't see any reason not to use it until the end of the year. He grabbed a red marker and turned to June, where he circled the days of the tuxedo fitting, the rehearsal dinner, and the wedding. He had to make sure he had coverage, not only for himself but for Anita. He was sure Fred and Mabel wouldn't mind picking up an evening shift, and he'd also been training Kevin as a cook. The kid picked things up quickly, so he could probably cover the night of the wedding.

When he was finished, he put the marker back into the desk and opened up the laptop he'd brought from home this morning. A website that specialized in selling coffee machines and supplies appeared on the screen. He surfed for a minute then sat back in the chair, thinking about Anita again. He hadn't seen her since Wednesday, and while it wasn't unusual in the past for them to go a whole week without talking, he wanted to see her. He'd thought he might after church on Sunday, but right after the service was over, she and Kingston had gone to their parents' house for lunch in Hot Springs.

I miss her.

He looked at the old landline phone on George's desk and thought about the cell phone in his pocket. If he called her, would she answer? Was she still upset with him about the kiss, and about telling Heather they were together? He'd never gotten a chance to explain.

Shaking his head, he went back to surfing the coffee supply site again. He had a lot of explaining to do on Wednesday, and after the meeting he could talk to her about what had happened with Heather. Then once everything was smoothed over, he'd ask her to be his assistant manager. That would make up for Heather. He was sure of it.

"Well, I can't tell you what's wrong with it. Not yet, anyway."

Anita frowned as Rusty stuck his head back

under the hood. She'd finally called him about the car this morning, and he had come right over. She'd hoped the problem would be simple, but if Rusty, who had practically been born with a wrench in his hand, couldn't figure it out right away, she was afraid it would be expensive.

He stood back up and shut the hood. "I'm plain bumfuzzled, Anita," he said in his good-old-boy southern drawl. "I reckon I'll have to take the engine apart."

She rubbed her index finger with her thumb. "Will that be expensive?"

"Won't know till I get in there." He gave her an encouraging smile. "I'll tow her for free, if that'll help ya out."

"Thank you, it will. Good thing you brought your tow truck with you." She glanced at the huge truck with *Rusty's Garage* painted on the side of it parked behind her car.

"Always do. Never know when someone needs a tow. I'll get her hitched up and out of here quicker'n a cat on a tin roof in June."

His words made her realize she hadn't seen Peanut this morning. She glanced up at the roof, although she was sure he wasn't there since he wasn't meowing for her to come get him. Actually, he hadn't been up there since Tanner had rescued her. She'd learned her lesson about getting on the roof when she was alone. Maybe Peanut finally had too.

"Can I get you some coffee or water?" she asked Rusty as he walked over to the tow truck.

"Coffee would be nice."

As she went inside to fix him a cup—two sugars, no cream, like he always ordered at Sunshine—she thought about Tanner. She hadn't seen or talked to him since Wednesday, and for the first time she had *expected* him to contact her instead of just *wishing* he would. He'd said he would explain why he had told Heather they were dating, but so far he hadn't. That irritated her, along with his staunch insistence that Jasper not say anything about seeing them kiss. She didn't want to be the talk of the town either, but he made it sound like it would be the worst thing in the world for him.

Then there was the way he'd kissed her. She still couldn't get that out of her mind, even as she eagerly waited for Harper to get the paperwork ready for her to sign. She'd never kissed anyone except Tanner, and maybe it wasn't that big of a deal for him. Maybe every girl he'd gone out with had been swept off her feet by his kiss.

Lucky girls.

She heard Rusty's truck start up, and she hurried out with his coffee. He wasn't kidding about being fast. He was already climbing into the truck when she walked out of the house, and she hurried to him as he shut the door.

"Much obliged," he said, taking the mug out of her hand.

She couldn't help but smile. Rusty was three years younger than her, and his accent was thicker than any of her classmates' had been. He was the definition of a country boy.

He held up the mug. "I'll get this back to you ASAP."

"No hurry. I've got plenty of them."

Rusty tipped his baseball hat, a bright-red one with the Rusty's Garage logo on the front. "I'll give ya a call when I figure out her problem. Thanks for the business."

She waved as he left, then went inside. Today was her day off, and she needed to get her mind off Tanner. If he hadn't gotten in touch with her by now, he wasn't going to, and she guessed he was eager to put the kiss and Heather behind him. She should do that too.

The midmorning was warm, and she decided to spend some time reading on her patio. Armed with *Beginner Business*, a cup of coffee, and sunscreen, she went outside and sat on one of the two plastic chairs she had purchased shortly after moving in, then propped her feet on the other one.

Meow.

Smiling, she glanced at the ground next to her. Peanut was on his hind legs and batting at her with his paw. She picked him up and sat him in her lap. She'd take an allergy pill later.

By lunchtime she had made it through one chapter of the book while Peanut napped in her lap. She glanced at her white legs, hoping she had gotten a slight tan. Her stomach growled, and she went inside for lunch and fixed herself a PB&J, heavy on the grape *J*.

Gloria Gaynor's voice rang out.

She grabbed her cell off the counter and took a bite of the sandwich, frowning slightly at the unfamiliar number. She considered sending the call to voice mail. If it was important, they would leave a message. But now that she was a soon-to-be business owner, she couldn't easily dismiss calls anymore. She slid her finger across the screen. "Hello?"

"May I speak to Anita Bedford, please?"

Anita frowned. Rusty had a southern drawl, but this man's accent sounded straight out of Mayberry. She would know; she'd seen every episode of *The Andy Griffith Show*. Oh, wait. This couldn't be who she thought it was.

I hope not. "Speaking."

"Well now, good afternoon, young lady. This is Mayor Quickel."

Sure enough, she'd been right. Why would the mayor be calling her? Or should she say *mayuh,* because that was the way he pronounced it. Before she could ask him, he continued.

"I hope you don't mind me calling you out of the blue, but your mother rang me up this morning and told me some wonderful news. I believe congratulations are in order."

Oh no. What had her mother done? "Thank you, *Mayuh,* er, Mayor." She winced.

"I'm always happy to welcome new businesses into the fold. We're all about growth here in Maple Falls, ya know."

She didn't know, and she wondered if he was being genuine. Farley Quickel had been the mayor of Maple Falls for almost a dozen years, and the town had gone in the opposite direction of growth during his tenure.

"Now that you're part of our business community, I'd like to invite you to our bimonthly business leaders' meeting tomorrow evening at six thirty in the basement of the town hall."

She hadn't even bought #3 yet. She'd stick out like ten sore thumbs at a meeting with all the other business owners. *Make that twenty thumbs.* "Uh, Mayor Quickel, I'm not sure I can attend—"

"See you tomorrow, young lady." *Click.*

She stared at the phone. Now she had to go, or she would look like she wasn't serious about her business. *Mother!* She scrolled through her Recents and made a call.

Mom picked up on the first ring. "Hello, sweetie," she said, muffled sounds in the background.

Don't "sweetie" me. Anita tempered her temper. "Where are you?"

"I'm in Little Rock at a custom paint store. There are quite a few people here. I guess Monday is a busy day."

Dread danced with her annoyance. "Why are you at the paint store?"

"I'm picking up color cards so we can select a scheme for the café. They have several lovely cream shades."

What was her mother's obsession with all things cream-colored? "I was planning to purchase paint from Hayden's store."

"The *hardware* store?" Mom clucked her tongue. "This paint is the best money can buy. You can't go wrong with quality paint."

"Price's has quality paint."

"Oh, I'm sure they have *good* paint. Trust me, honey, I know what I'm talking about."

Time to find my backbone. "Mom, I'm going to buy paint from Price's, and I don't want cream."

A pause. "All right. I'll put the cards back."

"Thanks, Mom."

"But if you don't find what you're looking for at Price's, then can we come here?"

That sounded reasonable. "Yes."

"Wonderful!"

"Mom," she said, needing to settle things right now. "Next time, let me know if you're going shopping for something for the café. Then I can either go with you or we can discuss it further. I don't want you wasting your time."

"That's thoughtful of you, and I'll try to remember to do that."

So far so good. "I heard from Mayor Quickel today."

"You did? I'm surprised he called you so quickly. I just spoke to him before I walked into the store. What did he say?"

"Why did you call him?"

"I thought he should know about your new business, that's all. I had some free time, so I gave him a little ringy ding."

Anita cringed. Sometimes her mother sounded older than Jasper.

"Mayor Quickel sounded excited that you bought the building, and when I said you were turning it into a gourmet coffee shop, he was thrilled."

"That's nice, but Mom, please let me tell everyone else, okay? I haven't even signed the contract yet. Remember, this is my business. I'm not ready for anyone to know about it yet."

Another pause. "I'm sorry," her mother said, sounding genuine. "It's hard for me not to take over. I don't realize how much I like being in control until I try not to be. I do wish you would have told me not to say anything, though. I've already told my garden club."

Great. Then again, she couldn't be mad at her mother, since she hadn't told her to keep the café a secret. Fortunately, the garden club was in Hot Springs, so Anita didn't have to worry about anyone else spilling the news . . . except for Quickel.

"Do you want me to call him back and tell him not to say anything?"

"No, that's all right." Hopefully Mayor Quickel wouldn't blab to anyone else before tomorrow's meeting, but she doubted it. Whenever he came into the diner, he always had a group of people with him listening raptly as he took control of the conversation. He also took his sweet tea with six sugars. *Blech.*

"Okay, I won't call him or anyone else. But can I at least do one thing for you?"

She steeled herself. "What?"

"Can I take you shopping for a work wardrobe? I promise I'll keep my opinions to myself. At least I'll try to."

Anita smiled. "Yes, Mom. Shopping would be great."

"Splendid! All right, I'll let you go now. I'm headed to the florist to discuss flowers for Paisley's shower."

"But the shower isn't until next spring."

"Spring and summer is wedding season, so I want to make sure we have the florist I want booked. She's very popular, you know. Ta-ta for now."

Anita shut off her phone, still smiling. She doubted Mom could keep her promise about not offering an opinion, especially when it came to clothes and shopping. But her mother was trying, and that was all she could ask for.

She'd just picked up her partially eaten PB&J when her phone buzzed with a text from Harper.

> Paperwork ready. Meet me at the title office Wednesday morning. Address below. <3

A jolt of nervous excitement ran through her. Harper was fast, and "Bob" must be eager to sell. Strange, since he'd held on to the building for so long. She couldn't believe it. On Wednesday morning she would officially own #3.

She polished off the sandwich and called the bank to make an appointment to talk about a loan. Then she sat down at her table, paper and pen in hand, and tried to figure out how much she thought she would need. Then she remembered the meeting at the diner. She could tell George about the café, along with the rest of the crew. Including Tanner. Maybe later he could answer some questions she had about accounting. Or even give her a tutoring session or two.

Maybe even another kiss.

Her smile disappeared. What was she thinking? They weren't kissing friends. Was that even a thing? If it was, it shouldn't be—in her opinion, anyway.

She and Tanner were friends. That was it. And as a friend, he was going to be as thrilled about her opening the café as she was. She might not be sure about anything else concerning this new adventure, but she was sure of that.

Chapter 18

Tuesday evening, Anita smoothed her pale-blue skirt and adjusted her headband as she headed for the meeting room in the Maple Falls town hall basement. She stopped a few feet from the door, anxiety pressing down on her lungs. She was running a few minutes late for the merchants' meeting, but she couldn't bring herself to go into the room.

She had no business being here—no pun intended. Yesterday she had been happy that things were going so smoothly, but now she was a wreck. It didn't help that her mother had called her right before she was leaving to come here, droning on about ten different kinds of quartz countertops and thirty styles of coffee mugs. Finally she'd had to remind her about the meeting. Of course her mother apologized, but Anita was so out of sorts she'd only grudgingly accepted it. Mom had made a passive-aggressive comment about her tone, and the call went downhill from there.

Somehow she had to shove that unpleasant conversation out of her mind and focus on her new role—almost-owner of #3. If she had half a brain, she'd turn around and leave. Let *Mayuh* Quickel scold her the next time he came to the diner. At this point she'd take a tongue lashing over trying to fit in with a group of business owners.

But she held her ground. Her urge to flee was more than familiar. She'd experienced this sensation before every big assignment and test in school, and somehow she'd graduated despite her fear. She would get through this meeting unscathed too. What was the worst that could happen—everyone snickering at her like the kids had in school?

We're all grown-ups here. All she had to do was sit there and speak when spoken to. Knowing how much the mayor liked to talk, she would probably be silent the whole time.

Unable to put it off any longer, she touched her headband again, drew in a deep breath, and went inside.

When she entered the room, she stopped short. Four rectangular tables were arranged in a square, all the seats filled except one. Farley Quickel sat at the head of the room, and sitting next to him was Granger Hendricks, the chief of Maple Falls' tiny police force. At another table sat Rusty, looking bored out of his mind as he picked at the grease embedded under his fingernails. She hadn't realized he'd be here, and she started to relax a little. Hopefully he had some news about her car, too, since she hadn't heard anything from him since he towed it off.

The rest of the group included Sophie Johnson from Petals and Posies; Jared Young, the pastor at Amazing Grace Church; Jasper Mathis, of all people; and Hayden, representing his hardware store. Sitting next to him was . . . Tanner? She realized he must be subbing for George, and she gave him a quick smile that faded when she saw his confused expression.

"Ah, Ms. Bedford." Mayor Quickel stood, always the southern gentleman with his pale suit and ever-present white hat lying on the table beside a loose sheaf of paper. "Glad you could join us. A gentle reminder, though." He dipped his head and gave her a pointed look. "We begin our meetings at precisely 6:30 p.m."

"Yes, sir," she mumbled.

When Jasper motioned to the empty seat next to him, she hurried and sat down. She was directly across from Tanner, who finally nodded at her before looking away. A knot of dread strangled her stomach as she realized he was going to find out about #3.

Calm down. Not a big deal. He was simply going to find out before she signed the paperwork. After the meeting she would ask him not to say anything to George until the deal was final.

She placed her brand-new notebook and pen on the table and stared at the bright-pink cover as the mayor sat back down.

"Let's continue," Quickel said. "Hayden, you

266

were saying that you're also representing Knots and Tangles tonight."

"Yes, sir," Hayden said with a nod. "Riley's busy with wedding plans—"

"Congratulations," the mayor interjected.

"Thank you. And thank you for saying that last month too." Hayden grinned, a sliver of his blond hair falling over his eyebrows.

"Where is Ms. Erma?" Quickel asked, his expression stern. "I left four messages on her voice mail last week. She hasn't been to one of these meetings in months."

"More like years," Jasper whispered to Anita.

"Well, uh . . ." Now Hayden looked uncertain, which was unusual for him.

Mayor Quickel's thin eyebrow arched. "Yes?"

Hayden paused. "Um, she said to tell you that she would rather kiss a rattlesnake than come to one of your meetings."

Jasper snorted and leaned toward Anita. "She's not wrong," he said, his whisper twice as loud this time.

"Ahem." Mayor Quickel adjusted his red bow tie. "You got something to say, Jasper? I'll remind you that you're a guest at these meetings out of courtesy."

Jasper straightened and looped his thumbs in his suspenders. Unlike George, he didn't need them to keep his pants up, but he was never without them. "I ain't got nothing to say, Farley."

"Fine. Then let's get down to business."

Anita opened her notebook and took notes, listening as everyone talked about their businesses and Maple Falls in general, all the while trying not to glance at Tanner. Hayden was called on again, and he started pushing for the reinstatement of the Too Darn Hot Parade, a Maple Falls original and mainstay until it was canceled two years ago.

"We don't have the funds to do the parade this year," Mayor Quickel said, not sounding a bit disappointed. "Maybe in two or three years—"

"The parade doesn't have to be big," Hayden insisted. "Just a small one, with a few antique cars, the police cruiser, and the elementary school students marching or making a float. Everyone will be taking on their own expenses."

The mayor shook his head, one of the four strands of hair covering the top of his bald head slipping loose. "That hardly seems worth the trouble."

"But—"

"Next item," Mayor Quickel said.

Anita glanced up to see him waving a dismissive hand toward Hayden. Hayden remained silent, but his mouth was pressed into a white line as he strangled his ballpoint pen.

"What a blowhard," Jasper muttered.

"Beg your pardon?" Quickel fixed a pointed look on Jasper.

Jasper waved his hand in imitation of the way Quickel had dismissed Hayden.

The mayor's cheeks turned red, and he cleared his throat. "Mr. Castillo, as the owner of Sunshine Diner, do you have anything to contribute?"

Huh? Anita frowned, her eyes shifting from Tanner to Quickel. "Um, Mr. Quickel," she said.

"Is there a problem, Ms. Bedford?" Quickel tapped on his pad of paper with the end of his pen.

She couldn't believe he'd made such a simple mistake, considering he was the mayor and had been going to Sunshine for ages. Before she could stop herself, she said, "Tanner is the *assistant* manager of the diner, remember? George is the owner."

The entire room went silent. Anita froze. No one was looking at her, not even Jasper. When she turned to the mayor, he had a smirk on his face.

"It seems you're out of the loop, Ms. Bedford. Mr. Castillo recently acquired the diner."

" 'Acquired'?"

"I bought the diner, Anita."

She fell against the chair back, unable to speak. Tanner wasn't looking at her now. Instead, his attention was directed at Quickel.

"Mr. Castillo, you have the floor."

Tanner addressed the mayor, his expression

now impassive, his tone calm. "I want to add my support to Hayden's proposal of reinstating the Too Darn Hot Parade."

"Me too," Sophie said.

"Y'all got my vote," Rusty drawled. "I always have a bunch of fun at the parade. Have since I was knee high to a grasshopper."

"And y'all can have fun again," the mayor said, his brow flattening. "In two to three years."

The room again went silent. Officer Hendricks had his head down. Sophie's arms were crossed over her chest, her simple wedding band glinting under the lights. She had married the Maple Falls football coach, Joe Johnson, last summer. Rusty was giving Quickel the stink eye, although the mayor seemed oblivious.

Quickel smiled. "Well, since I pride myself on being a man of compromise, we'll table the topic for the next meeting."

"But that's in June," Hayden pointed out. "It will be too late to plan anything."

"And you tabled it last month." Sophie glared at Quickel.

"Next meeting, Mr. Price." His gaze scanned the room, landing briefly on every single person there, including Jasper. "I realize a few of you are new business owners, so I'm obliged to let you know that we run things a certain way around here."

"You mean your way?" Sophie frowned. "I'm

not a new business owner, and I've been to these meetings for years, Mayor. You seem to kick the can down the road a lot."

"Like a regular politician," Jasper muttered.

The mayor looked stunned, then regained his composure. "You're free to look at our budget anytime you'd like, Mrs. Johnson," he said. "We're stretched thin as it is. Or would you like to cut our police-force hours in order to make your little parade happen? Maybe we can suspend trash pickup for the summer? Or that pothole in the middle of Main Street can wait so the elementary school children can trip over it when they march?"

"But I just said that there's no expense involved," Hayden groused.

Quickel ignored him. "The next order of business is—"

At that point everyone started talking at once, except for Anita and Tanner. They stared at each other as the rest of the room verbally duked it out. She tried to figure out his expression, but it was completely blank.

He'd bought the diner and hadn't told her? She couldn't believe it.

"Excuse me," Jared said, raising his voice enough that Anita heard him, although no one else seemed to. "Hey!"

Everyone turned to the mild-mannered pastor, who was in the same age group as Anita, Tanner, and Hayden. "We're getting nowhere bickering like this," Jared said.

Quickel rapped his knuckles on the table. "Order!" he exclaimed, as if he were the one settling everyone down, not Jared. "We have seven minutes left, so our discussion of the parade will continue during our next meeting, and that's final."

"Who said the meetings have to last an hour?" Tanner asked.

Anita saw Officer Hendricks shake his head at him.

"Our meetings are *precisely* one hour," Quickel said with a lift of his chin. "Y'all shouldn't have wasted your time arguing."

She thought Jasper was going to jump out of his seat. Quite a feat, considering his advanced age.

"Farley, what's left on the agenda?" Officer Hendricks asked, getting the meeting back on track.

The mayor consulted the papers in front of him. "Ms. Bedford is going to tell us about her new café."

Tanner's jaw dropped. When he'd first arrived tonight, the meeting had started exactly like Hayden said it would. "Quickel is a pain in the backside," Hayden had grumbled before they walked into the room. "This will be my third meeting, and I can see why nothing gets accomplished in this town. The best I can do is grin and bear it until the next election."

But no one was grinning now, least of all Tanner. He waited for Anita to correct Quickel about the café, the way she had corrected him about the diner. When she'd first showed up, Tanner had been confused. Then he'd been sidetracked by the realization she would find out about Sunshine, and he'd spent much of the meeting fighting to maintain his composure. When she did find out, she looked baffled. And a little lost. He'd still wondered why she was here, though.

And now he knew.

Anita didn't correct the mayor. Instead she said, her voice barely above a whisper, "I'm still in the planning stages."

It was true? "Where is this café going to be located?" he blurted out.

"In the old Trimble Building." Quickel leaned back in his chair, a grin plastered on his doughy face.

Anita had bought #3? He thought back to last Wednesday, when she'd had to leave after her phone call, then seeing Harper's Mercedes in the parking lot.

Wait, Harper was in on this too?

"Young lady, I'm pleased as punch that you bought that old place. I can't think of a better business in this town than a fancy gourmet coffee shop."

"It won't be too fancy," she said, her gaze glued to Quickel.

She looked like a frightened baby deer, but any compassion he had for her was fading at warp speed. Did she realize they were going to be in direct competition now? She would usurp all the customers for his coffee bar. His plans were going up in smoke because of her, and she didn't even know it.

"How could you do this to me—to Sunshine," he quickly corrected. But he could see Anita had caught his slip, and now she was staring at her bright-pink notebook.

Quickel turned to Anita. "What kind of coffee will you be serving?"

"Um, organic." She still wasn't looking at Tanner.

"Will you have lattes and cappuccinos?" Sophie asked, looking interested.

Anita nodded.

"Any donuts?" Hendricks added.

"We'll be serving pastries. I think. Like I said, I'm still in the planning phase."

"Will you have Wi-Fi?" Jared asked. "Sometimes I like to work on my sermons in a different location than my office at church. A change of scene helps writer's block."

"We have Wi-Fi at the diner," Tanner ground out.

"I know." Jared grinned. "I've been there a few times. But it's nice to have options."

"Specialty coffees, pastries, Wi-Fi." Quickel nodded his approval. "Sounds like a fine addition to Maple Falls. Let me know if you need anything from my office, Anita. I'm more than happy to help." His grin widened, his teeth slightly stained from all the coffee and tea he drank. "Make sure your momma knows that I'm available too," the mayor added. "I really *enjoyed* our conversation yesterday."

Gross. Everyone, including Hendricks, shifted uncomfortably in their chairs.

Quickel checked his watch then picked up his hat. "Meeting adjourned." He and Hendricks headed out of the room while everyone else went over to congratulate Anita on her new adventure.

Tanner didn't move. He couldn't. The pile of bricks sitting on his chest didn't allow him to. He'd been wrong to wait to tell her about buying the diner, but she was stabbing him in the back—and pocketbook—by opening up her café and not even giving him a hint about it. And he couldn't even argue against the fact that her plans sounded good for the town. Anita's café would be special, despite her saying it wouldn't. Anything would be fancier than Sunshine.

He shook his head. He'd even put in an order for gourmet coffee before he came to the meeting tonight, the brew three times as much as the coffee they usually served. He'd wanted to whet the appetites of his customers, along with letting them know he was making some changes for the better at the diner.

His stomach churned. Anita would ruin him. She had to have known that when she decided to open a coffee shop—

He stopped. She hadn't known until tonight that he'd bought Sunshine. His hypocrisy wasn't lost on him, but he didn't care. Apparently, she hadn't minded ruining George either.

"What's the name of the café?" Sophie asked.

"We don't have a name yet." Anita had somehow managed to physically shrink her appearance in the chair.

Tanner knew she hated all this attention, but he couldn't feel sorry for her. If running a café was what she wanted, then she would have to deal with everything that went with it. He shot up from his chair and stormed out of the room, almost physically ill.

"Hold up," Hayden called as Tanner headed for the exit.

He ignored him, but by the time he got outside, Hayden was right behind him. Finally he slowed down. This wasn't Hayden's fault. He turned to his friend.

"Did you know about the café?" Hayden asked.

His fists balled at his sides, he said, "No. She never said a word."

"Wow, way to keep a secret. I wonder if Riley knows."

Tanner didn't care if Riley or any of Anita's crew knew, although Harper obviously did. He had to regroup and figure out how to keep his business afloat. He needed to retain all his customers and keep making a profit in order not to lose his shirt.

"You okay?"

Tanner keyed in on Hayden and nodded. "Yeah. Sure. Good for Anita."

"You don't seem all that happy for her."

"Why should I be? The last thing Sunshine needs—that I need—is competition."

"How would she be competing with you? All she's doing is serving coffee and snacks."

Might as well fess up about his decimated plans. "I'm putting in a coffee bar at the diner. I already ordered the machines."

Hayden grimaced. "Oh. Yeah, I see what you mean. Hey, I told Riley I'd pick up dinner tonight, but I can call her and tell her I'll be late, if you want to talk this through."

That was the last thing he wanted to do. "Go home," he said. "I'll figure something out."

Hayden nodded. "Thanks for backing me up on the parade. We'll get that thing going eventually. Elections are a year and a half away. It's obvious we need more than just a parade to change Maple Falls."

Hayden was right, but Tanner wasn't focused on Maple Falls right now. His livelihood was at stake, and he didn't know if he could save it.

Anita gasped for air as she opened her front door. She made it to the kitchen counter and leaned over, her lungs burning and sweat sliding down her back. After that fiasco of a business meeting, she'd run all the way home. Now she wanted to puke, and not totally because she had sprinted a longer distance than she had since gym class her junior year. She'd seen the anger in Tanner's eyes before he shot out of the meeting room, and she didn't understand why he was so upset. She was the one who should be angry. And she was. He had never said a word about buying Sunshine, or that he even wanted to. She was a long-term employee of the diner. Did he think she wouldn't care about a change that big? Or was she just a lowly waitress who didn't need to know the background workings of the diner?

When she finally caught her breath, she grabbed a drink of water and collapsed onto the couch, squeezing her eyes shut. When exactly had he planned to tell her he was her new boss? Did everyone else at the diner know except her?

"I Will Survive" sounded abruptly.

That's it. She was burning her phone. She kicked her shoes off, flinging them across the room, then dug into her purse and looked at the screen. *Mom.* Dear Lord, no. She could *not* deal with her mother right now.

But as soon as the phone went silent, it started singing again. Her mother would call at a minimum five times before she would stop, and sometimes more than that. Anita swiped the screen. "Hello."

"Hello, dear. Just calling to see how the meeting went."

It was a horror show. Next month she was taking Erma's cue. Quickel was insufferable, and that crack he'd made about her mother . . . She shuddered.

"Fine," she managed to grind out.

"Lovely. I'm so proud of you, my business-owning daughter. I also want you to mark your calendar—you do have a calendar, right?"

"Yes, Mom," she said, sliding down from the couch and onto the floor, her skirt hiking up her legs to midthigh. The air felt nice and cool on her still-hot skin. Too bad it did nothing for her hot temper.

"Terrific. Make a note for next weekend. We're going to Dallas!"

"Why?" She was almost scared to ask.

"To shop for your wardrobe. You didn't forget your promise, did you?"

Anita pinched the bridge of her nose. Her world was collapsing, and her mother wanted to talk about fashion. "Can't we shop closer to home?"

she said weakly. "Hot Springs and Little Rock have nice stores."

"But not as many as Dallas. Your sister and I have been there three times so far."

Poor Paisley. Anita didn't know how her sister was able to handle law school with their mother bugging her all the time. "Mom, I can't go next weekend. I have to work."

"Where?"

"At Sunshine? You know, my job?"

"I thought you quit already."

"I need the money to make the loan payments."

Silence.

Anita cringed. Her mother was probably biting a hole in her tongue trying not to point out the loan had been unnecessary.

Finally Mom spoke. "When do you think you can leave Sunshine?"

That was a good question. "I'm not sure. Definitely not before next Saturday." When she did decide to leave, she needed to give two weeks' notice. She didn't want to put George in a lurch by having to find a new waitress in a short time.

Not George. Tanner. She scowled.

"Don't put it off too long. I don't want you to exhaust yourself trying to both open a café and work at the diner. Speaking of health, I did notice on Sunday that your skin was a little dry. I forgot to tell you about this cream I've started using. It works wonders on wrinkles."

"I don't have wrinkles, Mom."

"You will if you don't do something with your skin while you're young."

Anita leaned her head against the couch cushions and squeezed her eyes shut. "I have to go, Mom. Talk to you later."

"Ta-ta for—"

Click.

She tossed her phone onto the floor and yanked off her headband. She'd get an earful from her mother about hanging up on her, but Anita would tell her the phone was having technical difficulties. So was Anita, for that matter.

Exhaustion washed over her, and she slumped farther onto the floor. She hadn't been this tired or overwhelmed in a long time. In fact, she couldn't remember ever feeling this way. She was torn up about the café and Sunshine, upset with Tanner, annoyed with her mother, and now she had a headache from the too-tight headband she'd decided to wear tonight. Or maybe her head was pounding from stress. Didn't matter. Her temples were throbbing. She should get up and get some aspirin, but all she wanted to do was sit on the living room floor. She couldn't believe her mother had brought up wrinkles.

And I don't have dry skin.

She closed her eyes again, fully cooled down from her earlier run. Her anger was fading, too, as long as she didn't think about Tanner. She didn't want to think about anything, except maybe falling asleep right here . . .

"Anita?"

Her eyes flew open, and she turned her head. *Unbelievable.* She scrambled up off the floor and marched over to Tanner.

"What are you doing in *my* house?"

Chapter 19

Tanner stumbled back a step. He'd never seen her this angry before, and even though he was still furious himself, it gave him pause. Then again, he had just walked into her house. When he'd pulled into her driveway and seen her door ajar, panic had set in, and he'd hurried inside, only to find her sleeping on the floor. He also saw her skirt hiked up and showing more of her legs than he'd ever seen before. That included the white dress at Harper's party and the pajama shorts she'd had on last week, and those were plenty short. For a quick moment he'd forgotten why he was there. Unreal. Even when he was hopping mad at her, he couldn't stop being attracted to her.

"You left the door open," he said, forcing himself to remain calm. When she shrugged, however, he lost the last shred of composure he had. How could she be so cavalier about her own safety? "You're lucky it was me instead of some stranger," he snapped.

She frowned and crossed her arms. "I know everyone in this town. No one's a stranger."

That was true, not that it made any difference. He'd driven halfway home before turning around and heading for her house. He was still fuming, but since tomorrow morning was the meeting at the diner with all the employees, he and Anita needed to hash this out privately. The last thing he wanted was an emotional blowup in front of everyone, and the chances of that were high if they didn't talk tonight.

"You still haven't answered my question." She tapped her foot and glared at him. "What are you doing here?"

"We need to talk."

"It's a little late for that." She dropped her arms. "Why didn't you tell me you bought the diner?"

"Why didn't you tell me about the café?"

She opened her mouth then closed it again. "Why would I?"

He gaped at her. "What?"

"We're only coworkers—"

"I thought we were more than that."

"Oh, right." She was crossing her arms again. "We're *supposed* to be *friends*. That's why you told me about buying the diner, so I didn't have to find out in front of a bunch of our customers."

He shoved the stab of guilt aside. "Do all your friends know about the café?"

"Harper and Olivia do."

"Anyone else?"

"Do all of your friends know? What about all the employees? Or am I the last on your list to tell?"

He scowled. "Stop deflecting."

"I'm not. I've been working at Sunshine for ten years. Longer than you and everyone else except Mabel and Fred. Don't you think I had the right to know you were buying it?"

"I—"

"Forget it. You didn't think about me at all. Out of sight, out of mind. Just like always."

He moved closer to her. "If you'd let me finish a sentence, I can explain."

"Yeah, like you were going to explain about Heather. I'm still waiting for that."

Ouch. But even though he understood her anger, panic over his business bypassed common sense. "Did you think for a minute about Sunshine, or your coworkers, when you bought #3?"

"I haven't bought it yet."

She hadn't? Great, there was still hope he could talk her out of destroying him.

"Of course I thought about it," she said. "We're going to share customers."

Surely she wasn't that naïve. Then he thought about the book he'd seen on her nightstand the night he brought her home from Harper's party. *Beginner Business*. Now he knew why she was reading it.

"People will have coffee and pastries at the café, and they can eat their meals at Sunshine."

Good grief, she really didn't have any business acumen. "You truly think it would work out that way?"

"It did for Hayden, didn't it? He sent customers over to Sunshine from the hardware store, and we had our best day in years."

"Yeah, but they hadn't eaten at the hardware store. They were hungry. They won't be hungry after having coffee and food at your place. Maybe if the café were across town, but not when it's right next door."

"Did you ever think that the customers would be too full to eat dessert at my place?" she pointed out.

"If that's the case, then why would you open a café next to my diner? Anywhere else would have been better than the spot you picked."

She paused, looking surprised and a little hurt. He ignored that and gave her the final blow. "I'm opening a coffee bar at Sunshine," he said. "It's already in the works."

The color drained from her face. "I didn't know that," she said quietly.

"Now you do." He stuck his hands in the pockets of his jeans. "You'll have to figure out something else to do with #3."

Anita prayed she appeared serene on the outside, because her insides were quaking. She also felt stupid. She had been inspired by Hayden's marketing ploy, and she'd still believed there could be a way for her and Tanner to share customers instead of dividing them . . . if he didn't have a coffee bar. She couldn't believe they had come up with basically the same idea and had never talked to each other about it.

His normally easy, open expression was shuttered, and she couldn't read him at all. "You want me to give up the café," she said, his words sinking in.

"Yes. If you want to work at the coffee bar, you can be a barista. I'll hire a waitress to take your place."

How condescending. "Oh, wow. Thank you, sir." She performed a sarcastic curtsy.

"Anita," he said, his tone tight and strained. "I've spent years saving to buy Sunshine. It means everything to me."

More than she meant to him, that much was clear. And it was also clear that in his eyes, his business was more important than hers.

"It's not too late to change your mind," he said. "You haven't signed the papers yet. You can always back out of the deal, and no one would judge you for it." He moved closer to her, so close she could detect the faint scent of his cologne, the one that turned her thoughts to mush. "Don't open the café, Anita. Please."

She met his gaze, blank a moment ago but now filled with pleading and, unbelievably, something that made her toes grip the carpet. He was right. She could back out of the deal. She could give up owning her own business and continue to be a waitress. Or a barista. Occupations she would enjoy doing. Above all, she would make Tanner happy, something she also enjoyed.

Her new life would be over before it began.

"No," she said, backing away from him. "I'm signing the papers tomorrow, and I'm going to open my café."

He pressed his lips together. Then he said, "You owe me, remember?"

She frowned and she realized he was referring to rescuing her from the roof. "You're calling in that card now?"

"Yes."

Oh, that was low. She always tried to keep her word. This time, though, she was being manipulated. She'd had no idea Tanner could be so devious. "Do you realize what you're asking me to give up? This is my chance to prove to my parents that I'm not less than my siblings. That . . ." She started to choke on her words. "That I'm not a failure."

He glanced away, not saying a word.

His silence told her what she needed to know. She hardened her emotions and moved away from him. "Like you said before, I don't owe you anything."

His eyes narrowed, and then he was blank again. "So where do we go from here?"

That was a painful but easy question to answer. "We go our separate ways. You have your business to run, I have mine. It's not like there's anything between us . . . right?" She stared at him, trying to see any flicker of emotion in his eyes. Despite her anger and frustration, she held on to the last thin thread of hope that he would tell her what she wanted to hear. That there was more between them than a superficial friendship.

"Right," he finally said. "There's nothing between us."

Her heart turned to ice. "Then we have nothing else to say."

Tanner nodded, his jaw set. "Give me enough time to find someone to take your place."

Pain pierced her. He was all too eager to get rid of her now. All she could do was nod.

He turned and walked out the door, slamming it behind him.

Numb, she moved to the couch and sat down. She had expected the final nail in their relationship coffin to hurt more than this. Maybe telling herself that she didn't have feelings for him anymore had helped prepare her for this moment.

After a few minutes she got up and took a Post-it note and a pen from the junk drawer in her kitchen. She scribbled a few lines:

Official notice: 2 weeks. Anita Bedford

She stuck the note on her fridge. That way she'd

remember to take it with her when she worked her next shift. She wouldn't bother going to the meeting. She knew what he had to say. She also didn't want to change her mind. She could have used the money she'd make at the diner until the café was ready to open, but she couldn't work there anymore. Not with Tanner as her boss. Not when she knew he thought so little of her, so little of her right to have her own plans and dreams.

She tried to put a positive spin on things. She could get a bigger loan. She could focus on the café without any distractions and open the coffee shop sooner. She could discuss some ideas for cross-promotion—something she'd read about in the marketing section of her book—with Knots and Tangles and Petals and Posies. Even Hayden would be open to talking about it. Tanner would be sorry he'd kept his mind closed.

She clenched her fists. He would also be sorry he'd let her go.

For the next three weeks after the Maple Falls business meeting, Tanner threw himself into his work. Fortunately, he'd been able to cancel his coffee orders and get most of his money back. No point in serving special coffee now. He'd also picked up two more catering jobs and had put an ad in the paper to hire more waitresses who could also cater. He'd barely seen or talked to his mother. They were both so busy working, their schedules never matched up. If he had been burning the candle low before this, he was burning both ends now.

He was also still angry with Anita. She hadn't showed up to the Wednesday meeting. Not that he expected her to. After he'd met in the kitchen with the staff, who were all happy about the news that he'd bought the diner, he went back to the office and found Anita's Post-it note notice. He couldn't believe she was so petty. It was as if he didn't know her at all anymore.

Beyond pissed, he crumpled the note and threw it way. Then he marked her off the schedule, leaving his own note on her time card: *Employment terminated as of today.* A low blow, but she had her own business now. She obviously didn't need a measly waitress job.

To throw salt in the wound, his own staff was abuzz with the news that Anita was opening a café. "I can't wait to try the coffee," Bailey had said two days after the meeting—the length of time it had taken for the news to spread.

"We all figured this place would end up being yours someday." Fred poured batter into the waffle maker. "The real shocker is Anita."

"You're not mad she didn't tell you about her café?" Tanner had asked.

"Why would I be?" he said. "I'm happy for both of you. A café will be good for Maple Falls."

"Anything she serves will be better than our

swill." Mabel piled the top of a cherry pie high with meringue. "I've been after George for years to change it. Now it won't matter."

Tanner had gone back to the office, frustrated. Everyone was happy with this situation except for him. Not only had he lost the best waitress he'd ever have, but he'd also lost her friendship, for good. He refused to play back their last conversation in his head. Like she'd said, there was nothing left for them to talk about.

At the end of the day, he finished cleaning up the diner after closing, having sent Pamela home a little early. He hadn't closed the diner in a while, and like the last time he'd worked second shift, he thought about that evening when Heather had showed up. He hadn't seen or heard of her since then. But thinking of Heather made him think of Anita, and this time he couldn't stop.

He leaned against the mop handle and scanned the empty diner. Everything here reminded him of her. Like the time it was Jasper's eightieth birthday, and she had encouraged the entire diner to sing the birthday song to him, which they did. The old man had grinned for a full hour after that. Or the time three Girl Scout troops had come into the diner and all sat on her side. She'd worked hard to serve all of them, and she didn't complain once. Like she never complained when she had to serve Mayor Quickel, who always kept her hopping and was a lousy tipper.

Tanner gripped the mop handle and went back to scrubbing the floor. It would take time, but eventually he could be here without thinking about her—or about what she was doing at #3. The sale had gone through, and he had heard some of the customers talking about construction starting there, but he'd avoided checking it out himself, not wanting to run into Anita.

He was starting to realize how much of a jerk he'd been to her the other night. She'd told him about feeling like an outsider in her family, and he knew that having her own business would elevate her in their eyes. Still, his anger and panic over losing even one customer had overridden common sense and decency. She was furious with him, and she had the right to be.

But that didn't change the fact that one of them had to give in—and it wasn't going to be him.

Quickly he finished closing and took the trash out to the dumpster. He was about to get into his Jeep when a red sports car zipped into the lot and stopped in front of him. There was still some daylight left, along with a lot of humidity. Sweat ran down his back as the window rolled down and George poked his head out. "Hey, Tanner."

"George?" His old boss was the last person he'd expected to see driving a sports car.

"Like my new wheels?" When Tanner nodded, George added, "It's a '59 Alfa Romero." He patted the door affectionately. "My dream car.

Thanks to you I was able to buy it at an auction on Saturday. Just picked it up two hours ago."

"Nice." He surveyed the car. What a sweet ride. "Get in."

Tanner looked at him. "What?"

"I'll take you for a spin around the block." The corners of George's eyes crinkled as he grinned up at Tanner.

"I'm pretty sweaty."

"I've got seat covers. Brand new. Came with the car."

"All right, take me for a ride." He frowned a little at his choice of words. Technically, George had already done that when he sold him the diner.

He climbed into the passenger seat, his knees touching the dashboard. That was the thing with little cars like this. They looked great on the outside, but inside they were uncomfortable to ride in. He'd take his Jeep anytime.

George peeled out of the parking lot like a teenager who had just gotten his driver's license. "Lots of exciting stuff happening in Maple Falls," he said, making a sharp right toward Main Street. "My new car, your new business, Anita opening a café."

"So you heard about that."

"Listen to that motor purr." George shifted into second gear. "I'm not completely unplugged from the town. I'm glad to hear she's starting a new chapter in her life, like we are."

Tanner hadn't been aware she'd been unhappy with the old one. He sure hadn't been. The only big change that had happened when he bought the diner was a little more responsibility and a lot more personal-finance budgeting. But he realized George was right—Anita was heading out on a totally new adventure.

"Yeah, exciting times indeed. Maple Falls is going to return to its former glory." The tires squealed as they flew by Amazing Grace Church on the corner and made another turn. George glanced at Tanner. "Guess I'll have to read about her grand opening in the paper, though. I'm having it forwarded to my house in Florida."

The surprises kept on coming. "You're moving to Florida?"

"Yep. Me and my baby here." George patted the dashboard. "Already got a condo in a retirement village. Lots of single ladies in that village too."

"How do you know?"

"I asked, of course."

So he was embarking on a new adventure too. "I'm happy for you, George. Just behave yourself. You took all my bail money."

George laughed as he made the last turn and drove into the diner parking lot, the whole trip having taken all of four minutes. He pulled to a stop and looked at the diner. "You know, there was a time when I called this place my baby. I spent most of my life here, first as a kid working for my father and then as an adult. It strained my marriage, although Gloria rarely complained. She was sweet and patient until the day she passed away." His voice sounded thick as he turned to Tanner. "You remind me a lot of my younger self. Full of ambition and committed to being successful. But don't make the same mistake I did. Don't let this place become more than it should be. This is a job, not a life."

He clapped his hand on Tanner's shoulder. "What I'm trying to say is that you need to get married and have a family and then spend time with that family. If you don't . . . Well, you might end up like me. Alone, with only a car to keep me company. Although what a beauty she is."

Bemused, Tanner got out of the car. George didn't seem to mind. "See you on the flip side!" He waved a goodbye as he sped off.

Tanner watched him go, pondering his mentor's words. First his mother wanted to marry him off, and now George. What they didn't know was he was further from getting married, or even dating, than he had been a month ago. He was struggling to get over Anita as it was, and she had never even liked him as anything other than a coworker or friend. Now they were neither.

Dating, much less marriage, was so far down the road he couldn't see it. And with Anita out of his life, he didn't want to.

Chapter 20

The café was a disaster.

About three days into the renovation, Anita knew she was in over her head. Not only did she have to answer dozens of phone calls from the contractor—and the interior designer she had agreed to hire after caving to her mother's request—but she also struggled to figure out the finances that had plagued her from the start.

Three weeks after construction started, she sat on the floor in her office—or what would eventually be her office, a small room walled off from the rest of the building activity outside—trying to make sense of the accounting book she'd bought. Next to her, stuffed beside the wallet in her purse, lay a pile of receipts from various purchases. She didn't know what to do with them. And when she had talked to the bank officer about a loan, she'd felt like a fool.

"I'll give you the loan," the bank president said, "because I've known you and your family for a long time, and I'm sure your parents won't let you default."

Ouch. But she had to have the loan, so she'd agreed. When he asked her about incorporating her business, she'd told him she would get back to him the following week. That had been two weeks ago.

Things had gone downhill from there. Shortly after construction began, she'd gotten a call from her mother. Mom, who had been so entrenched in the café plans that Anita couldn't pry her loose, had a crisis with Paisley's wedding—a real one this time.

"She's getting cold feet!" Mom had exclaimed over the phone. "She can't get cold feet, Anita. We put the deposit down on her dress and the reception hall."

"I'm sure she'll be fine." Anita hadn't had time to talk her mother down. She was supposed to be at a meeting with the contractor. Rusty had fixed her car two days after he towed it and had even given her the Maple Falls family discount that was available to everyone living in Maple Falls. She was grateful for any break she could get. But having a working car had meant she was driving when her mom called. She'd been trying to figure out directions and needed her phone screen.

She glanced at the phone, fastened to a hands-free mount. "Can I call you back? I'm trying to find this guy's office—"

"This is a catastrophe," her mother had wailed. "I'm sorry, Anita, but Paisley needs me right now."

"All right. Call me back when you can, then."

"I'm going to Waco tomorrow night. I'm not sure when I'll be available."

Anita frowned and realized she'd missed taking a left turn. Crud. "She's not going to like you crashing her last semester of school."

"I still can't believe she had to take summer classes to graduate. I finished my bachelor's in three years. Did I ever tell you that?"

"Mom, let Paisley work this out."

"I will, when I get to Waco."

Her mother was serious about this. Anita started to panic. "But what about the café?"

"Oh, honey, you'll handle things. You wanted to do this on your own, remember?"

She couldn't tell if that was a passive-aggressive dig or if her mother was stating a fact. At that moment she hadn't had time to figure it out. "I have to go, Mom. I think I'm lost."

"Did you use your GPS? I always use my GPS."

"I'm talking to you on my phone. That's my GPS."

"You should have a separate GPS. I'm never without mine. I'll text you the name of the one I use. They have a less expensive version, although it doesn't have the functionality of the deluxe model, which is the one I own."

Anita had about lost it. She'd started counting to ten.

"I'll be out of pocket for a while, dear. Paisley needs my complete focus. Oh, and please don't bother your father. He's been overwhelmed with patients lately. Ta-ta for now."

Anita had finally managed to find the contractor, and shoving her mother and Paisley out of her mind, she'd listened as he talked about plumbing, carpentry, ordering supplies, one-third down, and other things that made her head spin. On the way home she'd tried to process everything the guy had told her, but she had forgotten most of it and kicked herself because she should have been taking notes.

Now she stared at the *Accounting for Dummies* book. Although she'd read the same page four times, she still didn't comprehend the information. Her mind kept stewing on all her problems, which were coming in droves lately.

Her ringtone sang out "I Will Survive" again.

She wasn't sure she was going to survive at this rate.

She picked up her phone and answered it. "Hello?"

"Ms. Bedford?"

"Speaking."

"I'm calling on behalf of Mendelsohn Interiors to let you know that the check you wrote to us last week came back as 'insufficient funds.' As you know, we require a down payment before we can implement the design plans we developed for your café."

Her check had bounced? How? Had she

forgotten to write down the amount in her check ledger? Or had she used her debit card for the plans? She couldn't remember.

"Ms. Bedford?"

Maybe she didn't need a designer. She'd save money if she could design the café herself. How hard could it be? "I'm sorry, I've changed my mind. I won't be needing your services."

"We still require payment for the plans, regardless of whether we implement them."

"How much are they?" When the woman told her the amount, she almost threw up. "That much?"

"The cost of the plans is listed in the quote."

She either hadn't noticed that or had forgotten about it. "All right. I'll send another check."

"Please use another form of payment. Do you have a credit card?"

She did, but she thought it was maxed out. Guess she would find out for sure now. She grabbed her wallet and gave the receptionist her card information.

"Thank you, Ms. Bedford. I'm sorry we couldn't do business together. You can pick up the plans in our office at your convenience."

"Can you just mail them to me?"

"We'd be happy to, for a thirty-dollar fee."

For crying out loud. "Never mind, I'll come get them." She hung up the phone, feeling stupid and a little duped, not to mention broke, something she'd never been before. Leaning her head against the drywall, she tried not to cry. She was so exhausted she felt she could fall asleep right there. She hadn't slept well since Tanner fired her. She was still angry about that.

The sound of hammers and buzz saws breached the thin wall. The noise wasn't helping, so she got up and went outside. She resisted the urge to look at the diner. Right now she craved a piece of Mabel's peach pie and a glass of sweet iced tea. But she didn't want to risk seeing Tanner again. It was bad enough she was paired with him for Riley's wedding. When Riley had talked to her, shortly after her fight with Tanner, about matching them up in the wedding party, she had told her friend not to worry about anything. She and Tanner were fine, she had lied. They were far from it, but she knew even he wasn't a big enough jerk to ruin the Riley-Hayden nuptials.

Just a big enough jerk to fire me.

She walked in the opposite direction of the diner, to the end of the sidewalk. The sky was filled with clouds, and the air felt like a damp, heavy blanket. The one time she really needed her mother, she wasn't available. She tried not to resent Paisley for that. If her sister was thinking about not going through with the wedding, that was a problem. She and her sister weren't close, so she wasn't surprised that she'd had no idea how Paisley felt about getting married, but she didn't want her sister to be unhappy. The world didn't need another Bedford sister down in the dumps.

Anita didn't know what to do. When she'd first told Olivia about the café, her friend had offered to help. But as expected, Olivia was busy with summer library programs that were in full swing and better attended than in the past. That was nice, and likely due to Olivia's complete revamp of the programs. She was also still in graduate school, and two Sundays ago Anita had caught her nodding off during Jared's sermon—and Jared always gave lively sermons.

That was the last time Anita had been in church. The café was taking up all of her time and energy, and she'd twice had to call in a sub for her class. She had always done everything she could to keep her word, and she hated that she wasn't fulfilling her commitment.

She stopped in front of Knots and Tangles, sweat beading on her forehead. Harper was busy with her job, and Riley had the store and wedding plans. Only Anita was incapable of handling her life.

The front door opened. "Hi, Anita," Erma said. "Riley's not here, if you were looking for her. She and Hayden took off for lunch in Hot Springs today. She'll be back this afternoon. Maybe." A sly look crossed her face. "Those two can barely stand to be apart from each other."

Anita sighed. Riley was so lucky.

"Land's sake, it's hot out there." Erma waved her hand in front of her face. "Come in and get cooled off. You can tell me all about the goings-on with your new café."

Anita hesitated. She needed to get back to the building site and work on her bookkeeping. She also had a few calls to return to kitchen-supply companies. Or maybe she should give up on buying reusable mugs and just go with paper products . . .

No. That didn't sit well with her. She didn't like the idea of unnecessarily adding more garbage to the landfill.

"Anita?"

"Sorry. Thank you." She walked into the shop, the cool air a welcome relief and the colorful hanks and skeins of yarn surrounding her a feast for her eyes.

Erma peered at her. "Are you okay, sugar?"

She wanted to tell her yes and pretend everything was perfect. She always enjoyed Erma's company, and the woman never failed to make her laugh. Riley's grandmother was a spry woman in her seventies and had been the assistant coach of the church softball team before she broke her leg sliding into third base. Anita thought about how Tanner, who had been up at bat and hit a double, had sped over to Erma to see if she was okay, his lean legs churning, his long ponytail flying behind him—

Darn it. Even Erma managed to remind her of him.

Anita didn't have the strength to pretend anymore. "I'm not okay, Ms. McAllister," she said, holding back a sob as moisture gathered in her eyes. "Everything's going wrong."

"Oh, honey, come on to the back, and I'll get you something to drink."

"I don't want to bother you." She wiped away the few tears that had escaped with the back of her hand.

"You're no bother. We've been slower than molasses running uphill today. The last thing people are thinking about on a hot summer day is knitting a sweater." Erma took her hand. "You look like you need some TLC."

Did she ever. Still, when she glanced down at Erma's canary-yellow T-shirt that said, *I'm not a hot mess, I'm a spicy disaster,* Anita couldn't help but give her a half-hearted smile.

After they were settled on the green couch with a bottle of water each, Erma said, "Now, tell me what's going on."

Anita revealed everything, from mismanaging her money to leaving the diner.

"You quit?"

"Yes. And no." She gripped the water bottle.

"Don't tell me that boy fired you." Erma's back straightened. "Because if he did, he's going to get a piece of my mind, and he's not gonna like that."

While it was nice to have someone stick up for her, she couldn't let Erma think Tanner was solely to blame. "I kind of asked for it," she said, acknowledging what she had refused to accept since she had read his words on her time card.

Erma shook her head. "I can't imagine you doing anything wrong."

Oh, she had done many things wrong, especially lately. "I gave him my two weeks' notice on a Post-it note and left it on his desk."

"Ah. Well, I can see that getting his dander up. How long have you two worked together?"

"Three years." And four months and three days, but of course she was the only one who'd been counting.

"He's only been there that long? I thought he'd worked there for at least a decade."

"He fit in right away." As if he'd been born for the job, and she knew he had. The diner couldn't have a better owner than Tanner. That was something else she hadn't been able to acknowledge, even to herself.

Erma took a sip of her water. "Well, sounds like you've got yourself in a pickle or two."

Anita looked down at her lap. "I never should have tried to have my own business," she whispered.

"Why in the world not?"

"Because I don't know what I'm doing. I can't tell the difference between debits and credits, for starters. Mr. Swanson at the bank asked me for a business plan, and I had to tell him I didn't know what he was talking about." She picked at the bottle label. "The only reason he gave me a loan was because of my parents."

Nodding, Erma said, "Who's helping you, sugar?"

Anita looked at her. "My mom, for a little while. Now she's in Texas with Paisley."

"Anyone else? Your father or Kingston, or your friends?"

"No."

Erma sat back against the couch. "That's part of your problem, then. Starting a business by yourself is difficult enough. When you don't have experience, it's like climbing Mount Everest blindfolded." Compassion filled her eyes. "Karen being in the mix couldn't have been easy."

"I love her, but . . ."

"She can be difficult. Remember, I've known your father since he was born. I remember his mother coming into Knots and Tangles and buying skeins of reduced and clearance yarn because she couldn't afford the regular price. She needed that yarn to make sweaters, hats, and mittens for her sons. Sometimes my mother threw a few skeins in there for free. Neither woman ever mentioned it."

Anita nodded. She knew her father had grown up impoverished and had worked his way through college and medical school, along with getting scholarships. He'd met Mom their senior year of college, and her background couldn't have been more different—upper middle class, school paid for by her parents, a happy life in Hot Springs.

"We were all surprised when he married Karen and decided to live here," Erma said. "But we weren't that surprised when they moved after Paisley's graduation. Life is slow in Maple Falls. I don't think Karen ever really felt like a part of the community."

Erma waved her hand. "Sorry to take a detour with your mother. Let's get back to how we're going to solve your café problems. I'm sure Harper and Olivia wouldn't mind helping. Riley, too, once she gets back from her honeymoon. She has lots of business experience now."

Anita shook her head. "They're busy with their lives. I don't want to be a bother."

"Are you sure that's the only reason you're not reaching out to your family and friends?"

She frowned. "Yes. That's the reason."

"Or is it just part of the reason? Perhaps the other part is that you feel you have something to prove." Erma got up from the couch. "Think on that while I go to the little girl's room. This is my third bottle of water this morning. My doctor would be happy, but he's not the one answering nature's call every thirty minutes."

As Erma headed for the back of the shop, Anita

thought about what the older woman had said. Did she have something to prove? She remembered what her mother had said almost a month ago—that she'd had to prove herself to Grandma.

Maybe I'm more like my mom than I thought.

When Erma returned and sat back down, Anita spoke. "School was so hard for me. I was in special classes, and I had to get tutors. I almost didn't graduate." She hadn't told anyone that, even her parents, and fortunately they both had been so busy they hadn't paid much attention, other than writing the checks to the tutors. "It took me a while to learn how to make change, and even now, if I'm under pressure I sometimes mess up. And my writing skills aren't great either. Everyone I know is doing what they love and succeeding. I'm the only one who was in a rut."

"Did you love being a waitress?"

"Oh yes. I've always enjoyed that. But being a waitress isn't the same as a doctor or a lawyer or a business owner."

"That sounds like Karen talking," Erma mumbled.

"Mom said I was being foolish for not letting them help me. They were right. And now I'm in a big mess."

Erma paused for a moment. "What about Tanner? If anyone can advise you about the food business, he can."

"He fired me, remember?" Anita sighed,

pushing back her bangs. They hung over her eyes, and the rest of her hair was growing out too. She didn't have time or money to get a haircut.

"He's also mad at me, and I'm not exactly thrilled with him right now either." When she saw the alarm in Erma's eyes, she said, "Riley told me Tanner would be my escort. Don't worry, I won't let my personal problems affect the wedding. I'm sure he won't either."

"Surely you two can work things out before then."

She explained what had happened at the business meeting. "We had a fight after that, then I turned in my notice, and then he fired me. We haven't seen or talked to each other since."

Erma tapped her bottom lip. "When you love someone, you can work things out."

Anita froze. "What? I don't love Tanner." Right now she didn't even like him.

Erma's eyes widened. "Oh, never mind. I must have you two mixed up with someone else. Anyhoo—"

"There's no love between me and Tanner," Anita whispered. "Even though I wanted there to be."

Erma's heart was breaking for this poor child. Her relationship with Tanner, whatever that was right now, her insecurity, and her insistence that she take on the huge task of opening the café by herself—just one of those things would bring a person down. Anita was a peach and one of Riley's closest friends, and Erma was determined to do what she could to help the young woman out.

She was also one hundred thousand percent sure that Tanner had feelings for Anita, and she'd thought that even before Jasper had told her about the sizzling kiss he'd seen between them a few weeks ago and how the two of them had insisted it was nothing. "You'd better not tell anyone else, Erma Jean," he'd said after he had come into her store and spilled the romantic beans.

"Land's sake, Jasper," she huffed. "Why did you tell me, then?"

"Because I had to tell someone." He chuckled. "You like trading tales more than anyone else in this town."

Other than you. But she didn't say that. She was a little honored that the cantankerous coot had confided in her. He'd also sworn her to secrecy, and she'd almost blown it. But now Anita had admitted it herself, although Erma wasn't sure if she realized she had voiced those thoughts out loud.

The two of them were a perfect match, and while Karen got on Erma's nerves once in a while, she thought a lot of Walter. And of course she'd always liked Rosa Castillo, enough that she wasn't giving up on the woman joining the

Bosom Buddies. There was no reason Anita and Tanner couldn't be together other than they were both sabotaging themselves. Although she had to admit the two of them not telling each other about their plans had been a big mistake.

A thought occurred to her that she immediately dismissed. *I refuse to get involved.*

She had tried to manipulate Riley and Hayden when Riley first returned to Maple Falls, and while she had been correct that they were meant for each other, it wasn't until she backed off that they started growing closer. She wasn't taking credit for their relationship, but she knew her decision to stay out of their personal lives had made things a tad bit easier on everyone. The best way she could help Anita was not to interfere. But she could at least give her some business advice. Decades of running Knots and Tangles had made her an expert.

"Do you have an accountant?" Erma asked.

Anita lifted her head. "Yes."

"Have you talked to him about your finances?"

"No. I'm too embarrassed. I was hoping I'd get things together before I scheduled a meeting."

"All right, here's what you're going to do. One, call your accountant and don't be embarrassed about talking with him. If he's worth his salt, he'll guide you. That's what you pay him for."

"He's going to think I'm stupid," she said.

"Sugar, you're not stupid. You're just uninformed, that's all. And if the accountant gives you attitude, kick him to the sidewalk."

"I think you mean the curb, Ms. McAllister."

"You can do that too. Second, you're going to swallow your pride and get advice from Tanner."

Her eyes widened. "I can't do that."

"Do you want your café to succeed?"

She paused as if she was thinking over the question. Then she lifted her chin. "Yes, I do."

"Then he's the person you need to go to. Everyone in town knows he's been running that diner for the past year or so anyway, so he knows all the ins and outs of running a restaurant. A café isn't the same thing, but there are things he can teach you that you can apply to your business."

Anita's confidence faltered. "What if he refuses to help me?"

"Then he's not the man I thought he was, and you can kick him to the curb and sidewalk too. Better yet, I'll do it." When Anita laughed, Erma knew she had broken through to the young woman. "Three, I'm tangled up in wedding plans, but once that's over, I'll help you with whatever you need. I can guarantee that your friends will too. You just have to ask."

She nodded. "I understand. All right, I'll do one and three."

"What about talking to Tanner?"

"I have to think about that."

Fair enough. Greece wasn't built in a day. Or

was that Rome? She'd never been good at world history. Anita was willing to accept help. That was the point. And Erma would bet her crochet hook that once she solved some of the business issues, she would be able to talk to Tanner. Hopefully that conversation wouldn't be *all* business.

The bell rang over the front door. "I'll be, we actually have a customer," Erma said, rising from the couch. Every joint in her body protested, but she was used to that.

This getting-old thing is getting old.

Anita stood. "Thank you so much, Ms. McAllister." She gave her a hug. "I feel better."

"That's what I want to see—your sweet, smiling face. Anytime, sugar. Anytime."

"Once the café is open, your coffee is on me."

Erma grinned. What a peach. Tanner would be a fool to let Anita get away. She would say an extra prayer at bedtime tonight that he wasn't.

Chapter 21

On Friday evening, a month after Anita had joined her and Tanner for lunch, Rosa returned home from the bottling company to find a note from Tanner.

> Working late tonight at Sunshine. Be home later. Tanner

She managed a half-hearted smile. Today had been rough, and seeing a note from her thoughtful son shined a little beam of light on it. But it didn't help the nausea in her stomach or the fact she felt like she'd been run over by a truck. Usually she changed clothes before settling in to watch her prerecorded telenovelas, but tonight all she could do was plop into her chair.

Closing her eyes, she prayed for the nausea to subside. It wasn't unusual for her to be tired by the end of the week, but tonight the fatigue was more pronounced. She tried to ignore how she felt and failed, just like she had failed to refrain from worrying about Tanner and Anita. When he'd come home that Tuesday night after the business meeting, he told her that he'd bought the diner. She was thrilled, but she could tell he was upset. He quickly mentioned Anita opening up a new café, then hurried upstairs to his room. She didn't understand why he wasn't happy for Anita. Rosa was impressed that she was striking out on her own.

She didn't dare bring up the topic with him. He was working even more now than he had before, and she was worried about him. Then again, did a mother ever stop worrying about her son? On top of Tanner's problems, Lonzo and Molly had broken up. She hated that both her boys had broken hearts.

Her sour stomach subsided slightly. She hadn't eaten anything since breakfast, and that was probably the problem. A few saltines and a cup of tea should do the trick. She rose from her chair.

A heavy pain spread across her chest. She paused, taking in some deep breaths. This wasn't the first time that had happened, and usually if she took a moment to rest, the pain went away.

This time it didn't.

A heavy dread seized her. She managed to get to her purse. Find her phone. Dial 911.

"Nine-one-one. How may I help you?"

"I . . . can't . . . breathe . . ."

"This is nice, Anita. We haven't had dinner at the hospital for years."

Anita nodded. Her mother was still in Waco, and she realized she hadn't checked on her father since Mom had left. When she called him earlier in the day, he'd been at the hospital but said he could meet her in the cafeteria for an early supper.

"I'm glad you were free," she said, dipping a fry in a mix of ketchup and mayo, her favorite combination. These fries weren't as good as Tanner's, but she was starving, and they hit the spot.

"So am I." Her father speared a tomato from his salad. "How's the café going? Since your mother took off to Waco, I've been missing my hourly reports."

"Oh, you know. It's going." She shoved a plain fry into her mouth. "Is Paisley okay?" She'd been so caught up with her own problems she hadn't even thought about calling her sister.

"She'll be fine. You know how your mother is. Everything's a crisis. Having some doubts about getting married isn't uncommon."

"Did you have doubts?"

"Talk about a loaded question." He grinned. "I'll answer it anyway. Yes. I had doubts. So did your mother, although I didn't find out about them until years later."

That surprised her. "Really?"

"Yep. Even the best relationships are complicated. When two people commit to each other, there are a lot of variables to contend with. Personality clashes, for one."

"You and Mom are very different."

"In temperament, yes." He took a drink of

lemon-flavored water. "But we both wanted the same things. Careers and a family. It hasn't been easy, but thanks to your mother, we've made it work. We're proud of our kids."

Anita didn't think he would be proud if he knew how much she was struggling. "I think I made a mistake."

"About the café?"

She nodded.

He straightened. "I thought there might be something wrong. What do you mean?"

"I don't know if I can do this." She told him about her talk with Erma, leaving out the parts about Tanner. She still wasn't sure asking him for help was a good idea. "I felt better after I talked to her, but when I went back inside the building, I was overwhelmed again."

"Why didn't you say anything?"

"Because I wanted to prove to you and Mom, and everyone else, that I could do this." There. She had put it out in the open. "I've always needed help, and for once I wanted to do something on my own."

"You've done plenty of things on your own."

"Being a waitress and renting a tiny house isn't a grand accomplishment."

"Where did you get that idea?" He paused. "Never mind, I already know. Look, honey, you don't have to prove anything to me. Your mother would say the same thing if she were here."

"I'm not so sure about that."

"Then ask her when she comes back. If I'm right, you'll have to eat an entire plate of liver-wurst."

No way was she going to take that bet. She chuckled. "Okay, I believe you."

Dad touched her hand. "Do you like being a waitress?" he asked.

"Very much."

"How do you like being a business owner?"

"Not so much. But that doesn't mean I won't like it once I've learned what I need to know."

"That's my girl. Miss Optimistic. You've always gotten over your hurdles, Anita. You'll fly over this one soon enough."

"Thanks, Dad."

"Once your café is open, let me know. I'm due a vacation, and I wouldn't mind putting in some time serving coffee. As long as I get a lesson or two beforehand from a professional."

She laughed. "I'll be happy to teach you how."

His beeper went off. "Hang on a minute," he said, checking it. "I've got a patient in the ER." His expression changed from father mode to serious doctor. "Take your time finishing up. I'll talk to you later."

When he grabbed his tray, she said, "I'll take care of it. Bye, Dad." She watched him hurry out of the cafeteria and smiled. She was proud of him too.

A few minutes later she was taking the last bite of her BLT when she got a text.

Come to the ER. Dad.

Her parents still signed their texts, as if she didn't have them in her contacts. She gulped down her Coke and picked up her and her father's trays and put them on the conveyor, then hurried to the ER. Why would her father want her to meet him there?

When she arrived, her father met her at the inside entrance. "What's wrong, Dad?"

"Rosa Castillo is on her way."

Her blood ran cold. "What? Is she okay?"

"I don't know. Tanner arrived at their house right before the ambulance. He's on his way, too, but he has to drive separately. She's one of my patients, and I need to be there when she arrives. Tanner's going to need you, honey. Either way."

Anita could barely breathe, but she nodded and hurried to the waiting room. It was empty when she got there, and she sat down and waited.

A few minutes later, Tanner came running inside. He went straight to the reception window. "I'm here with Rosa Castillo," he said, sounding breathless.

Anita didn't want to interrupt them, so she sat and listened as he gave the receptionist Rosa's information.

"You can wait here until we call you back."

"How long will that be?"

"We'll let you know." The receptionist slid the glass window closed.

Tanner turned around, scrubbing his hands across his face. When he looked up, he met Anita's gaze.

Without a word she went to him—and he fell into her arms.

Anita tapped her knee with her finger in a nervous rhythm. Tanner had arrived forty-five minutes ago, and he still hadn't been back to see his mother. The receptionist had said Rosa was getting a scan done and that she should be back soon. Anita hoped so, because Tanner was ready to jump out of his skin, and she didn't blame him.

She glanced at him. He had been silent since he arrived, and other than hugging her tight when he first saw her, he had ignored her. She didn't take it personally, although she wished there was a way she could comfort him. His knee rapidly bounced up and down, and for the dozenth time he got up and paced the length of the empty waiting room.

He looked at her. "What's taking so long?"

"I don't know. I can call my dad again if you want." She had called when Tanner arrived, but it had gone straight to voice mail. She wasn't surprised her father didn't answer. But if Tanner wanted her to try again, she would.

Shaking his head, he sat and leaned back in the chair.

"Do you want some coffee?" she asked, feeling helpless.

"No."

A short time later the receptionist opened the glass window. "Mr. Castillo? You can come back now."

Tanner turned to Anita. "Will you come with me?"

His request surprised her, but she nodded, and they got up at the same time.

"I'll buzz you in," the receptionist said, then directed them to Rosa's room.

As they headed to the back, she saw her father come out of one of the rooms. "Dad," she said, and they both hurried to him.

"How is she?" Tanner asked.

"She's going to be all right. She has what's called unstable angina."

"That sounds serious."

"It is, but we have medications that can control it, along with a lifestyle plan. That's why I'm keeping her under observation. She was supposed to see me last month but canceled the appointment. Twice."

Tanner grimaced. "I'll make sure she goes to them from now on."

"Excellent." He paused and gave Tanner's shoulder a gentle squeeze. "I expect her to fully recover once we stabilize the angina. You can go in and talk to her. She's awake."

"Thank you." Tanner shook his hand then went inside the room.

Anita hesitated, unsure whether to follow him inside.

"Let's let them have some time alone," her dad said, putting his arm around Anita's shoulders. "We can get a cup of coffee."

As her father led her to a small seating area, she looked over her shoulder. She was glad Rosa was okay. She hoped Tanner would be too.

"Don't worry about me, Tanner. I'll be fine."

Tanner sat at his mother's bedside, holding her hand and holding in his anger. He was tired of her standard answer, tired of her not listening to him, and tired in general. She wasn't fine now. He was thankful she wasn't worse. "I'm staying here with you until they discharge you."

She shook her head. "I don't need a babysitter."

"Apparently you do. Dr. Bedford said you canceled two appointments."

She averted her gaze. "I was going to reschedule."

Yeah. Right. She was seeing a cardiologist, and he'd had no idea.

He looked at their clasped hands and realized

his was still shaking. He'd come home from a break at the diner to get the laptop he'd forgotten that morning and found her unconscious on the living room floor. The terror of thinking she was dead was still with him. He'd already lost his father. He couldn't take it if he lost his mother too.

"Tanner," she said, looking at him.

"Shh. You need to rest."

"I will, but I have some things to say to you."

"Mom, they can wait—"

"No, they can't." She sounded more firm than he'd thought she could manage. "First of all, I'm sorry. You've been after me to slow down, and I didn't listen. Now I'm paying for that. So as soon as I get home, I'm quitting the cleaning job."

"Thank God." He'd thought he'd have a fight on his hands.

"But I'm not the only one who needs to make some changes. You're working too hard too. You always have, lately more than ever." Tears spilled out of the corners of her eyes. "I'm worried about you. Do you want to end up like me, in a hospital bed? You might not have a heart attack now, but you could have one in the future when you're older. Or an ulcer, or—"

"*Mamá*." He hadn't called her that since he was a child. He took her hand again. "I'll cut back on work, I promise." Guilt bit at him. "I'm sorry I made you worry." Had he contributed to her heart condition? The answer had to be yes. He'd been angry that she wouldn't listen to him, but he was just as pigheaded.

Her eyes drifted closed. "It's okay. Promise me something."

"Anything." He squeezed her hand.

"Work things out . . . with . . . Anita."

He shook his head as she fell asleep. Even in the hospital she was thinking about him and Anita.

The door opened and Dr. Bedford walked in. "Good," he whispered. "She's sleeping." He crooked a finger, and Tanner followed him into the hallway.

Once they were outside of the room Dr. Bedford said, "We'll do a few more tests tomorrow, just to make sure there isn't any serious damage to her heart."

Alarm jolted through Tanner. "I thought you said she was going to be okay."

"She is, but I like to double-check everything."

Tanner appreciated that he was thorough. "Thanks."

"I want her to get as much rest as she can tonight, so I encourage you to go home. I'll be here to keep an eye on her."

It didn't feel right to leave her there by herself. "Are you sure I shouldn't stay?"

"Positive. I'll call you in the morning and give you an update."

"Thanks, Dr. Bedford. I appreciate it."

"No problem. I've always thought a lot of your family. Your father and I used to get a beer together every once in a while, before he passed away." He cleared his throat. "He would be proud of the way you take care of your family."

Tanner swallowed, unable to respond. He'd had no idea Anita's dad and his father had been friends.

"Anita should be back any minute. I've got to check on another patient, but I'll talk to you in the morning." Dr. Bedford smiled and walked down the hallway.

Tanner leaned against the wall as he waited for Anita, the tension that had gripped him for the past few hours finally easing. His mother was going to be okay. That was all that mattered.

When he heard footsteps coming toward him, he turned to see Anita. Rather than feel awkward, he was relieved. Everything that had happened between them since the meeting last month seemed inconsequential.

"Are you okay?" she asked, standing in front of him.

"Yes. Your dad ordered me to go home so Mom can get some rest."

"Then you'd better follow his orders."

"I will." He held her gaze. "I don't know how I would have handled this without you."

"I'm glad I was here."

They stood in silence in the hallway. Then she said, "I'd better get back home. I've got to meet the painter at #3 early in the morning."

He nodded. "Yeah, I've got an early shift too."

She hesitated, as though she wasn't sure what to do. Then, with a quick wave, she left.

Tanner almost called out after her but held back. His mother didn't have to make him promise to work things out with Anita. He should have done that long ago. Now he wondered if it was too late.

Chapter 22

"Hayden, I think this is the first time I've seen you nervous."

Tanner stood in the corner of the small Sunday school room where he and the other groomsmen were waiting with Hayden for the wedding to start. Harrison, Hayden's brother and best man, was right. Hayden, normally cool as a crisp autumn day, a former pro player who had pitched in front of thousands of people, was shifting back and forth on his feet and tugging on his gold bow tie. More than once he'd shoved his fingers through his hair, only to have Henry, his other brother, tell him that he couldn't get married looking like he'd just rolled out of bed. "Riley would have our heads," Henry said, smoothing down Hayden's dark-blond hair.

"Sorry." Hayden started to pace. "It's the waiting that's hard, you know?"

Henry, Harrison, and Spencer, Hayden's college roommate, all nodded. They did know since they were all married.

"I feel like I've waited all my life for this moment." Hayden blew out a breath. "The last few minutes are killing me."

Tanner, the only single guy in the room, didn't comment. What did he know about love, anyway?

He'd ruined the one female friendship he cared about, and over the past five weeks or so without her, he had been able to admit that what he felt for Anita was far more than friendship. He'd ruined that, too, and all because of business. He'd put Sunshine before everything in his life, and he was paying a steep price.

The door opened, and the wedding coordinator poked her head inside, her cloying perfume entering the room. "We're ready, gentlemen."

Hayden dashed to the door then turned around and grinned. "Thanks, y'all, for standing up with me."

Tanner grinned. Hayden was a good guy and his closest friend. He quickly walked over to him and clapped him on the back. "Sure thing, dude. Time to get you hitched."

As they walked down the hall to the sanctuary, he touched the knot on his gold-colored tie to make sure it was straight. When they reached the front of the church, he lined up behind Henry and Harrison. Spencer moved to stand behind Tanner. Jared, who was officiating the service, winked at Hayden, who had started to shift from side to side again. Harrison put his hand on Hayden's shoulder, and he finally settled.

Last night they'd had the rehearsal with supper afterward. The rehearsal itself had been easy, other than when Tanner and Anita had to walk down the aisle. She kept her distance from him, and he knew he would have to break that promise to his mother he'd made at the hospital. He and Anita were never going to work things out. Even during the supper in the church hall—barbecue provided by Hayden's parents—she hadn't looked his way.

Tanner glanced at the wedding guests seated in the pews. Amazing Grace wasn't a big church, but it wasn't small either. It seemed like the whole town of Maple Falls was here. Erma was seated next to Hayden's parents in the front row. She was wearing a sleeveless navy-blue dress with a lace jacket in the same color.

Looks like Riley got her way.

Of course the Bosom Buddies, Erma's squad, were seated behind her, every one of them dabbing their eyes with white handkerchiefs. And there was no division of families or friends. Riley had insisted on that. Every guest had the choice to sit where they wanted to. Because of that, she'd dispensed with the tradition of ushers.

The organ music began to play. Just like they'd practiced last night, Olivia would walk down the aisle first, then Anita, then Harper, and finally Melody, Riley's roommate when she lived in New York.

Olivia appeared, wearing a dusty-purple floor-length dress with a neckline that looked more like a tank top than a fancy gown. But the style suited her, and she looked pretty. She

330

moved to stand on the other side of Jared.

Then Anita appeared at the back of the church, and Tanner forgot to breathe.

From the waist up, her dress was different. It didn't have the demure neckline Olivia's had. Instead, Anita's gown was strapless and low cut in an elegant way, with sheer dusty-purple fabric from the neckline to her waist. As she neared, he noticed the same jeweled barrette she'd had in her hair at Harper's party. Her makeup was light and sophisticated. Her hair had grown out some since their fight, and he liked the length. A simple gold chain circled her neck, and he saw that the small gold charm dangling from it was a ball of yarn, a nod to Knots and Tangles. Tanner would have thought it was clever if he could think at all. He'd never seen anything more beautiful than Anita Bedford walking down the church aisle, and he couldn't take his eyes off her.

Anita thought she'd been prepared to see Tanner in a tux. She'd even imagined what he would look like so she wouldn't be caught off guard. But nothing, *nothing* her imagination came up with compared to the real thing.

She'd been determined to keep her attention where it should be today, on Riley and Hayden. But they were far from her mind as she stared at Tanner at the beginning of the aisle, taking in his black suit and gold necktie. All of her senses were on alert. The man had literally taken her breath away.

"Anita, walk faster," Pearl, the wedding coordinator, whispered loudly.

She stumbled for a second, then regained her footing, but not much of her inward composure. Nerves crackled along her spine. This was the first time she'd been a bridesmaid. The first time going down the aisle. And of all people, Tanner was at the end of it. So were Jared, Hayden, and Hayden's other groomsmen. But she only had eyes for Tanner.

She tried to ground herself in the sweet scent of the white and purple flowers Sophie Johnson had arranged, the soft, romantic music coming from the organ, and the sight of Hayden tugging on his gold bow tie for the second time since she started down the aisle. But she couldn't stop focusing on Tanner.

That had been her problem all along.

She gripped the white and light-purple rose bouquet with gold ribbon and walked over to the side of the sanctuary to stand in front of Olivia. She'd made it, finally.

Riley had surprised all of them with her traditional choices for her wedding, considering her mixed-media art was so colorful and abstract. But Anita loved every decision Riley had made, even the sweetheart neckline of Anita's dress. With Harper's help, Riley had done an amazing job choosing different styles for her attendants, and she'd even managed to find something Erma agreed to wear.

Harper made her way down the aisle in her asymmetrical off-the-shoulder dress, and Melody walked in last, her jewel neckline perfectly accentuating her slender frame and dark skin.

When Melody took her place, the organist changed to the "Wedding March," and everyone in the pews stood. Riley appeared, and Anita smiled. Her dress was gorgeous—white with a sweetheart neckline like Anita's but with sheer lacy fabric overlaying the bodice and the tops of her shoulders. Her hair was pulled into a loose updo, and she wore the same yarn-ball necklace they all wore. Anita and the rest of the girls had laughed when she presented them with the necklaces, but Anita would always treasure hers.

She glanced at Hayden as he watched Riley approach, saw the tears in his eyes, then had to force herself not to cry. The Bosom Buddies were doing enough crying for the whole church.

The ceremony was just as beautiful as everything else, and she did shed a few tears when she heard Riley and Hayden exchange their vows. When Jared said, "You may kiss the bride," Hayden didn't hesitate, giving Riley a long, deep kiss right in front of everyone.

"Get a room!" Erma shouted from the front row in a teasing voice.

"Already booked!" Hayden replied, putting his arm around Riley's waist. Her cheeks were fire-engine red, but she was also beaming as she and Hayden exited the sanctuary.

The ceremony over, Anita steeled herself for the difficult part: being close to Tanner. She tightened her hold on her bouquet as Melody and Harrison walked down the aisle, then Harper and Henry. Now she was face-to-face with Tanner. Or face to his offered arm since she couldn't bring herself to look at him. She slipped her arm through his and felt his bicep under her hand. His extremely *firm* bicep.

Darn it.

"Anita."

Without thinking she looked up at him, and he met her gaze. And there it was. The intense flame in his eyes that caused her pulse to fly off the rails, only more powerful than she'd ever seen—or imagined—it before.

"Tanner," Spencer whispered behind him. "Go."

They fell into step together, and Anita couldn't help but hang on to him. She caught Erma's wink, and her face turned hot. Tanner's strong bicep under her fingers and Erma's sassy expression were not what she needed right now.

When they exited the sanctuary, she removed her hand from his arm, and they went to stand in the reception line next to Olivia and Spencer, who had followed them out and were talking nonstop about some book Anita had never heard of. She wasn't surprised at their intellectual exchange. Spencer was a doctoral student at UCLA and working toward his PhD in anthropology.

Tanner leaned over and whispered in her ear. "That wasn't so bad, was it?"

She glanced at him, not having to look up as much as she usually did because of her high heels. They weren't as comfortable as the black ones Harper had given her, and her feet were already aching. "No," she admitted, although being so close to him in this romantic atmosphere wasn't that easy either. Neither had it been last night during the rehearsal dinner. Her anger with him had subsided for the most part, but her attraction to him hadn't. That would take time, she kept reminding herself. But they could never go back to the friendship they'd had before. They would go back to living parallel lives, like they had before he started working at Sunshine.

His eyes were back to their usual sage-green color. "Nice ceremony," he said to her as Pearl came out of the sanctuary.

"Yes." She smiled, relaxing a little bit, remembering that she had vowed not to let her personal feelings affect Riley and Hayden's special day. "A beautiful one." She turned to him again. "How's your mom?"

"Doing well. Lonzo is with her at home."

"That's good." When he didn't say anything

else, she touched one of the lavender roses in her bouquet. They smelled nice.

Tanner smells better. She winced at her own cheesy thought.

"Where are Riley and Hayden?" Pearl said as she scurried up. "We can't dismiss everyone without the bride and groom in the receiving line." She wrung her plump hands together.

"Off sneaking kisses," Harper teased.

Anita heard Tanner laugh, and she glanced at him again, catching his smile. Her heart leapt, but only a little this time.

Finally Hayden and Riley appeared from the other side of the church. From the blush on Riley's face, Anita wondered if they had been doing exactly what Harper joked about. They took their place in line next to Melody and Harrison, and the guests started pouring out of the sanctuary.

"When are you coming back to the diner, Anita?" Jasper said as he appeared in front of her and Tanner.

"I have my own business now, Mr. Mathis. Remember?"

"Oh, that dad-burned coffee shop or whatever. The coffee's just fine at Sunshine." He looked at Tanner. "Could use a little more salt on my pot roast Monday evening, boy."

"Yes, sir."

Anita took Jasper's hand and cradled it in both of hers. "I miss seeing you, Mr. Mathis."

The old man smiled, his deep wrinkles sinking farther around his thin lips. "I miss you too, Miss Bedford." He gave Tanner a sharp look, ignored his outstretched hand, and moved down the line.

"What was that about?" Anita said to him in a low voice.

"He blames me for you quitting."

She frowned. "That's not right."

Tanner's silence led her to wonder if he'd let Jasper think he was at fault. She decided she would correct Jasper at the reception. Right now she had to focus on greeting the rest of the guests.

As everyone in the wedding party continued to greet guests, Anita discovered Jasper wasn't the only one who wanted her back at the diner. Each of the Bosom Buddies stopped to tell her that Sunshine wasn't the same without her sweet presence, and one of her preschool students' mothers said no one made iced tea like Anita did. There were several others who voiced their sentiments, all within the earshot of Tanner. When she glanced to see his reaction, there wasn't one. He continued to smile, say hello, and agree that the wedding was lovely. If anyone's comments bothered him, he didn't let on.

Once they were finished, they all headed for the reception hall in Hot Springs. The groomsmen were in one limo and the bridesmaids in the other, while Riley and Hayden took a separate car. When Anita entered the limo and closed the door, Harper popped a bottle of champagne that sat in a bucket, almost getting bubbles on her dress. "Time to celebrate!" she said, pouring the drink into glasses.

"None for me," Anita said, holding up her hand. She'd had her fill of alcohol for a long, *long* time.

"Good choice." Harper grinned. When everyone else had their champagne, she handed a bottle of water to Anita. "I got your back."

Smiling, Anita clinked her plastic bottle to the glass flutes. "To Riley and Hayden," she said.

"Riley and Hayden!"

She sat back and sipped her water as the rest of the girls gushed about the wedding, but her thoughts moved in a different direction. She'd appreciated the compliments she received and had promised her former customers she would drop by Sunshine from time to time. All of them promised to visit her café when it opened. She was grateful to be appreciated and happy that people were already willing to give her business a chance. But she couldn't stop thinking about how their words affected Tanner. Like her, he had put his life savings into his business. It had to be hard for him to listen to what could be construed as complaints about Sunshine.

Olivia was sitting next to her in the limo. She leaned over and whispered, "You're looking pensive."

She didn't realize she was wearing her emotions

so publicly instead of focusing on celebrating the married couple. She turned to Olivia and smiled. "I'm thrilled for Riley."

"Me too." Olivia tapped her champagne flute against Anita's water bottle, and they both took a drink. "Now, on to the reception."

"Right. The reception." Her smile tightened. There was only one more thing to get through tonight, and that was her dance with Tanner. After that, they would go their separate ways . . . closing the last chapter of her old life.

"Ya might want to slow down with that punch."

Tanner looked at Rusty and then at the small glass cup in his hand. If there was any alcohol in the cranberry-flavored punch, he couldn't taste it, and this was his last glass anyway. "Thanks for the advice," he said, draining the cup and setting it down at the end of the table where all the used cups were.

"I prefer a cold beer myself," Rusty drawled, taking a sip from a glass filled with water. "None of that sissy punch for me."

He eyed Rusty. "Sissy?"

"Oh, I ain't callin' you a sissy. Just referrin' to the punch." Rusty grinned, his straight white teeth gleaming through his perpetually scruffy red beard. "Nice weddin', wasn't it? Looks like it's gonna be a pretty good reception too."

Tanner nodded absently, barely listening to

Rusty as he complimented the appetizers provided by the facility, a rustic yet updated barn nestled in a wooded area outside of Hot Springs. The apps were all southern—pimento cheese balls, Creole fried pickles, black-eyed-pea hummus, corn-and-green-tomato cakes, bacon-jalapeño deviled eggs, and mini chicken-and-waffle skewers. There was a variety of southern desserts too—banana pudding and pecan pie along with peach and blackberry cobblers. Normally he was the first one to sample the food, but he hadn't eaten a bite. How could he when all he could think about was Anita?

The moment she had held on to his arm, he'd lost his internal battle. He was tired of fighting his feelings, but he had to tread carefully. She was still tense, which was why he'd tried to lighten her up a bit when they stood in the reception line. When he saw her delighted expression as everyone told her how much she was missed at Sunshine, he'd had to keep from smiling. He'd heard all of it in the weeks since Anita left.

Correction, since I fired her.

The groomsmen had ditched their jackets and ties but kept their vests on while the women remained in their bridesmaids' dresses. Tanner had catered a few weddings, mostly casual affairs, and often the bridal parties changed into more comfortable clothes for the reception. But

Hayden had only slipped off his bow tie, and Riley still looked picture perfect in her wedding dress.

Many of the guests were finishing the appetizers, and Hayden and Riley were still greeting guests at the tables, since some of the attendees hadn't been at the wedding ceremony. He spied Anita at the edge of the dance floor, talking to Jasper again.

"Boy, she cleans up nice," Rusty said, tipping his cup in Anita's direction. He let out a low whistle. "She sure is pretty, don't ya think?"

"Yeah," Tanner ground out. *More than pretty. She's downright beautiful.*

"I'm thinkin' of askin' her to dance." Rusty took another drink of water. "But I got two left feet, so that might not be a good idea."

A spike of jealousy stabbed Tanner, but he couldn't expect Anita not to get asked to dance, especially the way she looked tonight. He grabbed another cup of punch and drained it dry.

"All right, ladies and gentlemen, it's time to introduce the bridal party." The enthusiastic DJ pressed a button on his soundboard, and a slow song sounded through the speakers. He turned down the volume as Tanner walked over to the bridal table. Anita was on the other end of the table, and by this time the entire bridal party was ready to dance. The jealousy he'd felt a minute ago switched to nervousness. More than likely this was their last chance to be together. After the wedding they would go their separate ways again, like she had said the night when everything had fallen apart.

"Olivia Farnsworth and Spencer Updike!"

Olivia and Spencer walked out on the dance floor. Spencer lightly put his arm around Olivia's waist, and they started to sway to the music.

This is it. Great, of all times for his palms to grow damp.

"Anita Bedford and Tanner Castillo!"

Tanner and Anita met in the middle of the dance floor. He sensed people looking at them, but all he saw was Anita. Without saying anything, he barely touched her lower back, then took her hand and held it as she laid her other hand on his shoulder. Luther Vandross' velvety smooth voice crooned a rendition of "Always and Forever."

Unable to stop himself, he drew her closer to him, grateful she didn't resist.

The romantic chorus played.

He didn't dare look in her eyes because he'd lose it if he did. She felt so good in his arms. So perfect. He didn't want the dance to end—

"And now the bride and groom, Mr. and Mrs. Hayden Price!"

He'd been so focused on their dance, he hadn't noticed the other couples were on the floor.

Anita stepped away from him and turned around, along with the rest of the bridal party, clapping as Hayden and Riley started to dance, their foreheads pressed together, not an inch of space between them.

He thought he heard Anita sigh.

He turned, gazing at her as she watched them dance. And just like that, their required interaction was over. He looked at his arms, still outstretched from holding her. They felt unbearably empty.

The song switched to another slow tune, and the DJ encouraged everyone to join Hayden and Riley on the dance floor.

Maybe it wasn't over. He turned to Anita. "Do you want—"

"Hey, Anita." Rusty inserted himself in front of Tanner. "Would you like to dance?"

Anita smiled. "Yes, I would. Thanks for asking, Rusty."

Rusty took her hand and led her farther into the group of people dancing together until Tanner couldn't see them anymore, leaving him alone.

He moved to the edge of the dance floor. He couldn't see Anita and Rusty, but he did see plenty of familiar faces having a great time. Jared was dancing with Myrtle Benson, one of Erma's friends. Harper was still dancing with Henry, and Kingston was leading Melody onto the dance floor.

"You surprise me, boy."

Tanner turned and saw Jasper standing next to

him. The old man had appeared out of nowhere. "I do?"

"Yep." Jasper rubbed his bulbous nose with a bony finger. "Didn't take you as the kind of man who would give up so easily."

"Give up on what?"

Jasper gestured to the dance floor. "Her."

Anita was dancing with Rusty, her face beaming. Rusty was a stocky man, and he and Anita were almost the same height. Another thorn of jealousy went through him. "I don't know what you're talking about."

Jasper scowled. "You didn't think I believed that bunk about nothing going on between the two of you, did you?"

"It's true."

"Keep on lying to yourself, then. You're the one who'll regret letting her get away."

Tanner watched the old man shuffle off, probably to annoy someone else. Then he looked at the dance floor again. There was something Jasper didn't know: Tanner was already filled with regrets.

He continued watching Anita dance with Rusty. While they both seemed to be having fun, there was something wrong with the picture.

She should be dancing with me.

Chapter 23

"Oops, I'm sorry. Again."

Anita forced a smile at Rusty. This was the third time he'd stepped on her foot, and not lightly either. Combine that with the ache from her shoes, and this was turning out to be a painful dance. "It's all right. You're a good dancer otherwise." Not exactly true, but her compliment brought a smile to his face.

"You're a real good dancer," he said.

His hands rested on her waist while hers were on his shoulders, and they had plenty of space between them. Unlike her dance with Tanner. She had refused to look at him when they danced together and was glad the dancing had been short. Now she could spend the rest of the night enjoying herself, dancing with whomever she wanted to, and not giving him another single thought. That was what she wanted . . . wasn't it?

"Can I cut in?"

Her brows shot up, and she turned around to see Tanner standing there.

"Sure," Rusty said.

"No," Anita said at the same time. Tanner had to be up to something. Maybe he wanted to try to convince her again to give up the café. She ignored him, keeping her gaze on Rusty. "This is our dance."

"Oh, I don't mind," Rusty said in his always genial way. "Might save you a few bruises." He drew away from her. "Thanks for the dance, Anita. I sure did like it."

"But—"

Tanner smoothly took her in his arms, not holding her as close as he had earlier, but not leaving a lot of room between them either.

"Why did you do that?" she asked, not hiding her irritation.

"I wanted to dance with you."

"We already danced."

He met her gaze. "I wanted to dance with you again."

Under the low lights of the reception hall he was almost ethereal.

Stop it. Remembering how he'd tried to manipulate her before, she knew she couldn't trust him. "What if I don't want to dance with you?"

Hurt flashed across his face. "Then don't."

"I won't." She moved out of his arms, ignoring his pained expression, and started to walk away.

"Anita, wait."

The music stopped the second he finished speaking. Thank God no one had noticed. A fast-paced country song played next—another surprise since Riley didn't like country—and even more guests poured onto the dance floor.

Tanner took her arm. "We can't talk here."

"What, are you going to drag me into a closet? How about another pantry—I'm sure they have a kitchen around here somewhere."

His brow flattened. "I was thinking about talking outside."

She was about to shake her head, and then she paused, remembering Rosa. Regardless of how she felt about Tanner, he'd had a huge scare recently, and she didn't need to pile anything else on him. She'd listen to whatever he had to say, and then she was moving on. "Lead the way."

He seemed to know where he was going, which was good because she had never been here before. She followed him down the hall-way, past the restrooms, and out the back into a small courtyard. A creek flowed behind it, and unlike the past week, the heat and humidity tonight were at a manageable level. Strings of white lights in the trees and on tall wooden posts surrounded them, casting a hazy, romantic glow.

"How's this?" he asked, facing her.

"Fine." She noticed a seating area. Thank the Lord. She sat down on the white metal bench and took off her shoes. *Ah, that's better.*

"Feet hurt?" He sat down next to her.

"Yes. I'm not used to pointy heels like these." She wiggled her lavender-painted toes.

"Nice pedicure," he said.

She sighed and glared at him. "Please tell me you didn't drag me out here to talk about my feet."

He shook his head, rubbing the back of his neck. Then he glanced at her. His mouth opened, then closed, then opened again. Finally he managed to speak. "I want to explain about Heather."

"Now?" When he nodded, she added, "Can't it wait?"

"No. It can't. When I met her after work that night she came into the diner, she was hitting on me, full-court press."

Were his cheeks turning red? Yes, they were definitely crimson.

"She wouldn't take no for an answer, so I panicked and said I was seeing someone. You were the first person who came to mind."

She was? She had always believed she was an afterthought in his life. But what a time for her to come first.

"It was dumb and cowardly of me, and I never should have put you in that position. If you haven't noticed, I don't do well when I'm caught off guard. Heather, finding out you bought #3, using the Peanut situation against you . . . even that time back in high school after we kissed in the closet. I blew it back then too." He angled his body toward her, the sleeves of his shirt rolled up to his elbows.

Dang. Even his forearms were sexy.

"Anita, I want to help you with the café," he said. "Whatever you need me to do to help you get your business up and running, I'll do it."

Her mouth dropped open. This had to be a joke. "Did Erma talk to you?"

"No." His brows slanted together. "Why?"

Then again, maybe it wasn't a joke. "I don't understand," she said, confused. "Why do you want to help me?"

"You were there for me when Mom was sick—"

Now the truth had arrived. She should have expected this. "You don't owe me, Tanner." She got up from the bench, frustrated. A light breeze wafted over her bare shoulders, along with fatigue.

Here we go again. She could see the train wreck coming. He was breaching her defenses like he always did. Any minute she would start to hope that he finally saw her in a romantic way, only to find out he didn't. Then she would be hurt for the umpteenth time.

"I can't do this anymore," she whispered.

"Anita," he said, coming up behind her.

Even his voice, low and sensual, was doing its magic. She couldn't blame him. He didn't know the effect he had on her. He was just being himself.

There was one way she could drive him away for sure.

Tell him the truth. Once he knew how she felt, then she would be free.

She turned around and faced him, meeting his eyes without faltering. Then she delivered the final blow. "Tanner Castillo . . . I love you."

Chapter 24

No, no, no, no. That wasn't what she had planned to tell him. She hadn't meant to use the *L* word. She'd only intended to say that she liked him as more than a friend. Even a hint of romantic talk would freak him out. More than anything, she wanted to snatch those words back.

But now he knew the real truth, the one she'd been dancing around all these years, unable to admit to herself. Her feelings for him weren't puppy love or simple infatuation. They were real, painful, and pointless.

It didn't help that Tanner wasn't saying anything. She had expected him to at least show some shock. Or maybe awkwardly laugh and tell her that he had to get back to the reception. Instead he kept looking at her, his gaze holding hers, his eyes growing intense . . .

Oh my.

He took one step closer. "Did you say you love me?"

She backed away. "Um, yes. I did. I love a lot of people, though. And things. Like Peanut. I *really* love Peanut."

"Your cat."

"My lovely cat. He's also good now. He hasn't been on the roof since . . ." Good grief. Not only was she an idiot, but she also sounded like one. A weird laugh escaped. "I'm a loving person, that's all."

"That's true." He inched closer.

"Forget what I said." She stepped back.

"That you love me?" His tender smile went straight to her heart. "That's not something a person easily forgets."

Now what was she going to do?

Escape. "Shouldn't we get back to the reception hall?"

"We will." He closed the distance between them. "Why didn't you tell me this before?" he said in a low, husky, insanely sexy tone.

She shivered, even though the temperature was in the seventies. Her heartbeat tripled. Might as well go all the way with the truth. "Because I know you don't love me."

He stilled, his eyes darkening. "I'm sorry."

Game over. She should feel relieved, but instead she wanted to cry. Shoot, shoot, shoot. Monday morning she was calling a therapist, because she was convinced she was a loony bird. Holding back tears, she said, "It's okay. You don't have to apol—"

He cradled her face in his hands and kissed her. Not once, not twice, but so many times she lost count, and when he finally stopped, they had somehow ended up entangled in each other's arms.

"I'm so stupid, Anita," he said, tucking a strand

of hair behind her ear. "It took me so long to see what's right in front of me."

"What's that?" Tears slipped from her eyes.

"You. I love you too. It took fighting with you, and then not having you in my life, to realize that." He brushed his thumb over her cheek. "I also realized that I put Sunshine ahead of everything else."

"It's important to you."

"Not as much as you are to me. That's why I want to help you. I know the café is important to you, and that makes it important to me."

The last of the barrier around her heart came crumbling down. "But what about the customers? The competition?"

"Sunshine will survive. It has all these years. And competition isn't bad." He lightly ran his palm over her bare shoulder. "But cooperation is more fun."

Oof. She was putty in his hands now.

He guided her over to the bench, and they sat down. "I'm sorry I waited so long," he said.

"Three years isn't bad." Although it had seemed an eternity. Even now she wasn't sure she wasn't having one of her fairy-tale dreams.

"Ten years is, though." At her questioning look, he added, "The kiss in my closet? That was ten years ago."

"You were always good at math." She leaned against him, pressing her cheek against his chest.

"But dumb as a post when it comes to love. I think I was a little in love with you back then, even. I was just too busy and had my priorities too upside down to realize it."

"We can't all be perfect."

Tanner laughed and pressed a kiss on top of her head. She heard the thumping of his heart against her ear, and she closed her eyes. After all this time, her world was right.

"Where do we go from here?" he asked.

She lifted her head and smiled. "Wherever we want."

"Finally!"

Anita jumped up from the bench and saw Harper, Olivia, Melody, and Riley standing there. All of them started clapping.

"What's going on?" Tanner stood and faced them, placing his arm around Anita and holding her close.

"We didn't think you two would ever figure it out," Harper said.

"Even *I* knew you were meant for each other. And I don't even live here." Melody smirked.

Riley beamed. "This is so romantic."

"We should get back to the reception," Harper said, then pointed at Anita and Tanner. "But not you two. Y'all can stay out here as long as you want."

"Don't worry," Tanner said, giving Anita a look that not only curled her toes but healed her heart. "We're planning on it."

Epilogue

Three months later

"Are you sure you don't need me to bring you another pillow?" Tanner handed his mother the remote control to the TV.

She sighed. "Stop fussing over me, Tanner. I've got my water, my crochet"—she held up a ball of orange-and-yellow yarn with a crochet hook stuck through it—"and plenty of pillows. I also got a gold star from Dr. Bedford yesterday, so you can finally quit hovering."

Tanner put the blue throw pillow back on the couch and perched on the edge. He had to leave soon, but there was something he wanted to talk about before he did. "I'm glad to hear you've impressed the taskmaster."

"And I'm glad you finally did something about those white things in your ears."

He resisted touching the two clear stitches in each of his earlobes. They were almost healed, and because the holes hadn't been that big, there wouldn't be much of a scar. "I kind of miss them, though."

"I don't. Now you look like a real business-man."

Tanner beamed. Things couldn't be better. His

mother had recovered from her unstable angina, although she would be on heart medicine for the rest of her life. But she had lost weight and had gone to part time at the bottling company in addition to quitting her second job. This left her more time to volunteer at church and hang out with the Bosom Buddies. He hadn't seen her this happy in years.

"Is Anita excited for her grand opening tomorrow?" Mom went back to crocheting the cowl she'd been working on, using the same pattern Anita and her friends had decided on for their charity project this year. They had already donated more than two dozen to the homeless shelter, most of them made by his mother. She had picked up the craft quickly after not doing it for so long.

"Yes, but she's nervous."

"I can't wait to see what the place looks like," she said. "You two have been so secretive about it."

"We want everyone to be surprised."

His mother stopped crocheting and looked at him, her eyes soft. "I'm so glad you decided to combine businesses."

"Me too." The Sunshine Diner was now next door to the brand-new Sunshine Café. After Hayden and Riley's wedding, he and Anita had started working together, and soon after, she had asked him if she could name the café Sunshine.

She had also returned to work at the diner, picking up a shift or two when she was able. "It's not work to me," she said one night when they were closing together and he'd wondered aloud if she was taking on too much. "I miss this place."

Everyone had missed her. Most of all him.

"There's only one thing left to do," Mom said as he got up from the couch.

"What's that?"

She winked at him and went back to crocheting.

He laughed. "See you later, Mom." He was still smiling when he got into his Jeep.

She has no idea.

"This coffee is amazing, Anita. What do you call it?" Riley took another sip from the plain white coffee mug.

"Jamaica Blue Mountain." Anita sat down at the table with Riley and Olivia, a latte in her hand. "It is delicious, isn't it?"

Olivia dunked her tea bag into her cup. "I prefer Earl Gray. I don't see how y'all drink coffee. It's too bitter for me."

"That's because you haven't had this." Riley gestured to her mug. "You should try some. It will change your life."

Shaking her head, Olivia set the tea bag on the saucer. "I'll stick with Earl."

Anita chuckled. Opening day was tomorrow, but she wanted to spend some time with her friends while she still could. If everyone who had said they would be there on the first official day of business showed up, she would have a huge crowd. Things would be busy, and she didn't want to neglect her friends.

"Any idea where Harper is?" Olivia asked. "She's ten minutes late."

"She said something about dropping her car off at Rusty's," Riley said. "The engine's making a funny noise."

"I didn't know Rusty worked on foreign cars." Olivia poured a small amount of milk into her cup.

"I guess he works on all cars. I'm sure she'll be here soon."

Anita picked up an orange-flavored biscotti and dipped it into her coffee. "What do you think of these? They were Mom's suggestion."

After making sure that Paisley's wedding was still on, her mother had returned to Hot Springs and immediately started *helping* again. Anita had welcomed her suggestions, although she didn't take most of them. Between her, Tanner, and Erma, she had been able to open the café on time and under budget.

"Delicious." Olivia took a bite, and Riley nodded. "She has good taste."

"That she does. And she'll be the first one to tell you." Anita chuckled.

"I'm sorry I'm late!" Harper hurried inside, the

high heels of her tall brown boots clicking on the tile floor. She sat down in the empty seat and set her large handbag on the floor.

"How's the car?" Riley asked.

"Turns out there was nothing wrong with the engine. I guess I'm hearing things." She turned to Anita. "Is it too late to get an Americano?"

"Of course not." She got up from the chair and walked over to the coffee station, where she started on Harper's drink. When she'd finished preparing it, she brought it to her friend, along with a biscotti on a small plate, then settled back into her chair.

"I've been thinking," Harper said, her French-tipped nails clicking against the mug as she picked up the coffee. "Remember how we discussed finding a name for our little group?"

"Oh yes," Olivia said, leaning forward. "We desperately need one."

"I wouldn't say 'desperately.' " Riley looked at Harper. "But it would be nice. Did you come up with something?"

"I did, and it's perfect." Harper grinned. "The Latte Ladies!"

Anita, Riley, and Olivia exchanged looks. "What?"

Harper's enthusiasm dimmed. "You don't like it? We're obviously going to be hanging out here a lot and having a lot of lattes. Or Americanos." She glanced at Olivia and scoffed. "Or tea."

"Um, it's nice." Riley took a quick drink of her coffee.

"Yes. Nice." Anita rubbed a small spot on the table.

"It's worse than the Four Musketeers."

"Don't beat around the bush, Olivia." Harper rolled her eyes.

"I like the 'latte' part," Anita said. "But the 'ladies' part makes us sound . . . old."

"I'm not ready to be a lady yet." Riley chuckled. "At least not that kind of lady."

Olivia nodded. "Next thing you know we'll start playing bridge."

"I actually like bridge," Harper said. She sighed. "Fine. I see your point. No Latte Ladies."

"How hard can it be to name a group?" Olivia said.

Harper looked at her. "Not that hard if *someone* wasn't so picky."

"I'm not picky. I'm discerning."

They all laughed, and Anita smiled. It was good to relax with her friends again.

When they finished their coffees, everyone started to leave. "We don't want to keep you," Riley said. "You have a big day tomorrow."

"Don't fib, Mrs. Price." Harper arched a brow. "We know you're in a hurry to get back home to your husband."

Riley blushed.

"Ugh, newlyweds. You should be over that

stage by now." Olivia turned to Anita. "Do you need help cleaning up?"

"No, it won't take me long. Thanks anyway."

"See you tomorrow."

A few minutes after her friends left, she'd started to clear away the coffee cups and dessert plates when the door opened. Her heart leapt. Tanner.

"I thought they'd never leave." He went straight to her and gathered her in his arms, not stopping to take off his jacket. Instead of kissing her on the lips as he usually did whenever they were alone, he nuzzled her neck.

"Tanner, what if anyone sees?"

"It's after eight. Ninety percent of Maple Falls is probably in bed by now." He winked and went to shut the door. "You need to lock this when you're the only one here, okay?"

"I will." She smiled, filled with love that made her feelings for him before they became a couple pale in comparison.

"Ready for tomorrow?" he asked, grabbing the rest of the dishes and following her into the kitchen.

"I think so." She set the mugs in the sink and turned to him. "I'm anxious, though."

"Everything will be great. Fred and Mabel have the diner covered, so I'll be here if you need me."

She went to him. "Thank you. I couldn't have done this without you."

He grinned and slipped his hand into the pocket of his jacket. "I got something for you."

She almost fainted on the spot. They'd been inseparable since Riley's wedding, but the *M* word had never been mentioned.

Oh my goodness. He's going to propose.

He pulled out a box, and she barely noticed that it was a little on the large side for a ring. "It's a little good luck for the opening tomorrow," he said.

She lifted the lid. Inside lay a delicate silver bracelet with two tiny coffee-mug charms hanging from it. "Oh," she said, irritated with herself that she was a little disappointed. She picked it up. "It's beautiful."

"Do you like it?"

"Yes. Can you help me put it on?"

He took the bracelet and fastened it on her wrist. She smiled, the little charms shining in the light of the kitchen. "Thank you. I love it."

"Whew. I was hoping you did." But when she reached up to kiss him, he put his finger on her mouth. "Wait. I almost forgot."

"Forgot what?"

From her phone, Whitney Houston's voice belted the chorus of "I Will Always Love You."

Tanner frowned. "Don't answer it."

She glanced at her purse on the counter. "It could be someone important."

"They can leave a voice mail."

"What if it's Mom?"

He paused, then rolled his eyes and stepped back. "You'd better answer it."

Sure enough. "Hi, Mom," she said, winking at Tanner.

"Hello, sweetheart. Are you all set for tomorrow?"

"Yes, ma'am." When she saw Tanner tapping his wrist, telling her to wrap it up, she added, "I'm busy now, though."

"This won't take too long. I want to discuss adding another coffee flavor to your menu."

"Now? It's too late for that."

Tanner walked over, pushed her hair aside, and whispered in her ear, "Tell her you have to go."

A pleasant shiver shot down her spine. "Mom—"

"The coffee is Parisian. Doesn't that sound divine? I sampled it when I was in Dallas with Paisley, and you simply have to serve it soon. I finally found a place you can order from."

"All right, I—"

Tanner took the phone from her. "Hi, Mrs. Bedford."

"Oh, hello, Tanner, dear. How are you?"

"I'm good, Anita's good, the café's good, and we'll serve Parisian coffee next month."

"But—"

"Ta-ta for now." He clicked the phone off and tossed it onto Anita's purse.

"That was impressive." She'd have to ask him for some pointers on how to put off her mother in the future.

"Now," he said, grinning. "Where were we? Oh, right. We were here." He opened his hand. A diamond solitaire ring lay in his palm.

Her hand went to her mouth, and she looked at him.

He took her hand and slipped the ring on her finger. A perfect fit. "Will you marry me, Anita?"

"Yes!" She hugged him. "You're a stinker, you know that?"

"I've heard you use that language with your Sunday school class. I don't know whether to be proud or insulted." He held her tight.

"Both." She whispered in his ear, "I love you, Tanner Castillo."

"And I love you, Anita Castillo." When she gave him a puzzled look, he added, "You might as well start getting used to it now."

She laughed, her heart full. Nothing had ever sounded so good.

Acknowledgments

A big thank you to Becky Monds for her exceptional editing skills on this book. She was key in helping to bring out Tanner's "swoony" side. ☺ Thank you also to Leslie Peterson for her valuable line editing, and Natasha Kern for her unfailing support. And thank you, dear reader. I hope you enjoyed Anita and Tanner's story as much as I do!

Discussion Questions

1. Anita feels she needs to change—not for others, but for herself. Has there ever been a time in your life when you needed to change something or yourself? How did you go about making the change(s) and what was the result?
2. Tanner panics when he finds out George is going to sell the diner. Do you think he did the right thing by buying the diner on the spot? What might he have done instead?
3. Tanner and Anita both had their reasons for not telling anyone about buying the diner and opening a café. Do you agree with their reasons? If not, what should they have done differently and why?
4. Rosa tells Tanner that he can always make time for the things he cares about. Do you agree with this statement, and how can you apply it to your own life?
5. Unfortunately, Rosa neglects her health to the point that she must be hospitalized. What are some ways people can balance work and self-care?
6. Anita believes she has failed her parents compared to her siblings and their successes. Discuss a time in your life when you thought

you were a failure. How did you handle that, and what advice can you give to someone who is struggling with those feelings?

7. It took almost losing Anita for Tanner to realize how he truly felt about her, and that he needed to change his priorities. Discuss a time when you discovered you needed to shift your priorities, and what the process was.

| Books are produced in the United States using U.S.-based materials | Books are printed using a revolutionary new process called THINKtech™ that lowers energy usage by 70% and increases overall quality | Books are durable and flexible because of Smyth-sewing | Paper is sourced using environmentally responsible foresting methods and the paper is acid-free |

Center Point Large Print
600 Brooks Road / PO Box 1
Thorndike, ME 04986-0001 USA

(207) 568-3717

US & Canada:
1 800 929-9108
www.centerpointlargeprint.com